The Ballad of YaYa

YaYa

Book 2: The Prisoner

Written by

Jean-Marie **Omont**   Patrick **Marty**   Charlotte **Girard**

Illustrated by
Golo **Zhao**

Created and Edited by
Patrick **Marty**

Localization, Layout, and Editing by Mike Kennedy

LION™
FORGE   MAGNETIC™

www.lionforge.com

WHEN THE JAPANESE BOMBED THE STREETS OF SHANGHAI IN 1937, MANY FAMILIES WERE SEPARATED IN THE CHAOS. ***YAYA*** WAS ONE SUCH LITTLE GIRL, HAVING RUN AWAY FROM HOME TO ATTEND HER PIANO AUDITION, UNAWARE OF THE DANGER THAT SURROUNDED THE CITY.

IN THE PANDEMONIUM, SHE IS HELPED BY A YOUNG STREET URCHIN NAMED ***TUDUO*** WHO WAS ALSO RUNNING AWAY FROM ***ZHU,*** THE WICKED GANGSTER WHO FORCED ORPHANS TO WORK FOR HIM ON THE STREET. UNFORTUNATELY, ZHU AND HIS HENCHMAN, ***OYSTER GRAVY***, CAPTURED YAYA AND TUDUO AND BROUGHT THEM BACK TO THEIR HIDEOUT...

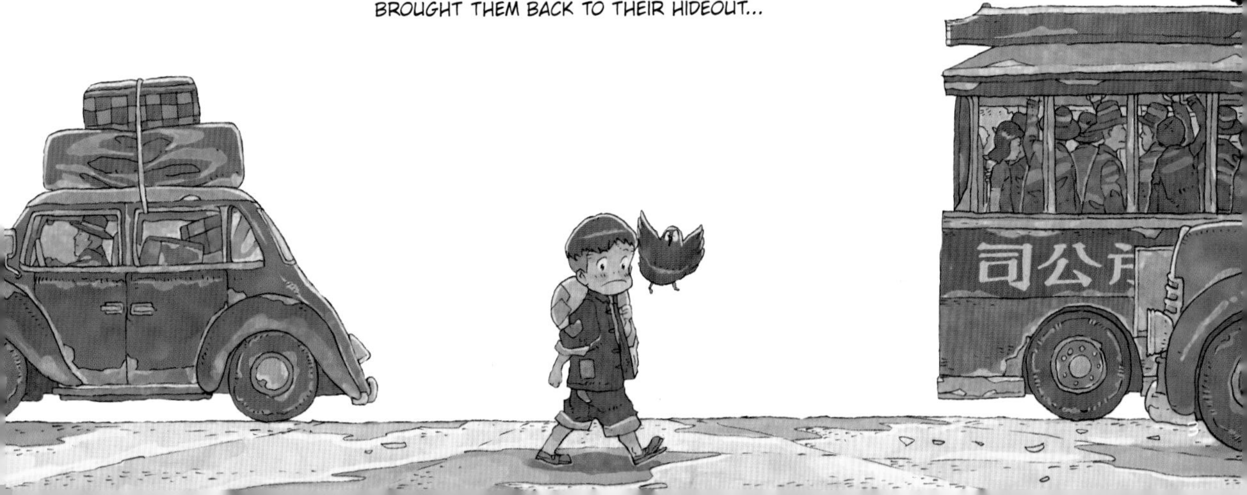

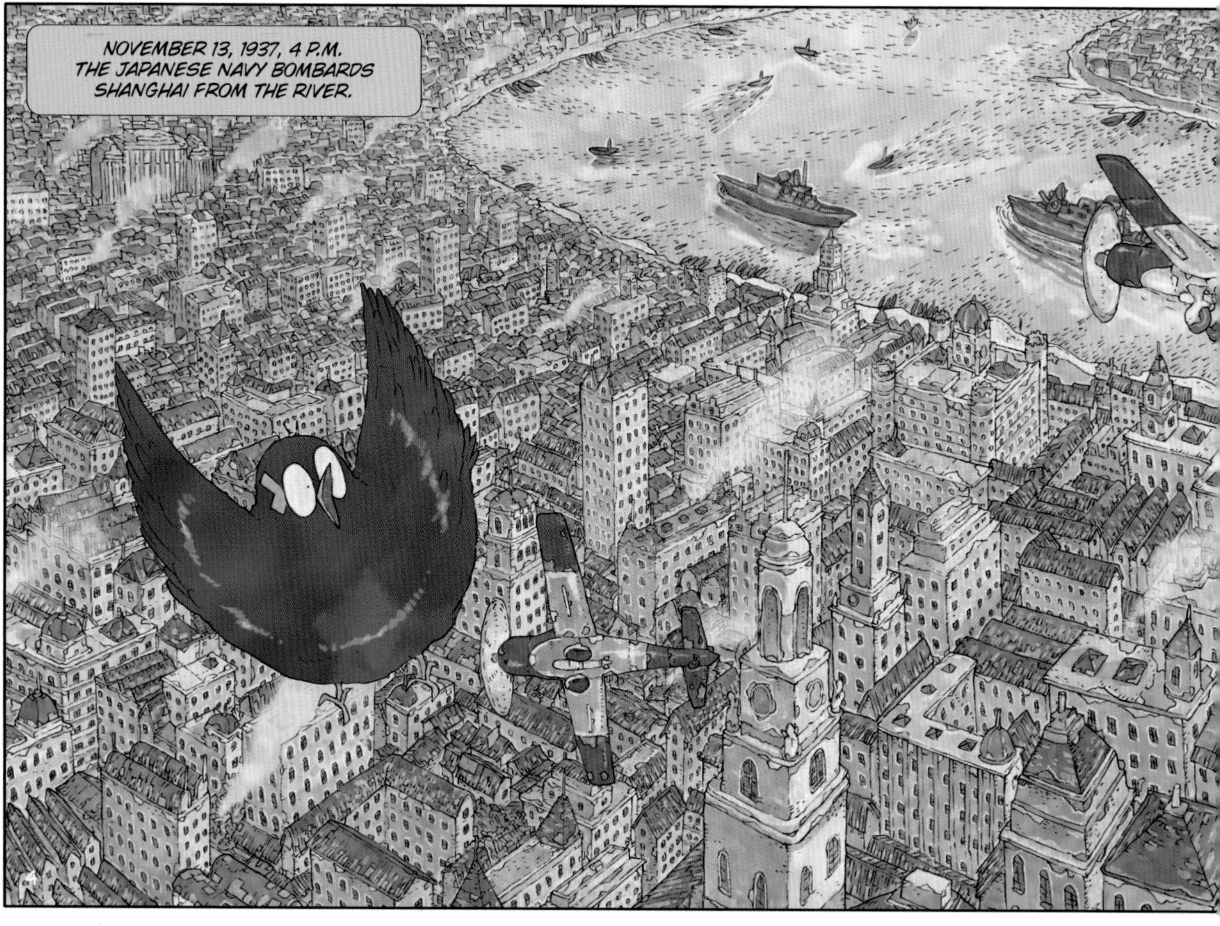
NOVEMBER 13, 1937, 4 P.M.
THE JAPANESE NAVY BOMBARDS
SHANGHAI FROM THE RIVER.

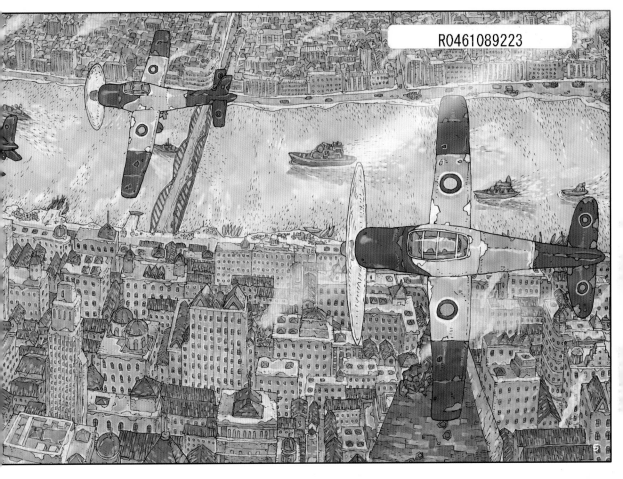

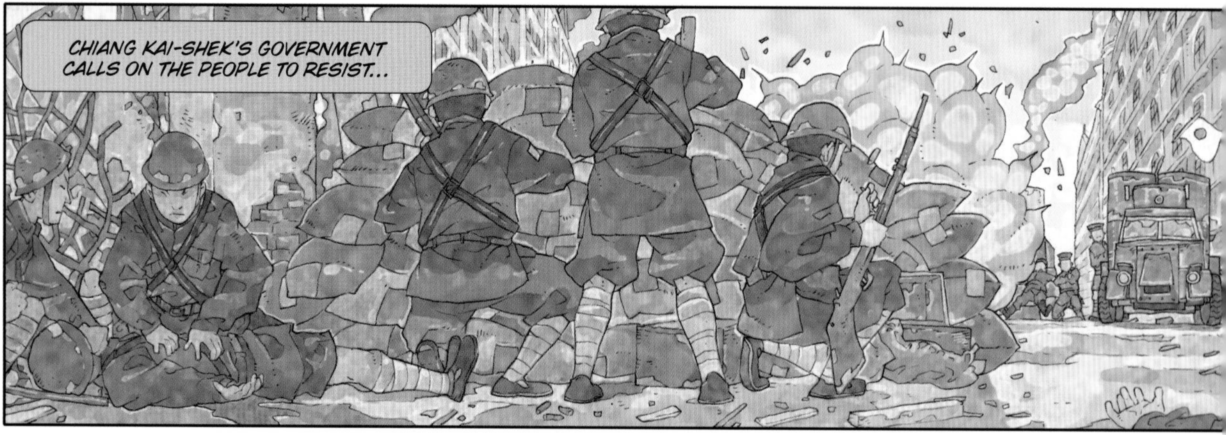
CHIANG KAI-SHEK'S GOVERNMENT CALLS ON THE PEOPLE TO RESIST...

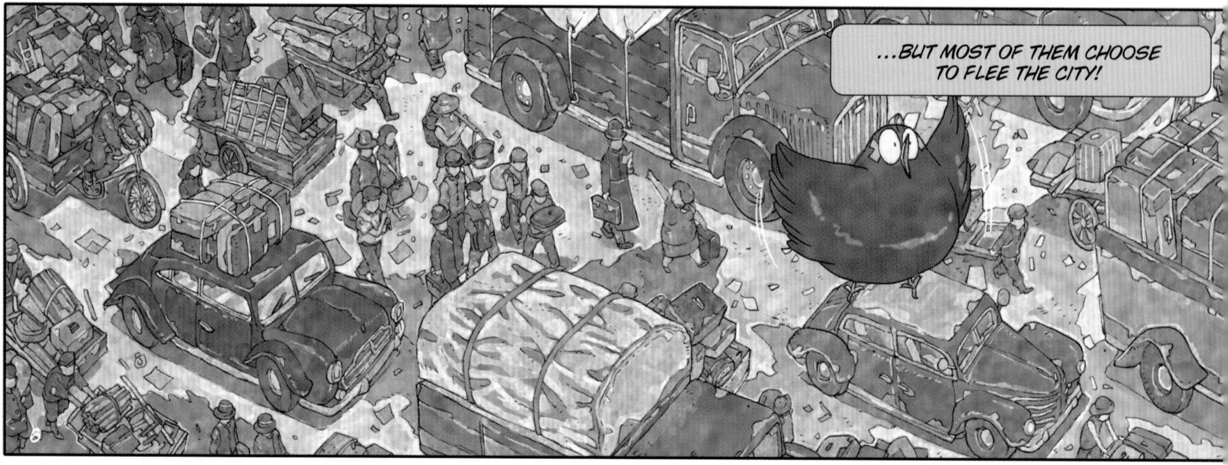
...BUT MOST OF THEM CHOOSE TO FLEE THE CITY!

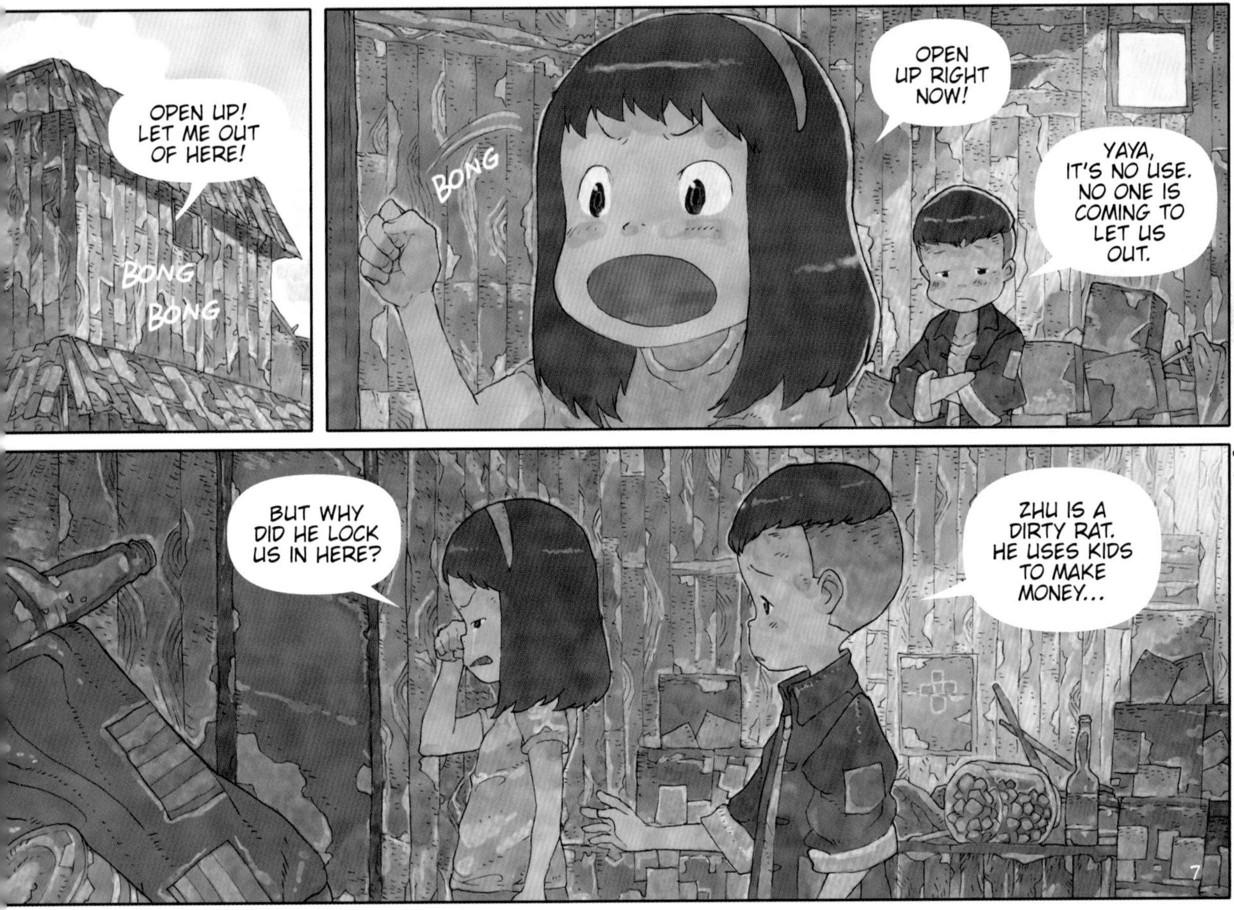
OPEN UP! LET ME OUT OF HERE!
BONG
BONG
BONG
OPEN UP RIGHT NOW!
YAYA, IT'S NO USE. NO ONE IS COMING TO LET US OUT.
BUT WHY DID HE LOCK US IN HERE?
ZHU IS A DIRTY RAT. HE USES KIDS TO MAKE MONEY...
7

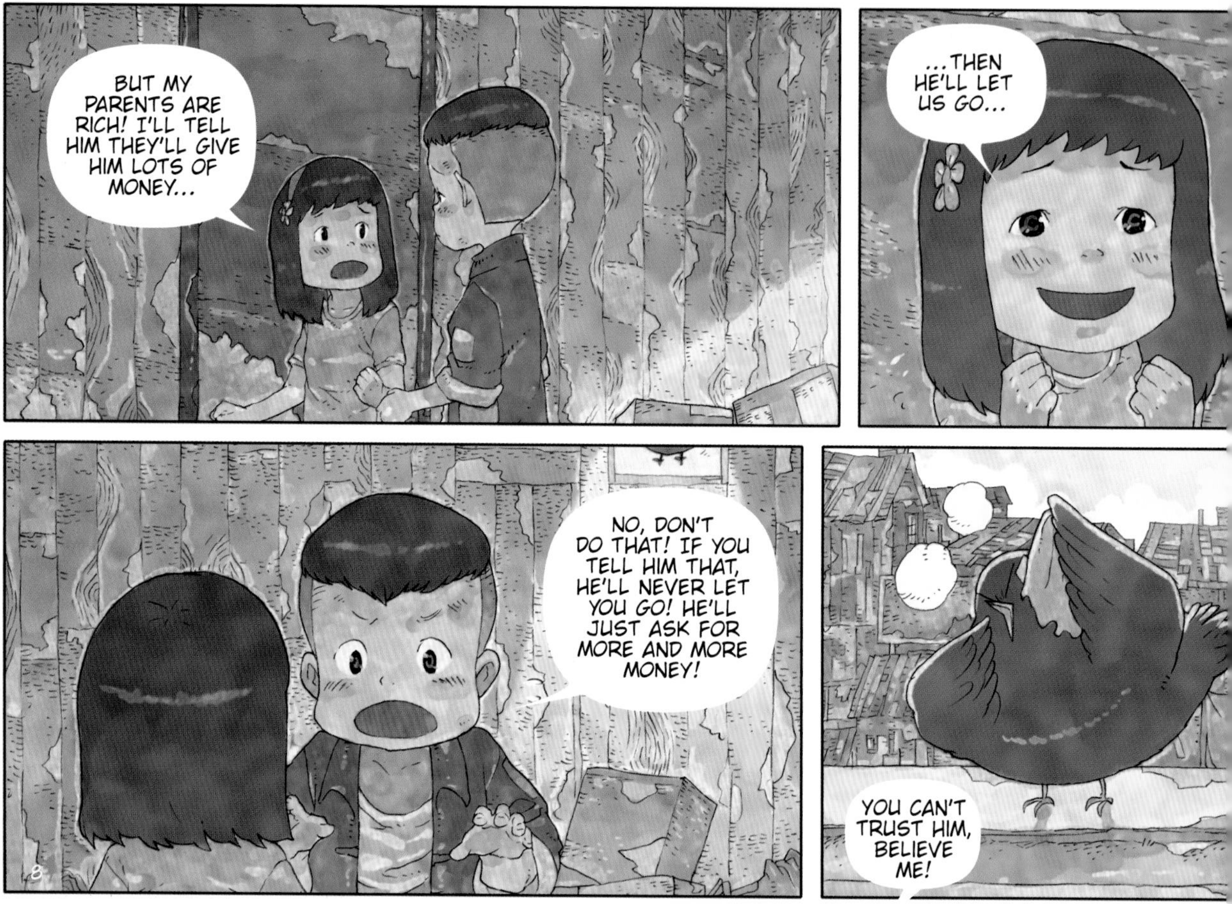
BUT MY PARENTS ARE RICH! I'LL TELL HIM THEY'LL GIVE HIM LOTS OF MONEY...
...THEN HE'LL LET US GO...
NO, DON'T DO THAT! IF YOU TELL HIM THAT, HE'LL NEVER LET YOU GO! HE'LL JUST ASK FOR MORE AND MORE MONEY!
YOU CAN'T TRUST HIM, BELIEVE ME!

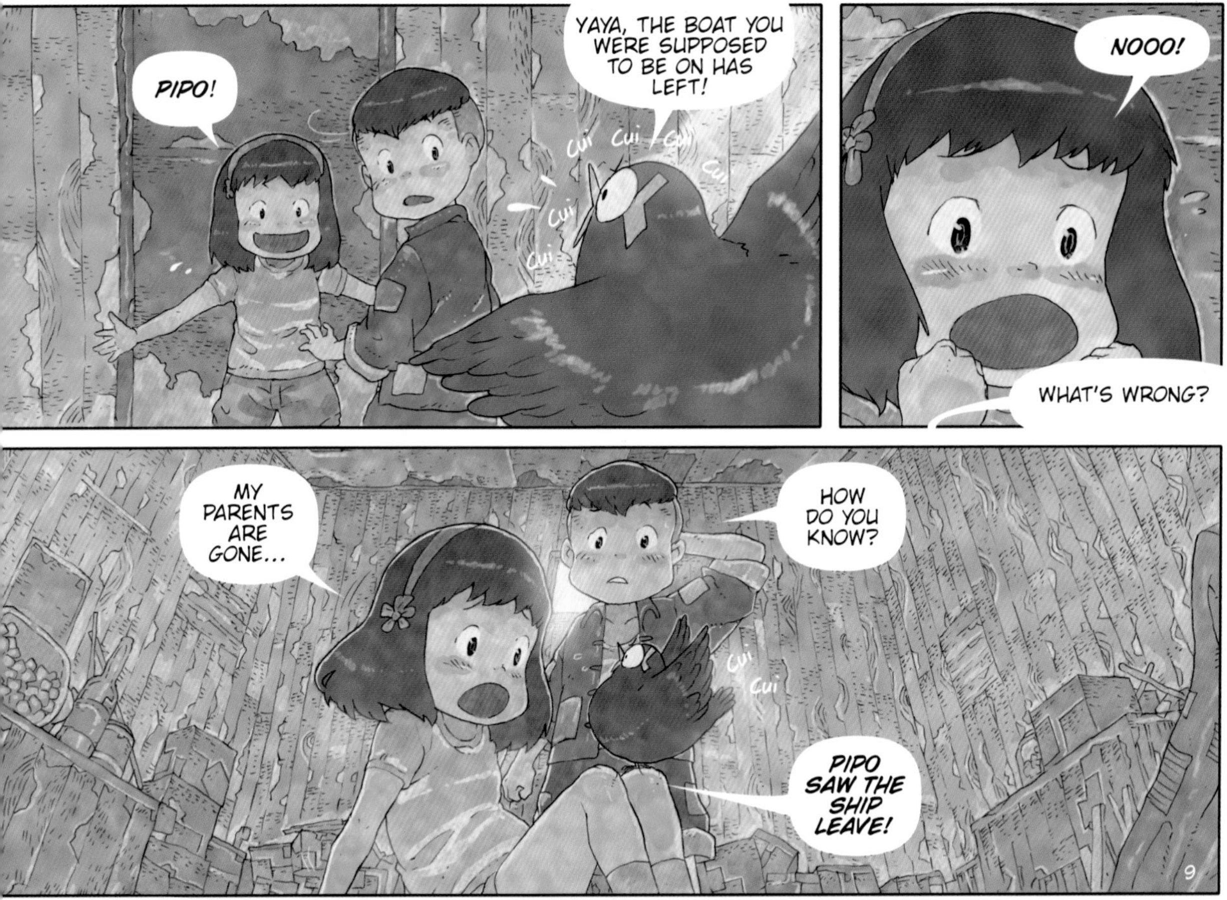
PIPO!
YAYA, THE BOAT YOU WERE SUPPOSED TO BE ON HAS LEFT!
Cui Cui Cui Cui Cui Cui
NOOO!
WHAT'S WRONG?
MY PARENTS ARE GONE...
HOW DO YOU KNOW?
Cui Cui
PIPO SAW THE SHIP LEAVE!

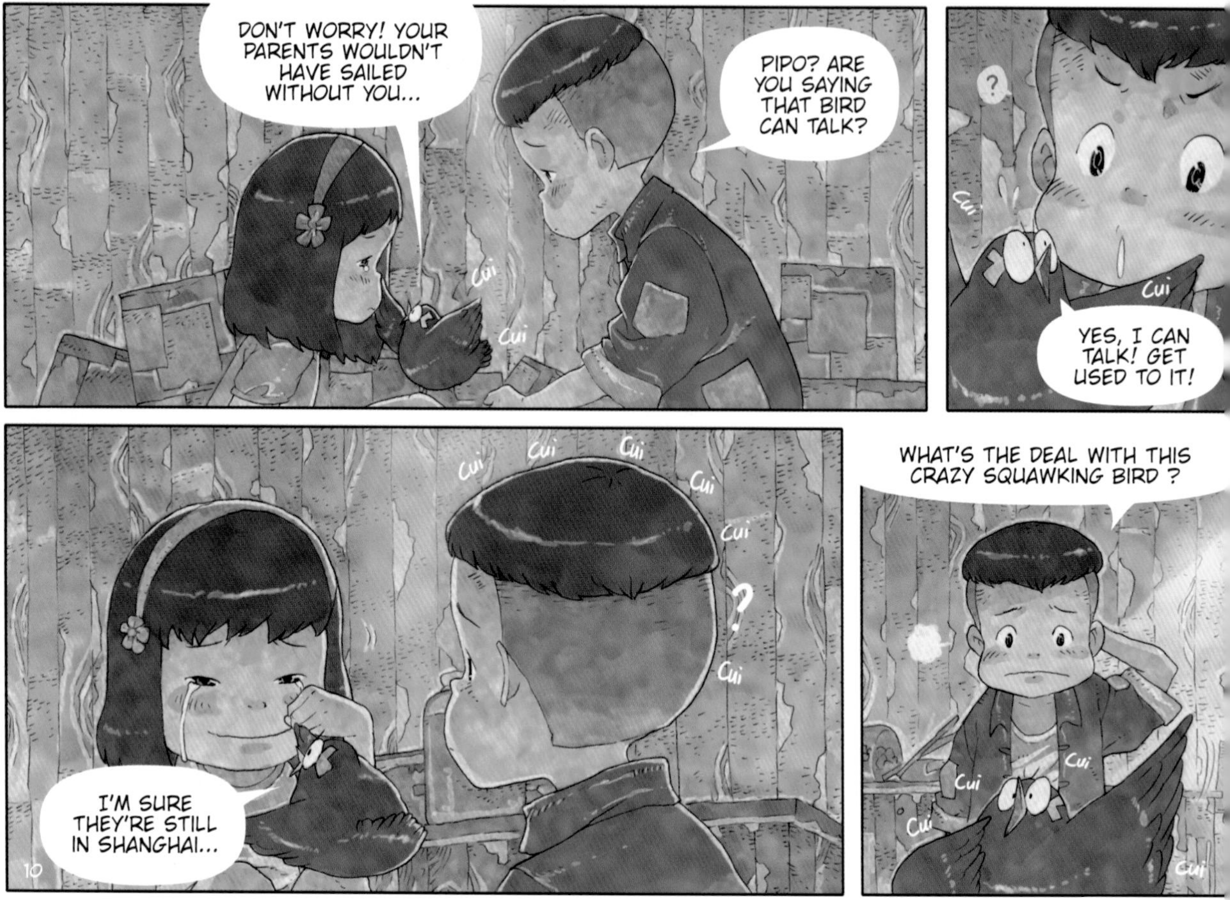
DON'T WORRY! YOUR PARENTS WOULDN'T HAVE SAILED WITHOUT YOU...
Cui
Cui
PIPO? ARE YOU SAYING THAT BIRD CAN TALK?
?
Cui
Cui
YES, I CAN TALK! GET USED TO IT!
Cui Cui Cui Cui Cui
?
Cui
I'M SURE THEY'RE STILL IN SHANGHAI...
WHAT'S THE DEAL WITH THIS CRAZY SQUAWKING BIRD ?
Cui
Cui
Cui
Cui

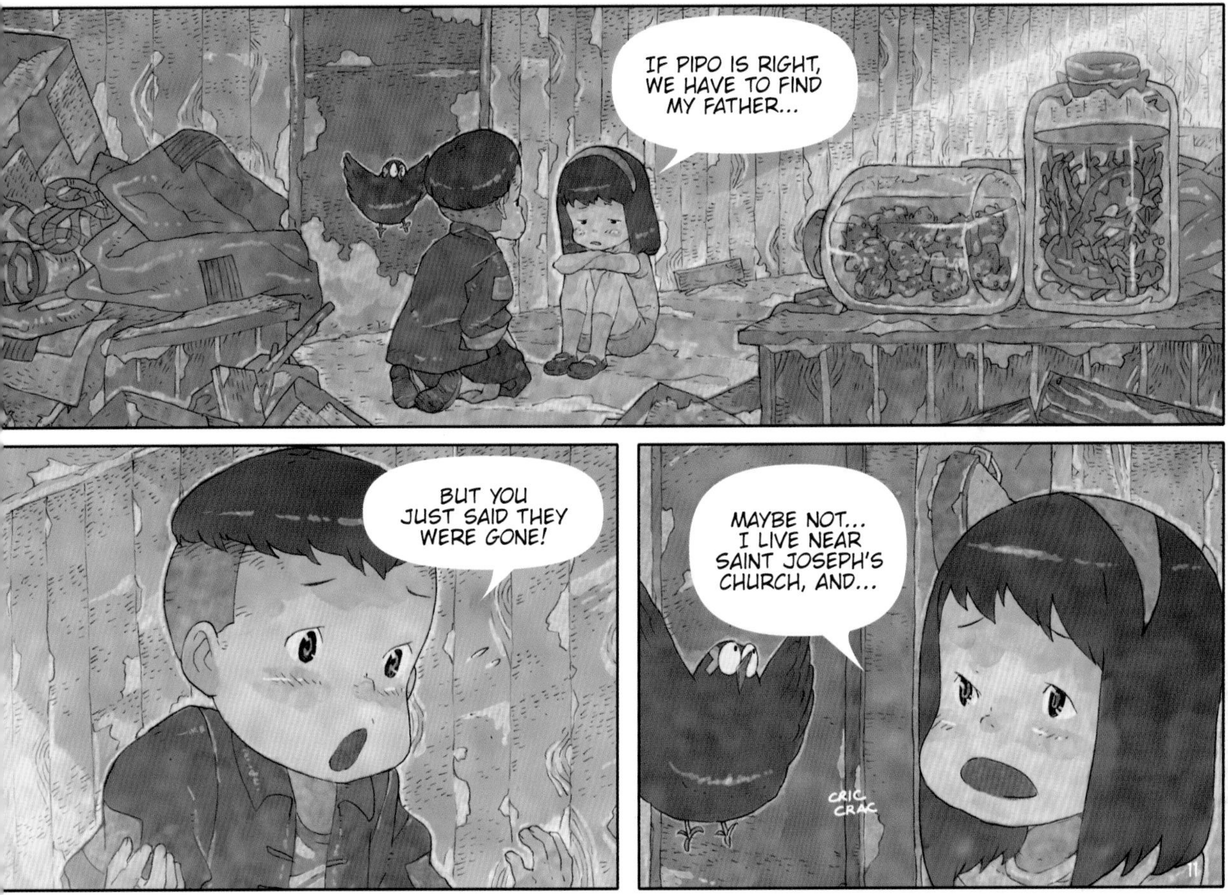
IF PIPO IS RIGHT, WE HAVE TO FIND MY FATHER...
BUT YOU JUST SAID THEY WERE GONE!
MAYBE NOT... I LIVE NEAR SAINT JOSEPH'S CHURCH, AND...
CRIC CRAC
11

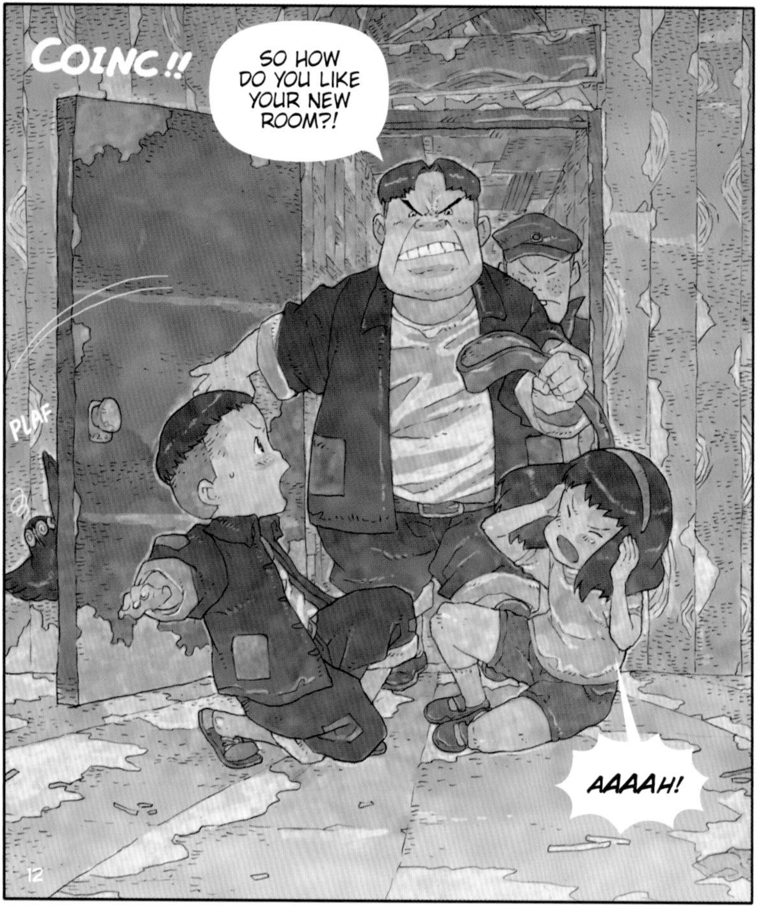
COINC!!
SO HOW DO YOU LIKE YOUR NEW ROOM?!
PLAF
AAAAH!

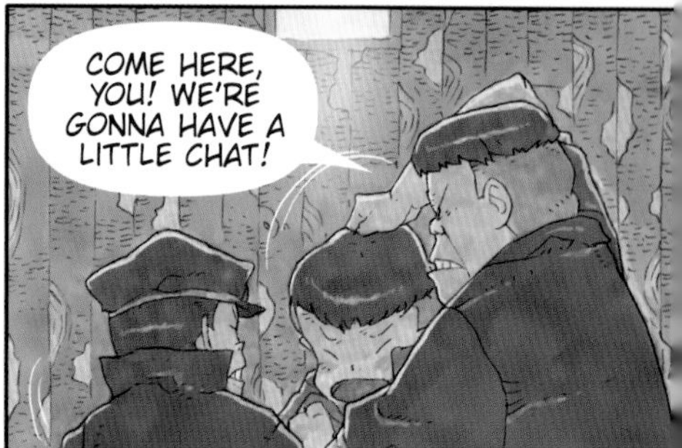
COME HERE, YOU! WE'RE GONNA HAVE A LITTLE CHAT!

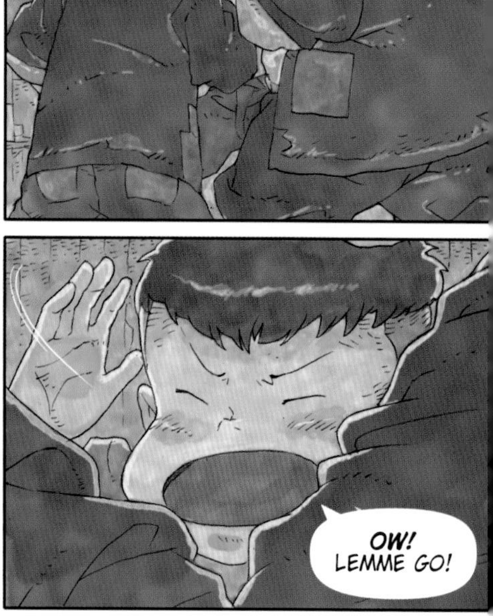
OW! LEMME GO!

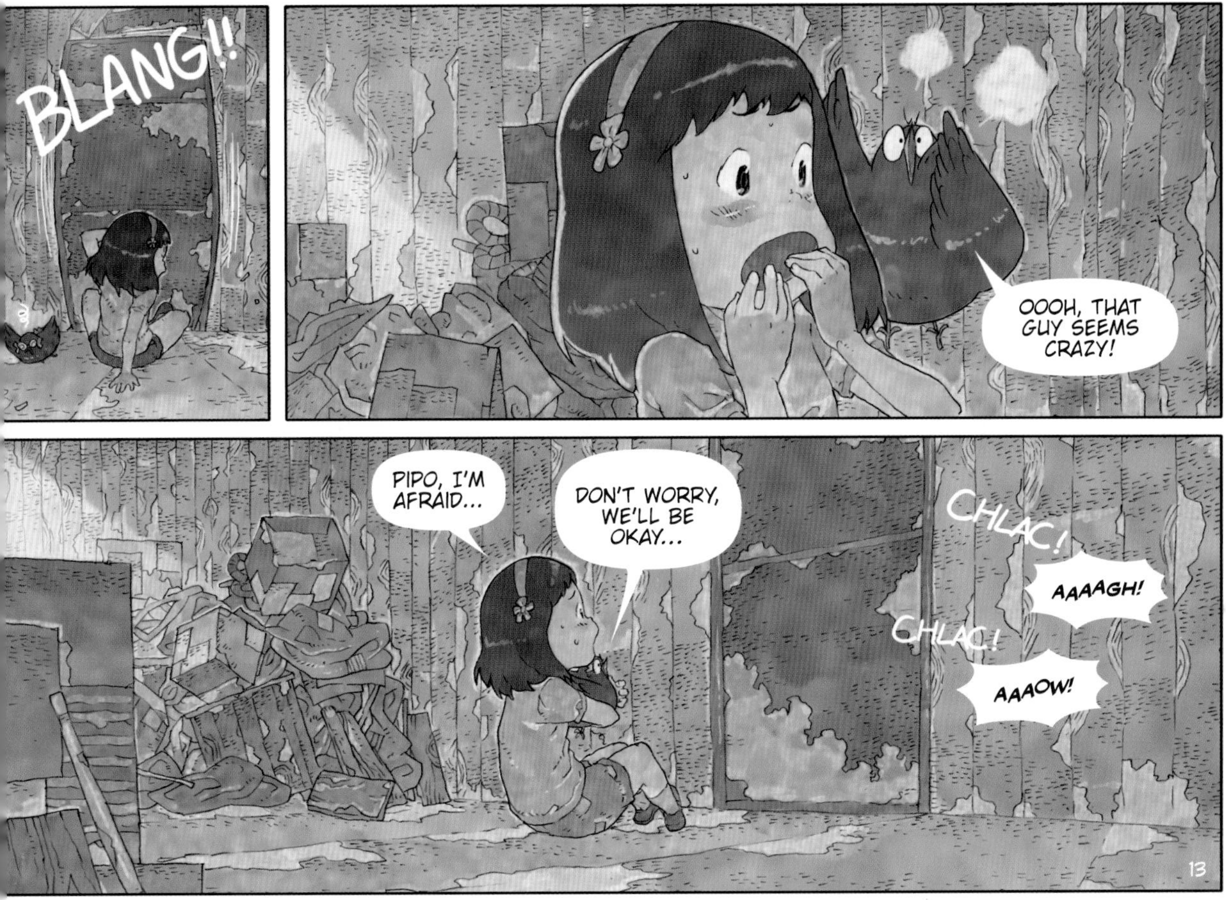
BLANG!!
OOOH, THAT GUY SEEMS CRAZY!
PIPO, I'M AFRAID...
DON'T WORRY, WE'LL BE OKAY...
CHLAC!
AAAAGH!
CHLAC!
AAAOW!

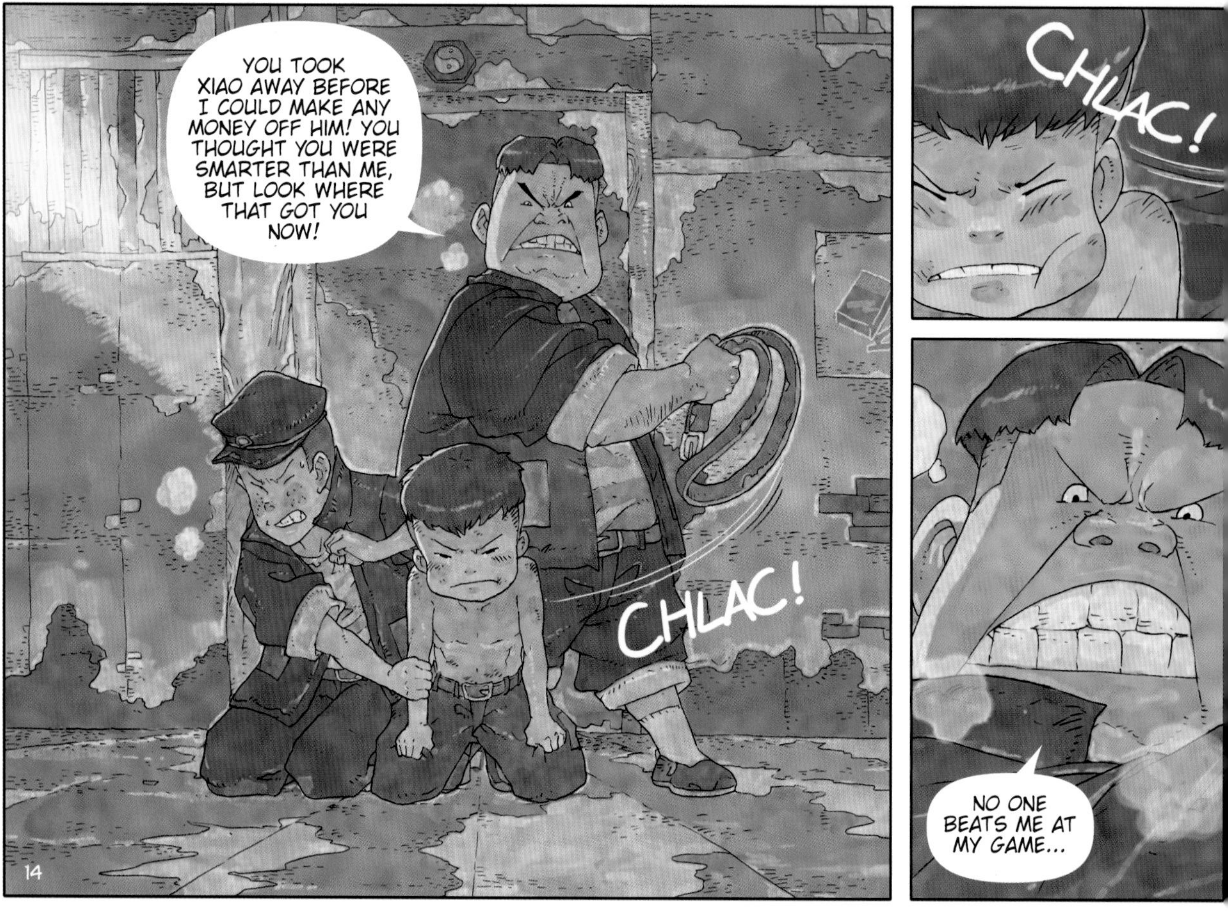
YOU TOOK XIAO AWAY BEFORE I COULD MAKE ANY MONEY OFF HIM! YOU THOUGHT YOU WERE SMARTER THAN ME, BUT LOOK WHERE THAT GOT YOU NOW!
CHLAC!
CHLAC!
NO ONE BEATS ME AT MY GAME...

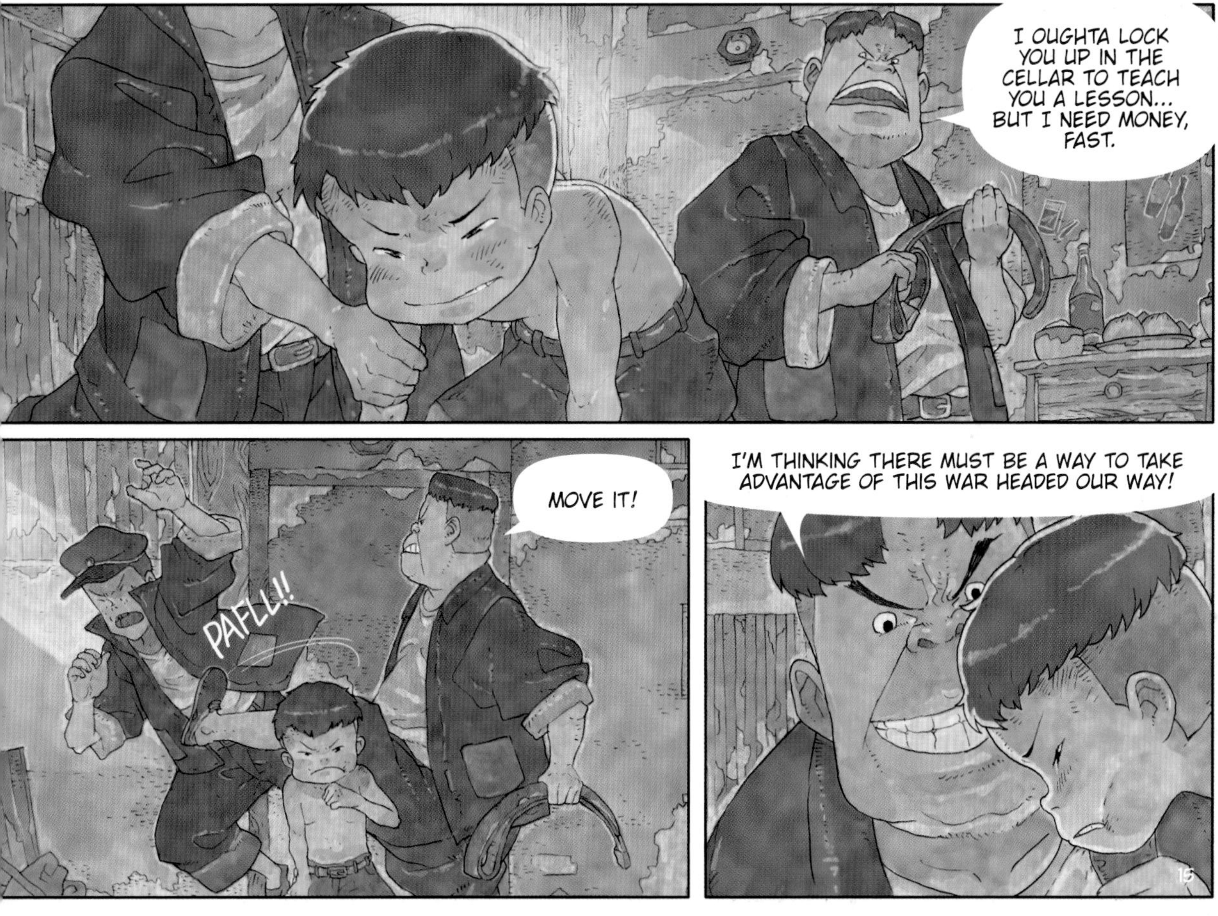
I OUGHTA LOCK YOU UP IN THE CELLAR TO TEACH YOU A LESSON... BUT I NEED MONEY, FAST.
MOVE IT!
PAFLL!!
I'M THINKING THERE MUST BE A WAY TO TAKE ADVANTAGE OF THIS WAR HEADED OUR WAY!

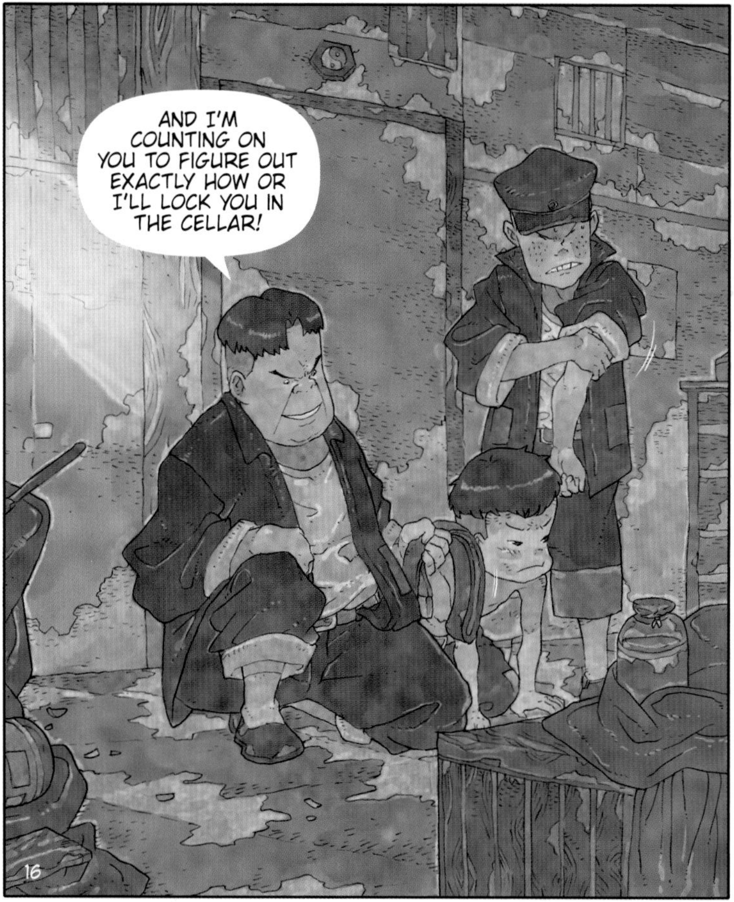
AND I'M COUNTING ON YOU TO FIGURE OUT EXACTLY HOW OR I'LL LOCK YOU IN THE CELLAR!

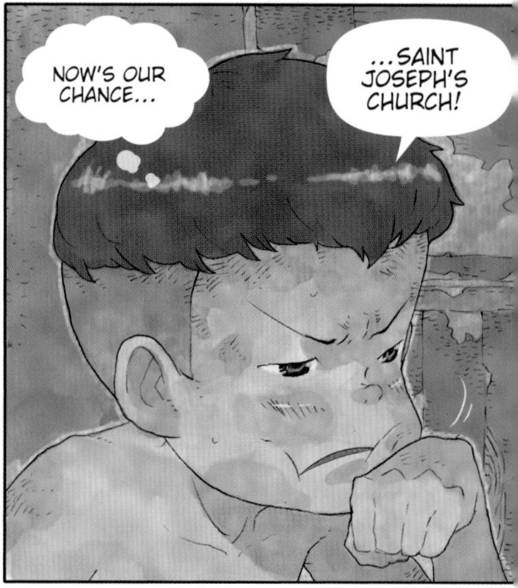
NOW'S OUR CHANCE...
...SAINT JOSEPH'S CHURCH!

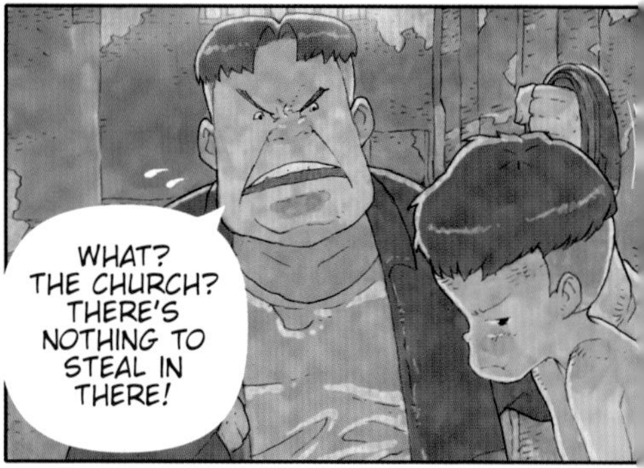
WHAT? THE CHURCH? THERE'S NOTHING TO STEAL IN THERE!

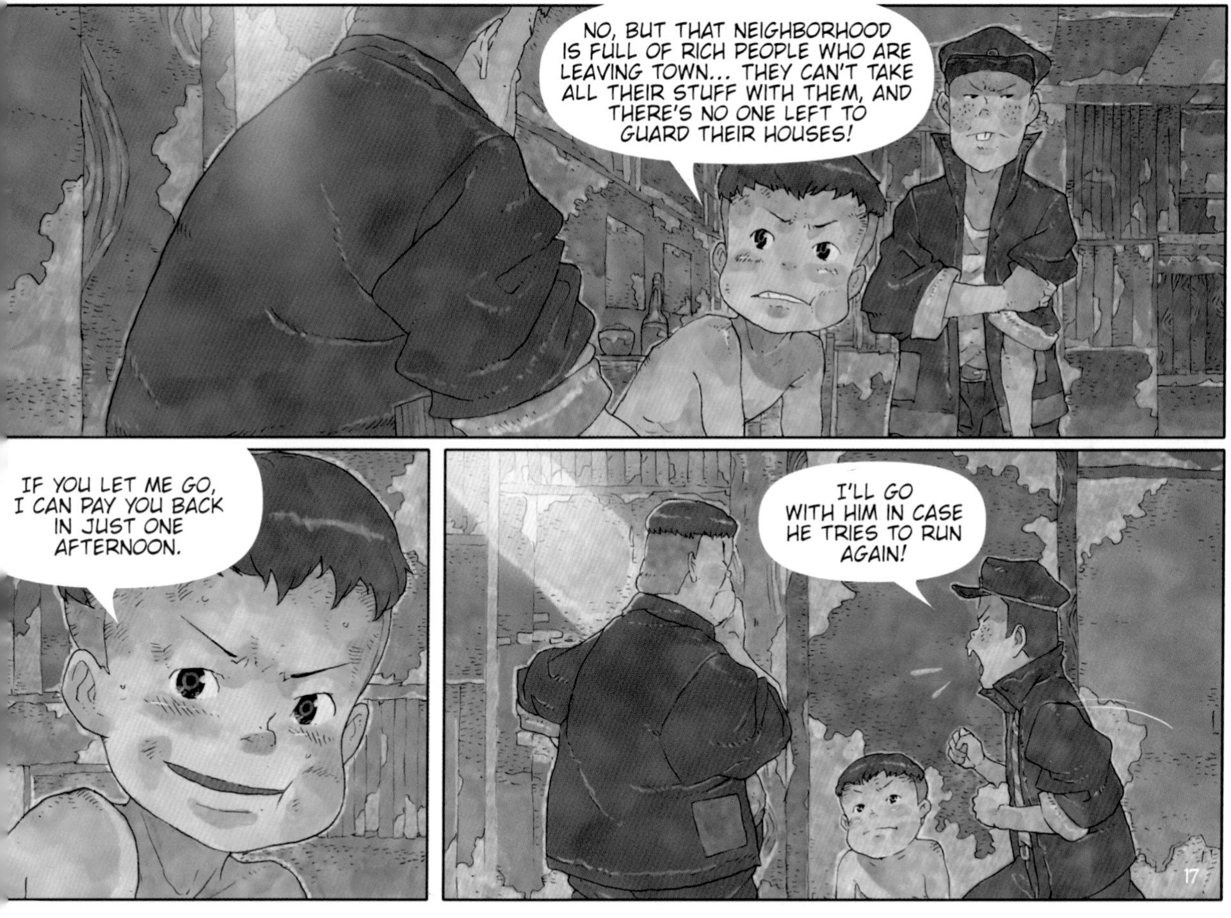
NO, BUT THAT NEIGHBORHOOD IS FULL OF RICH PEOPLE WHO ARE LEAVING TOWN... THEY CAN'T TAKE ALL THEIR STUFF WITH THEM, AND THERE'S NO ONE LEFT TO GUARD THEIR HOUSES!
IF YOU LET ME GO, I CAN PAY YOU BACK IN JUST ONE AFTERNOON.
I'LL GO WITH HIM IN CASE HE TRIES TO RUN AGAIN!

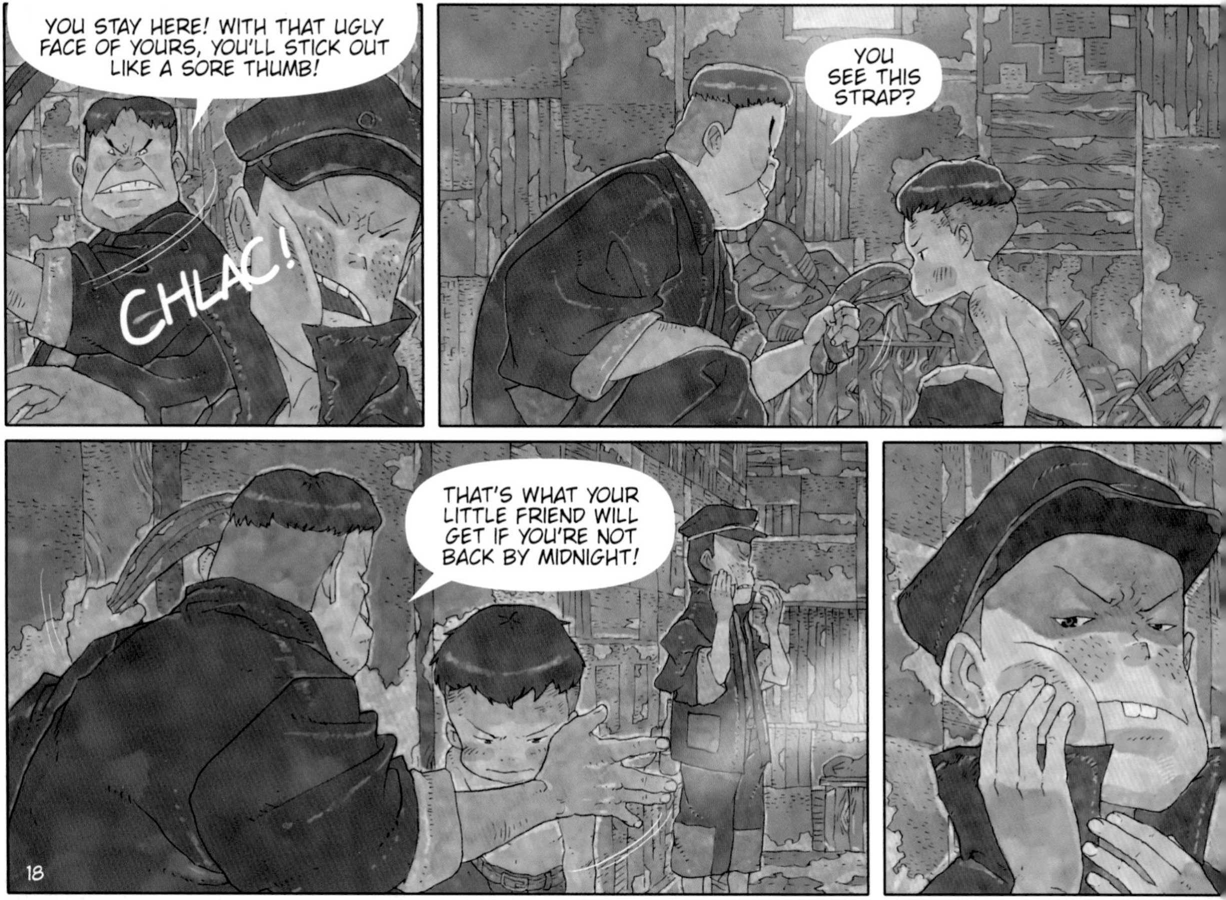
YOU STAY HERE! WITH THAT UGLY FACE OF YOURS, YOU'LL STICK OUT LIKE A SORE THUMB!
CHLAC!
YOU SEE THIS STRAP?
THAT'S WHAT YOUR LITTLE FRIEND WILL GET IF YOU'RE NOT BACK BY MIDNIGHT!

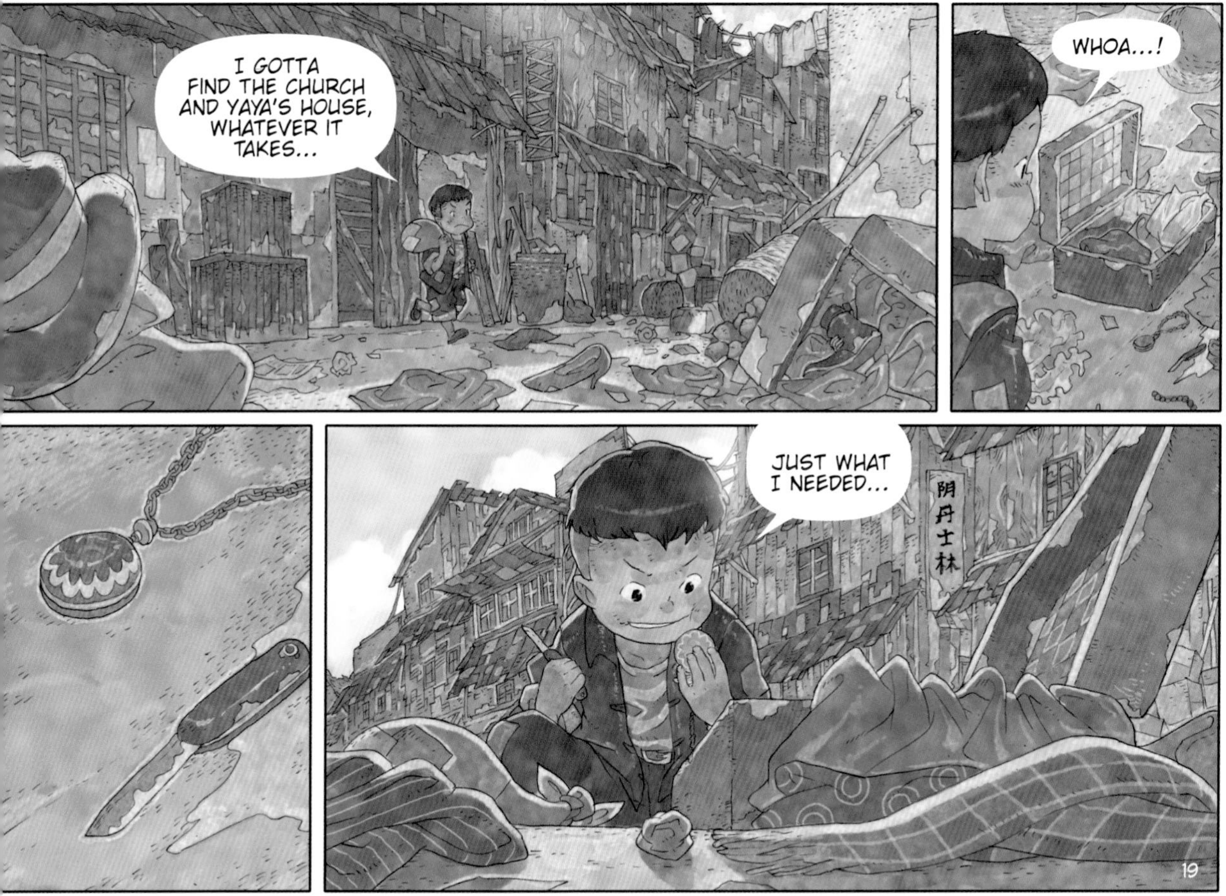
I GOTTA FIND THE CHURCH AND YAYA'S HOUSE, WHATEVER IT TAKES...
WHOA...!
JUST WHAT I NEEDED...
阴丹士林

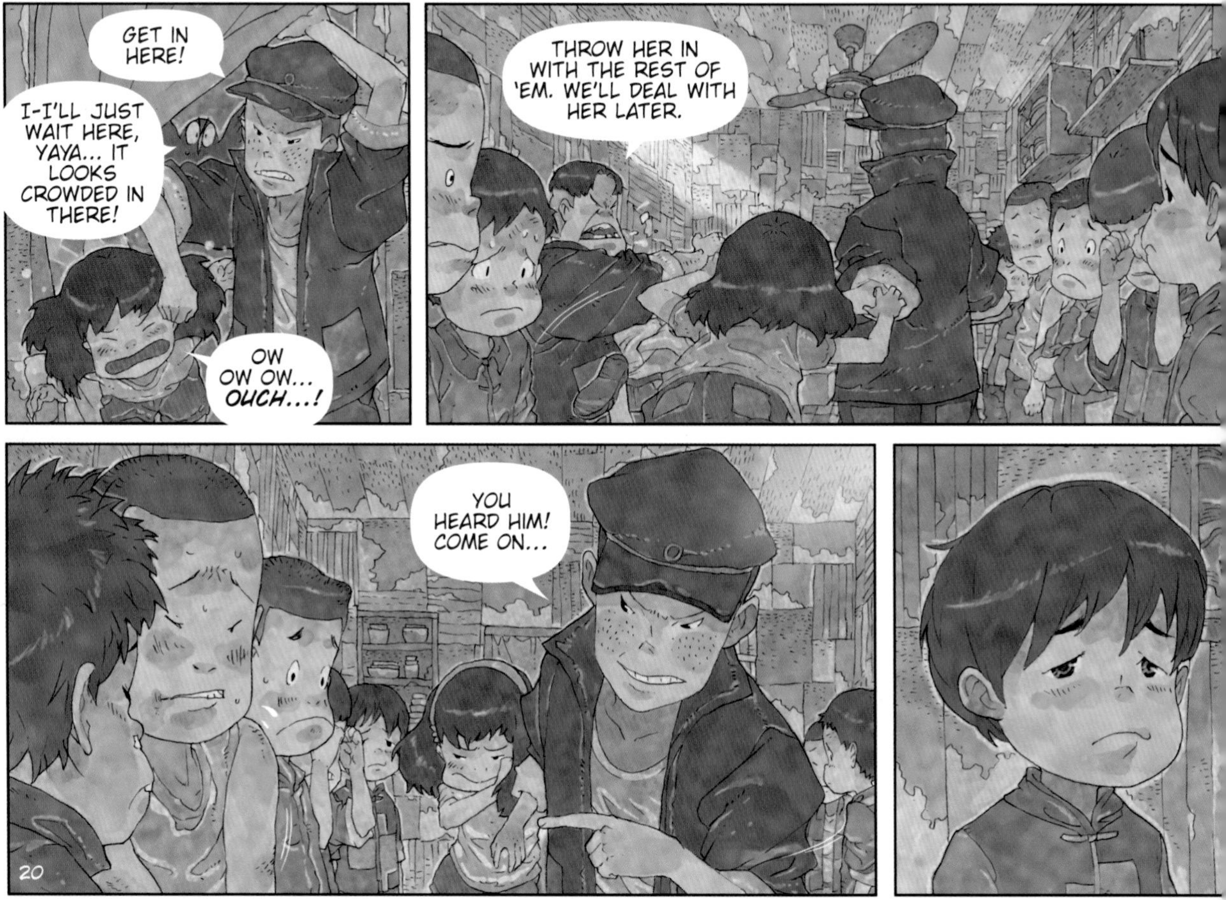
GET IN HERE!
I-I'LL JUST WAIT HERE, YAYA... IT LOOKS CROWDED IN THERE!
OW OW OW... OUCH...!
THROW HER IN WITH THE REST OF 'EM. WE'LL DEAL WITH HER LATER.
YOU HEARD HIM! COME ON...

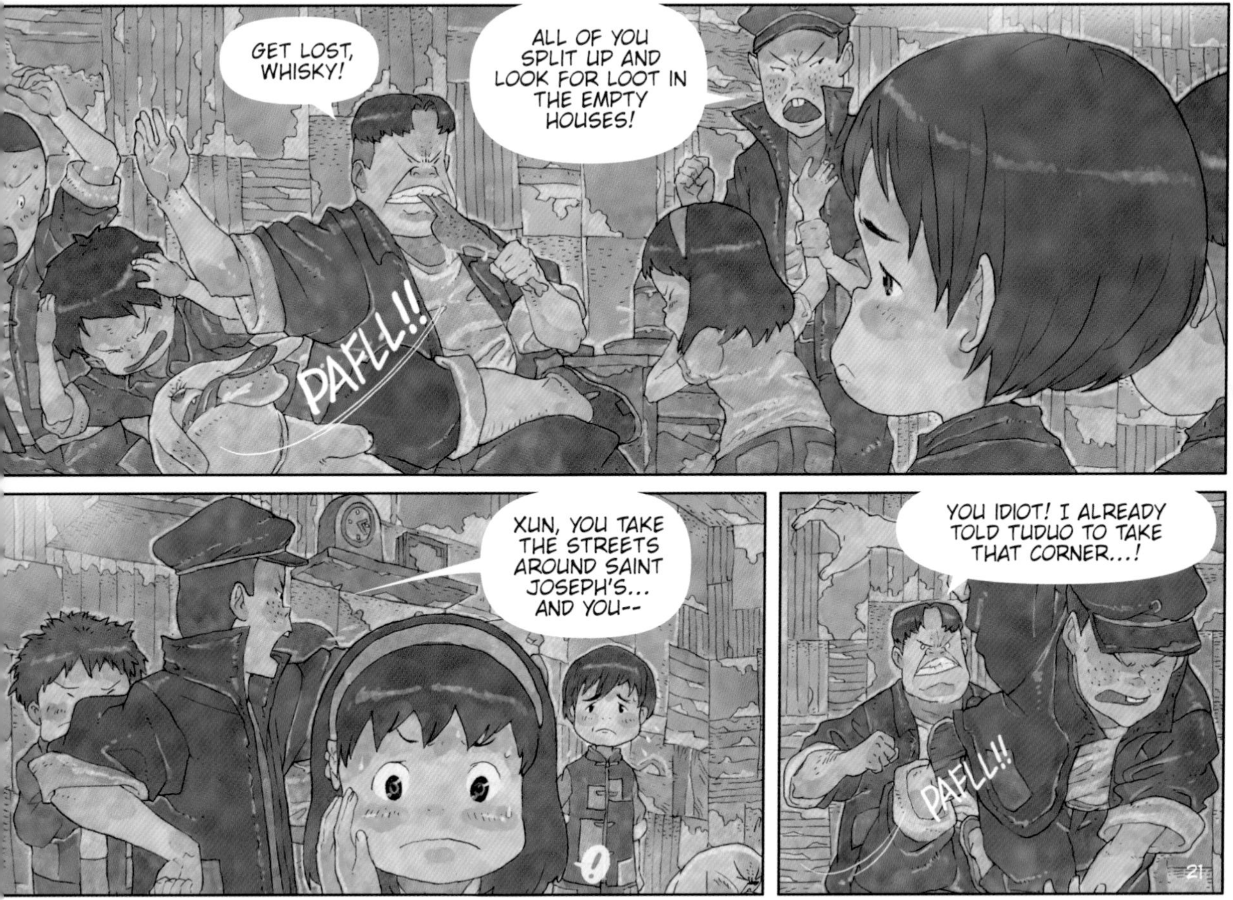
ALL OF YOU SPLIT UP AND LOOK FOR LOOT IN THE EMPTY HOUSES!
GET LOST, WHISKY!
PAFLL!!
XUN, YOU TAKE THE STREETS AROUND SAINT JOSEPH'S... AND YOU--
YOU IDIOT! I ALREADY TOLD TUDUO TO TAKE THAT CORNER...!
PAFLL!!

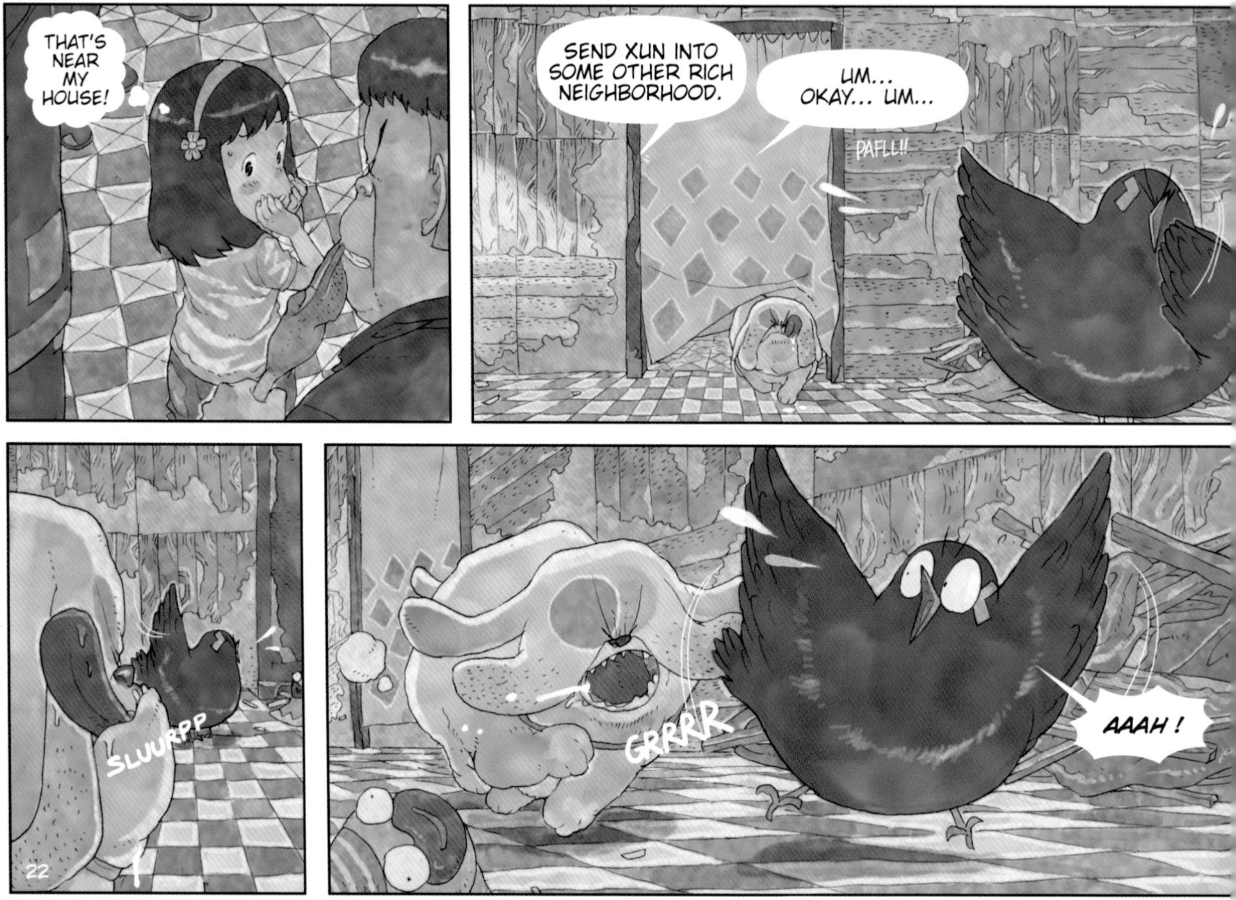
THAT'S NEAR MY HOUSE!
SEND XUN INTO SOME OTHER RICH NEIGHBORHOOD.
UM... OKAY... UM...
PAFLL!!
SLUURPP
GRRRR
AAAH !

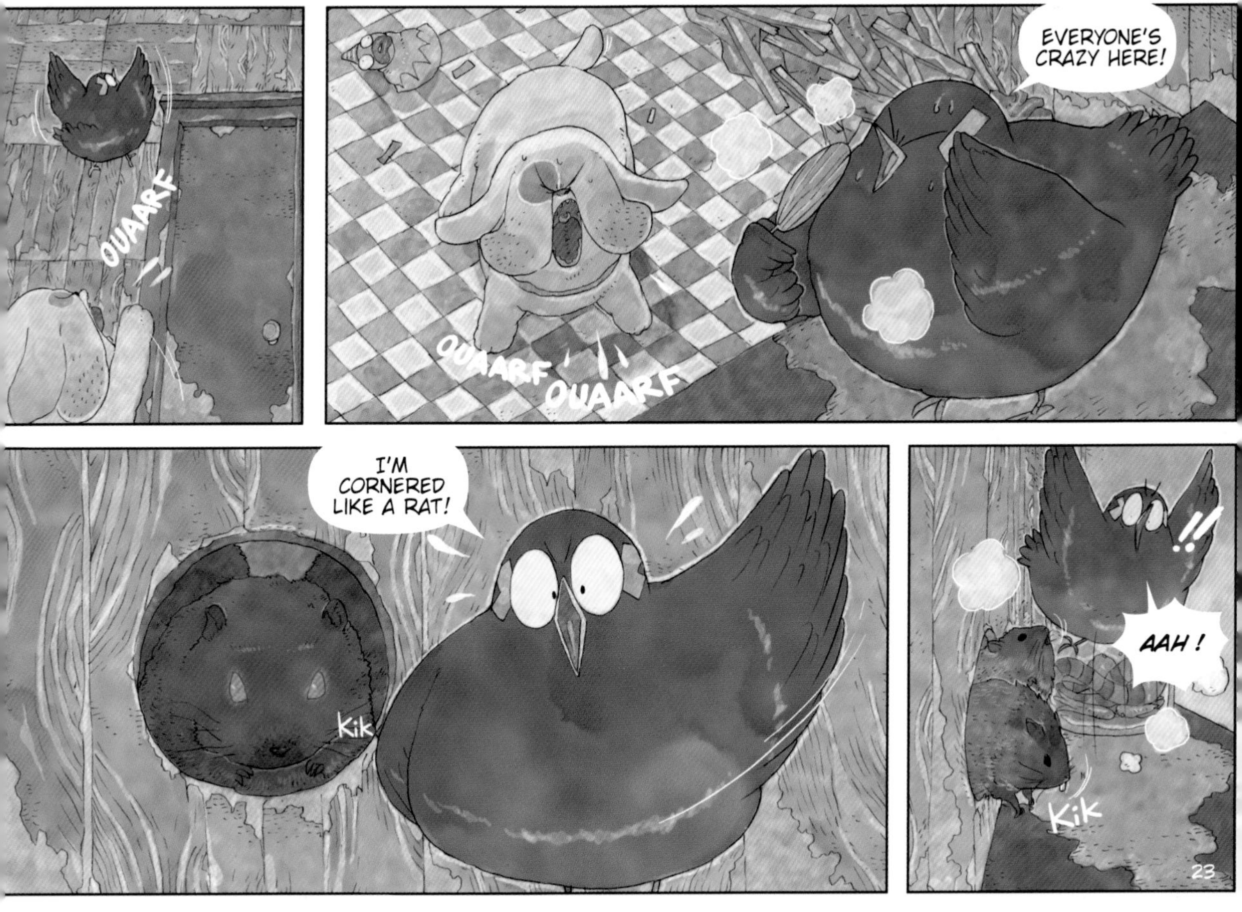
OUAARF
EVERYONE'S CRAZY HERE!
OUAARF
OUAARF
I'M CORNERED LIKE A RAT!
Kik
!!
AAH !
Kik

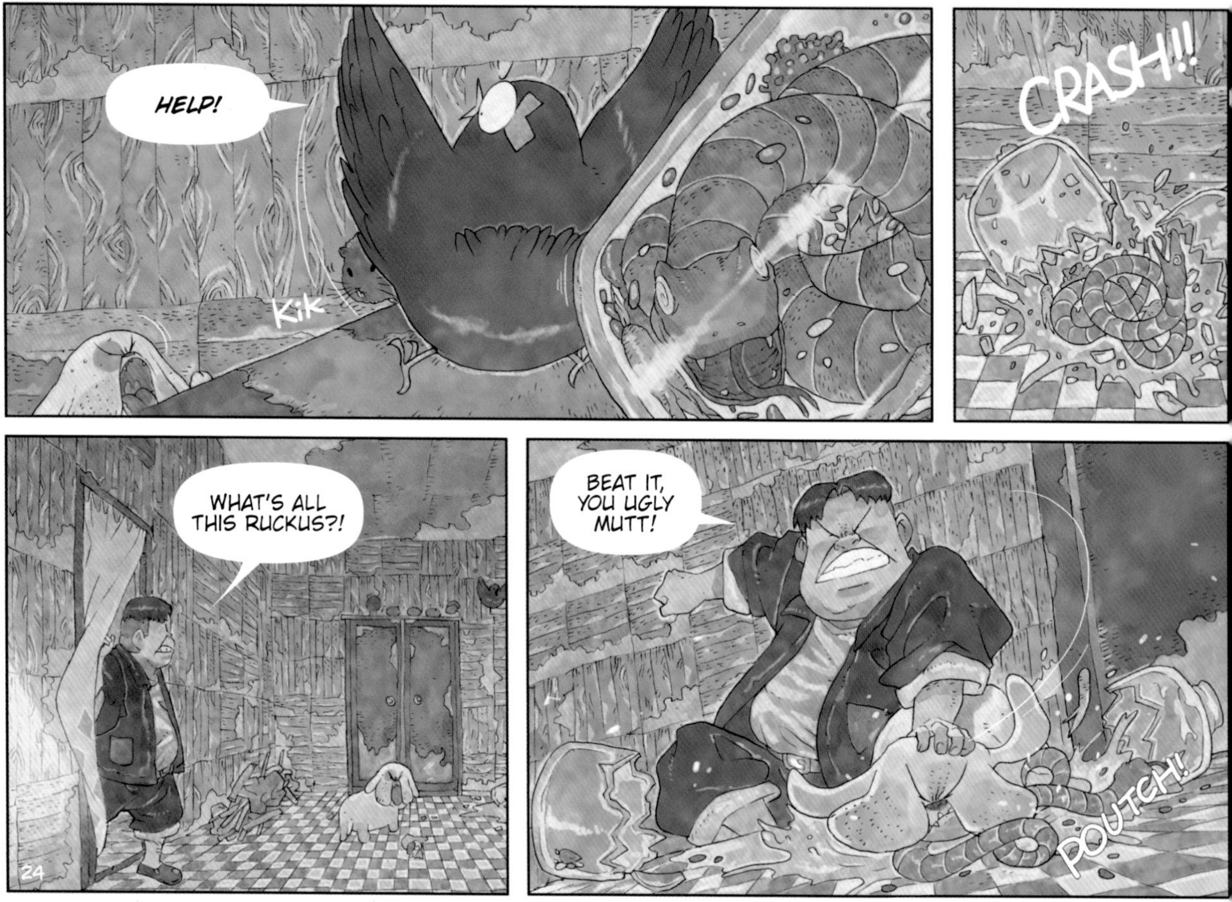
HELP!
Kik
CRASH!!
WHAT'S ALL THIS RUCKUS?!
BEAT IT, YOU UGLY MUTT!
POUTCH!

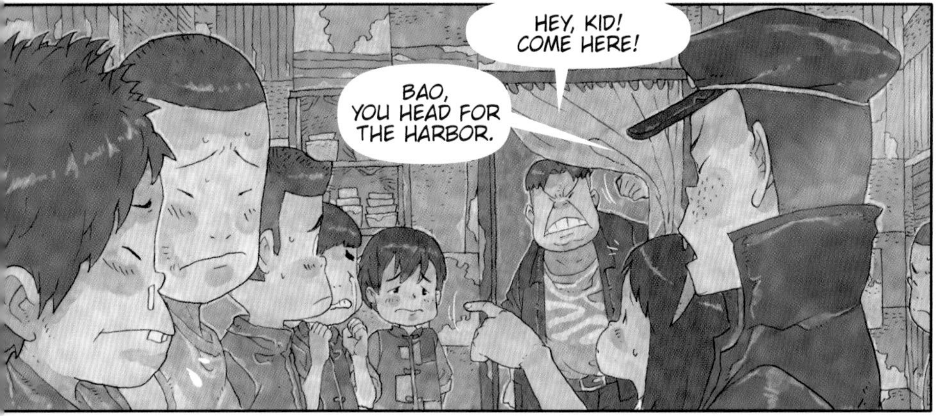
HEY, KID! COME HERE!
BAO, YOU HEAD FOR THE HARBOR.

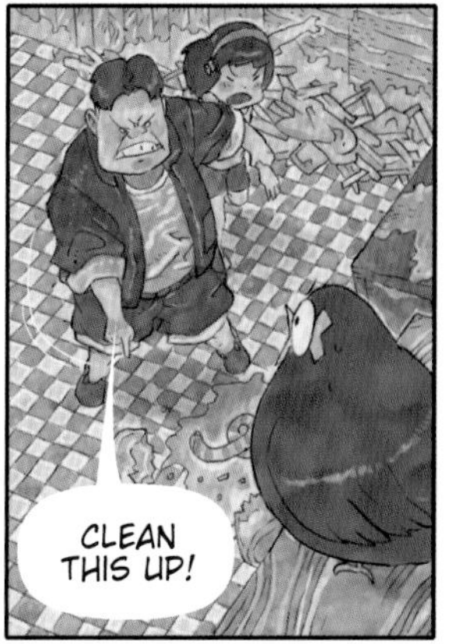
CLEAN THIS UP!

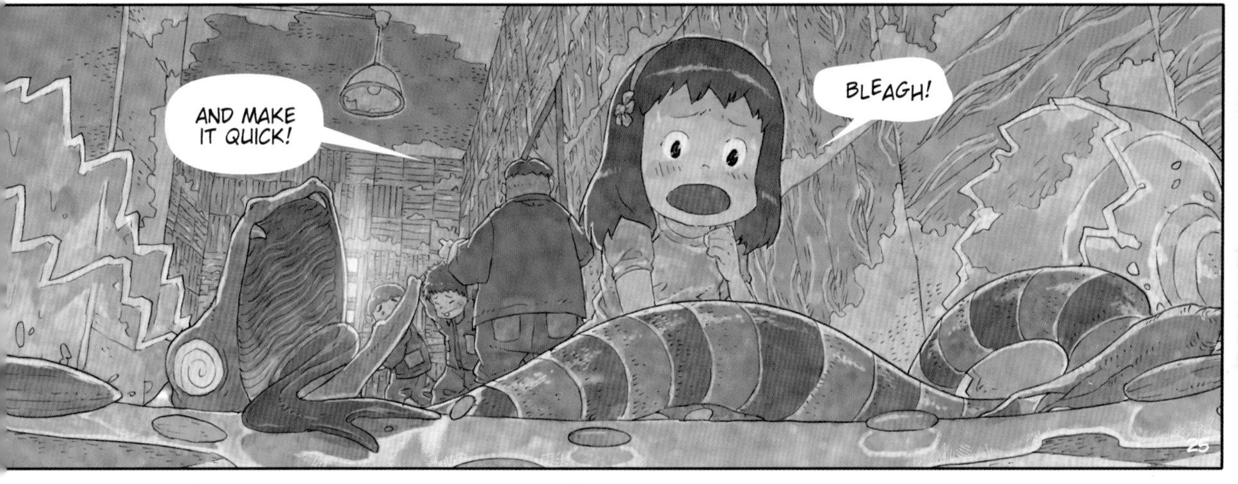
AND MAKE IT QUICK!
BLEAGH!

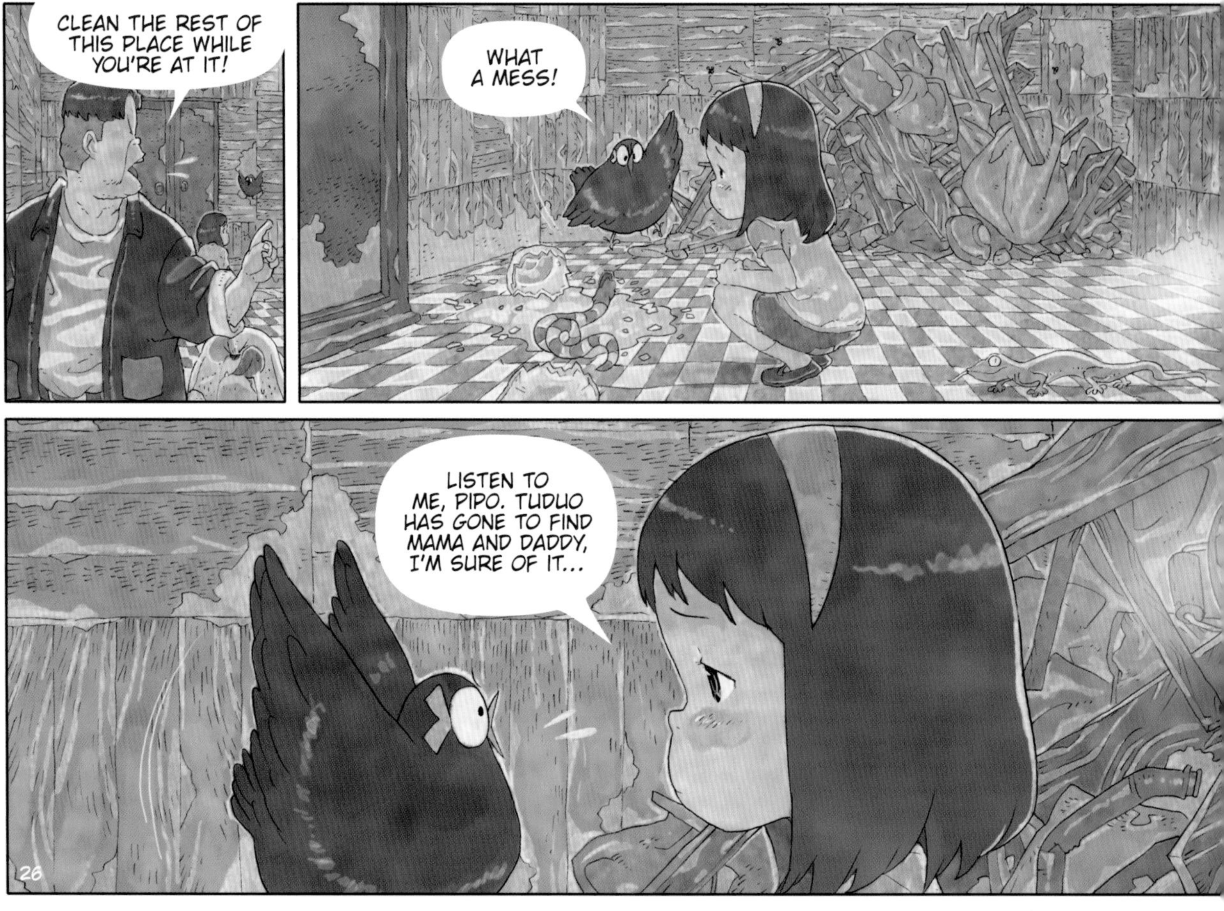
CLEAN THE REST OF THIS PLACE WHILE YOU'RE AT IT!
WHAT A MESS!
LISTEN TO ME, PIPO. TUDUO HAS GONE TO FIND MAMA AND DADDY, I'M SURE OF IT...

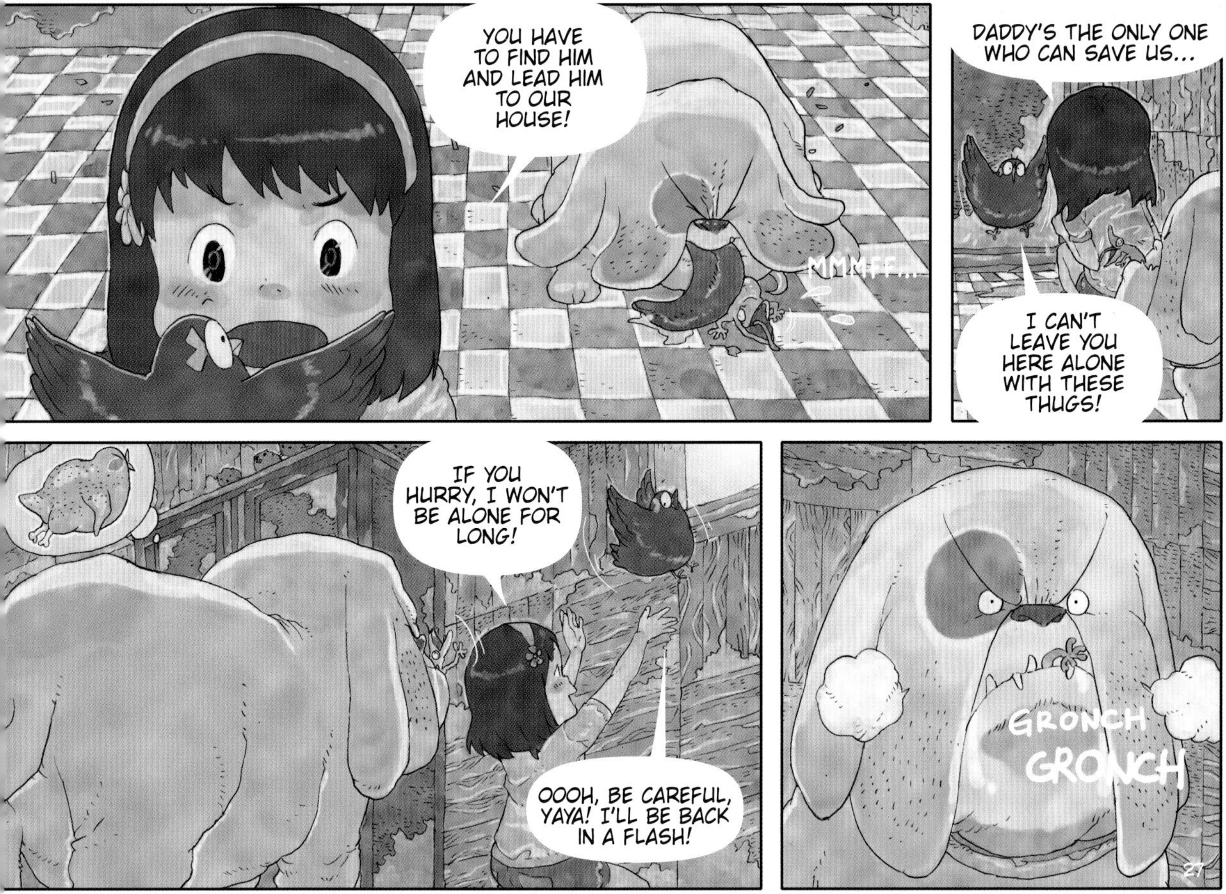
YOU HAVE TO FIND HIM AND LEAD HIM TO OUR HOUSE!
MMMFF...
DADDY'S THE ONLY ONE WHO CAN SAVE US...
I CAN'T LEAVE YOU HERE ALONE WITH THESE THUGS!
IF YOU HURRY, I WON'T BE ALONE FOR LONG!
OOOH, BE CAREFUL, YAYA! I'LL BE BACK IN A FLASH!
GRONCH
GRONCH

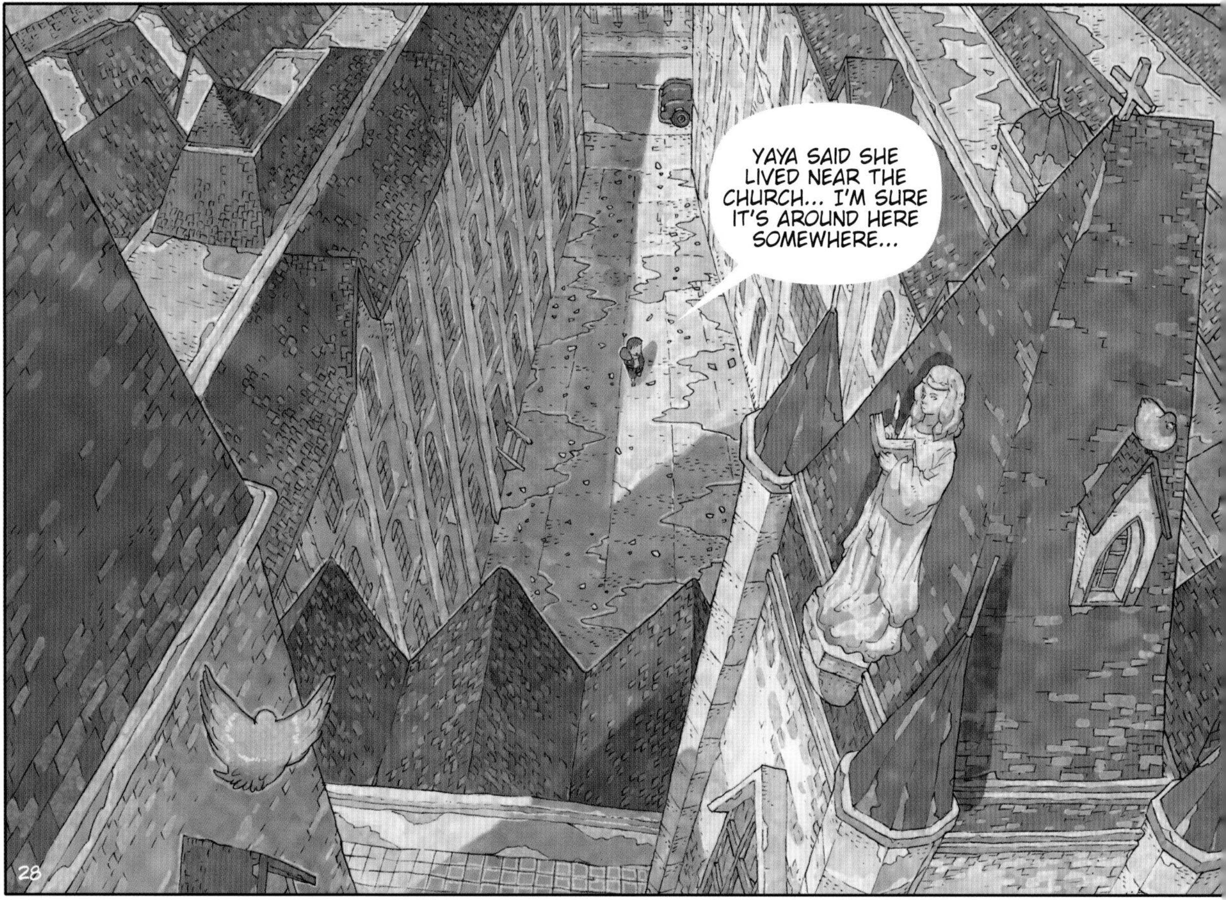
YAYA SAID SHE LIVED NEAR THE CHURCH... I'M SURE IT'S AROUND HERE SOMEWHERE...

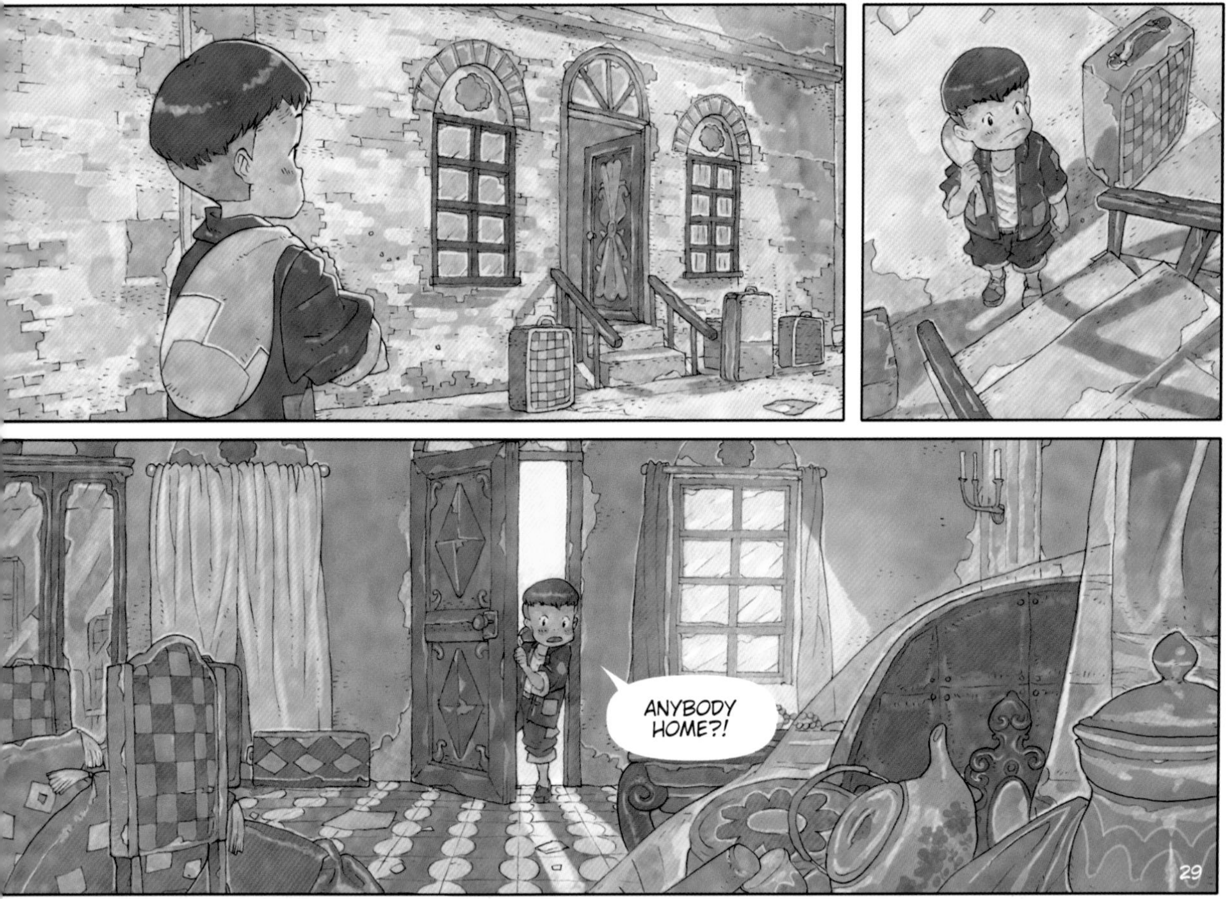
ANYBODY HOME?!

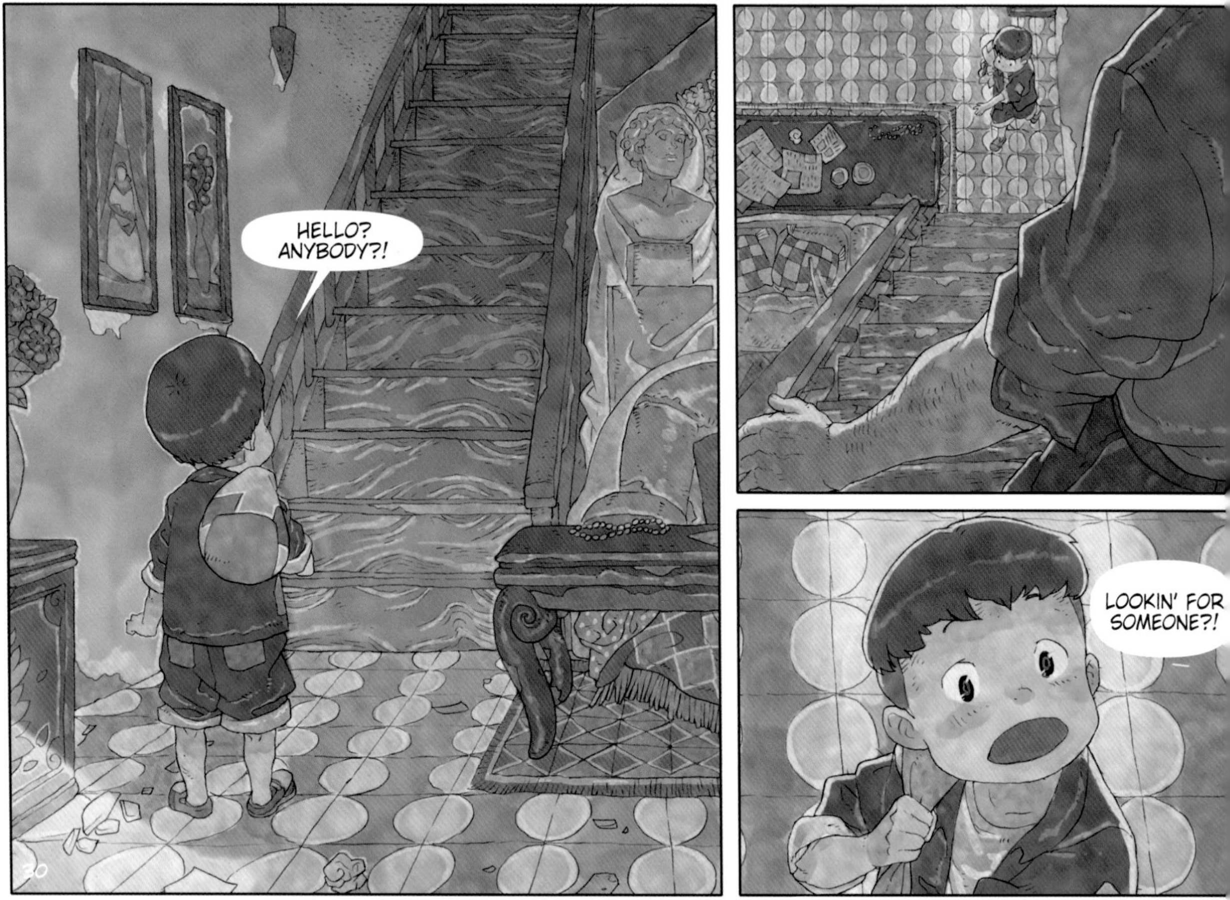
HELLO? ANYBODY?!
LOOKIN' FOR SOMEONE?!

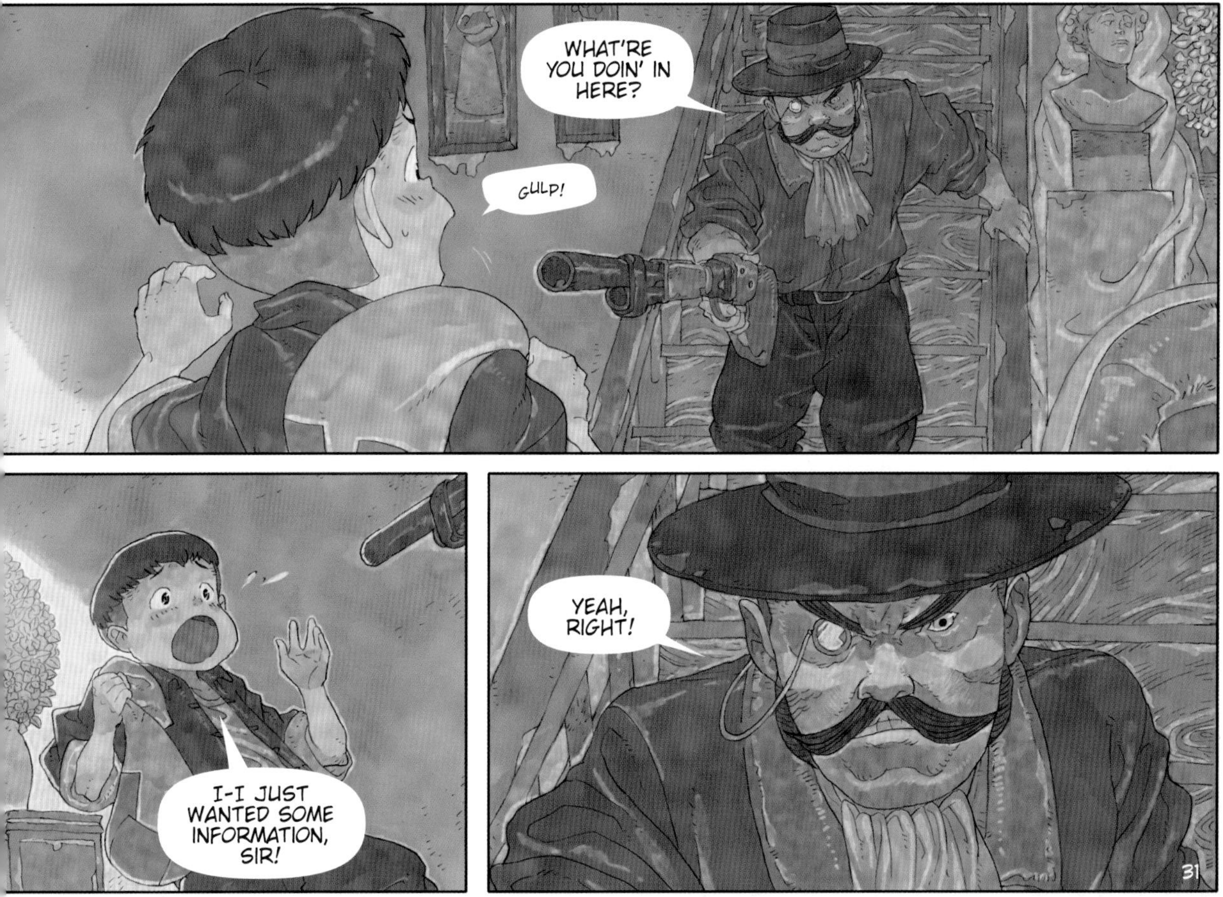
WHAT'RE YOU DOIN' IN HERE?
GULP!
I-I JUST WANTED SOME INFORMATION, SIR!
YEAH, RIGHT!

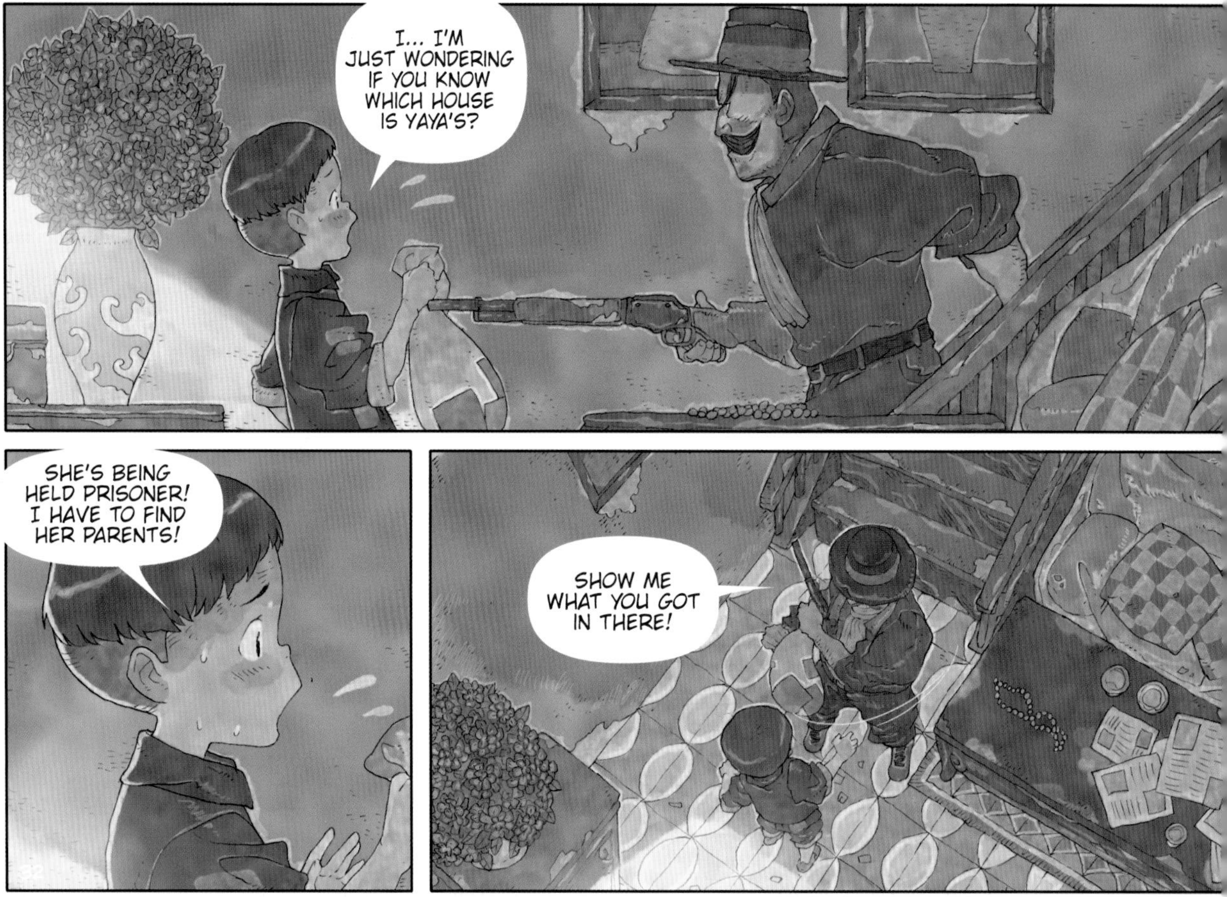
I... I'M JUST WONDERING IF YOU KNOW WHICH HOUSE IS YAYA'S?
SHE'S BEING HELD PRISONER! I HAVE TO FIND HER PARENTS!
SHOW ME WHAT YOU GOT IN THERE!

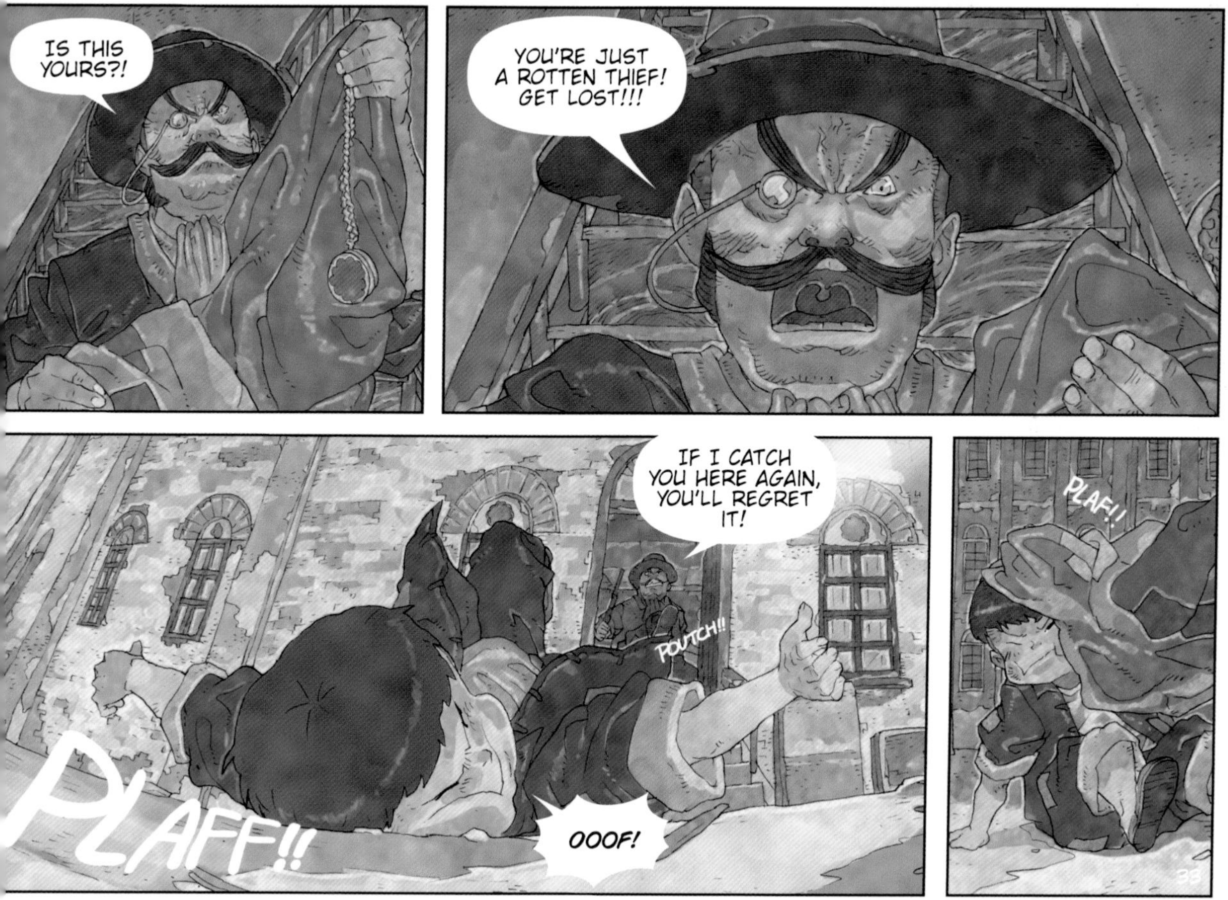
IS THIS YOURS?!
YOU'RE JUST A ROTTEN THIEF! GET LOST!!!
IF I CATCH YOU HERE AGAIN, YOU'LL REGRET IT!
POUTCH!!
PLAFF!!
OOOF!
PLAF!!

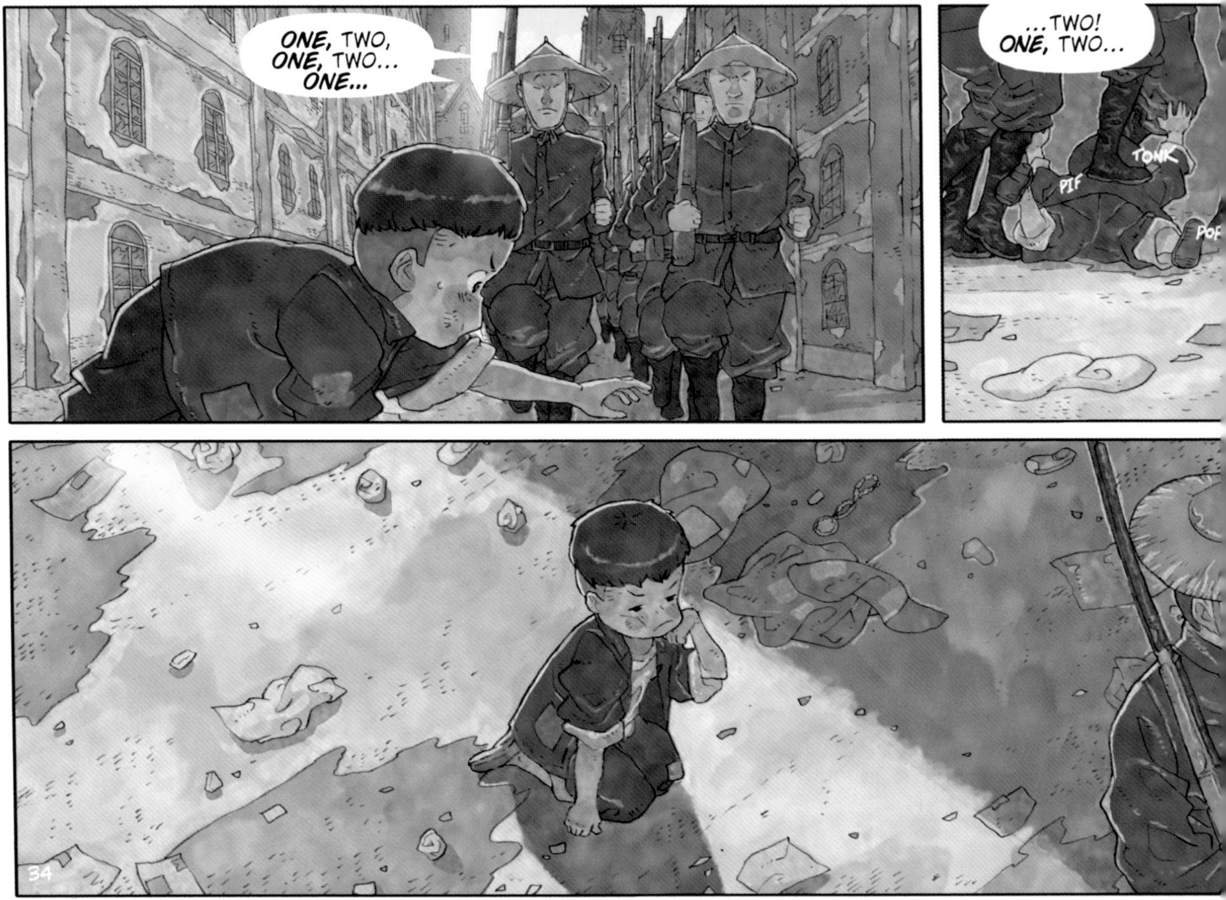
ONE, TWO,
ONE, TWO...
ONE...
...TWO!
ONE, TWO...
PIF
TONK

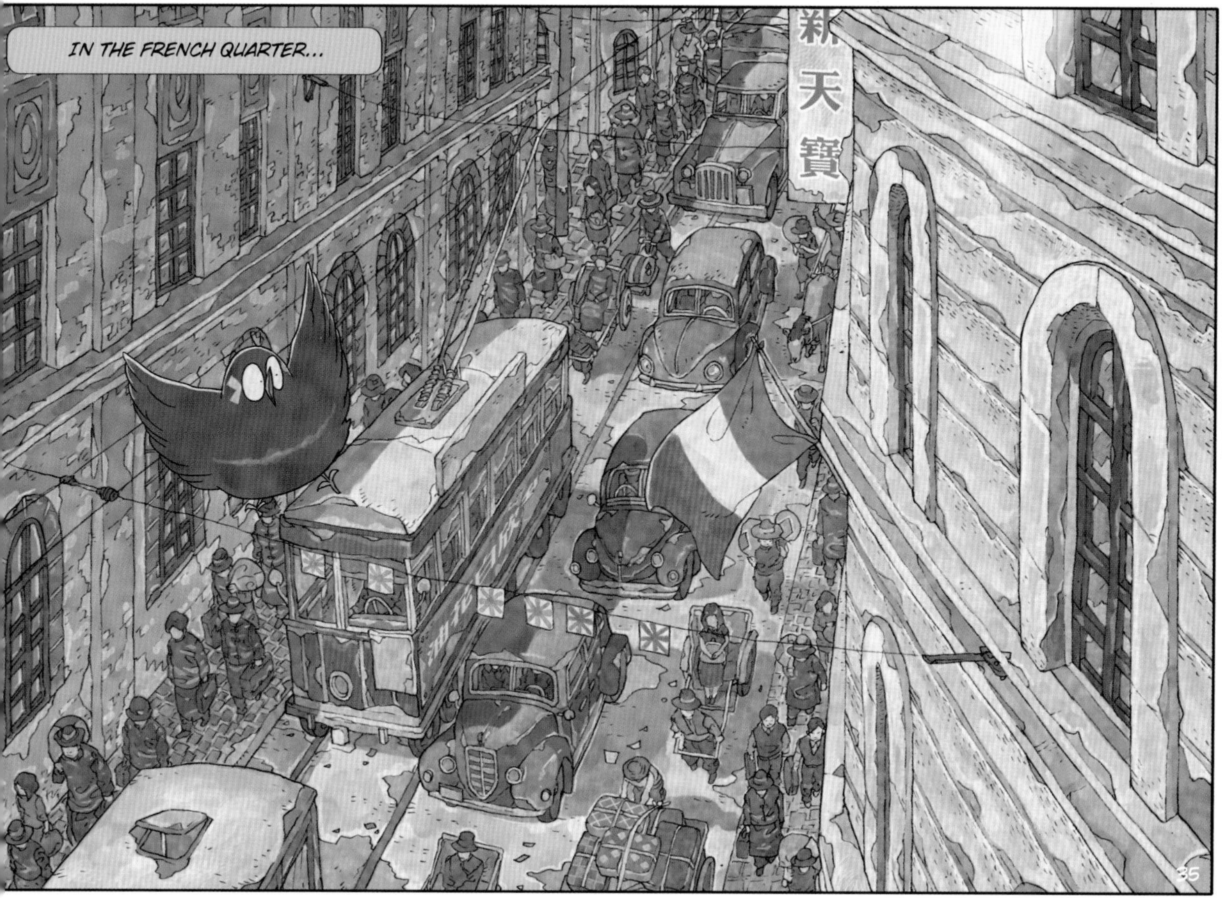
IN THE FRENCH QUARTER...
新天寶

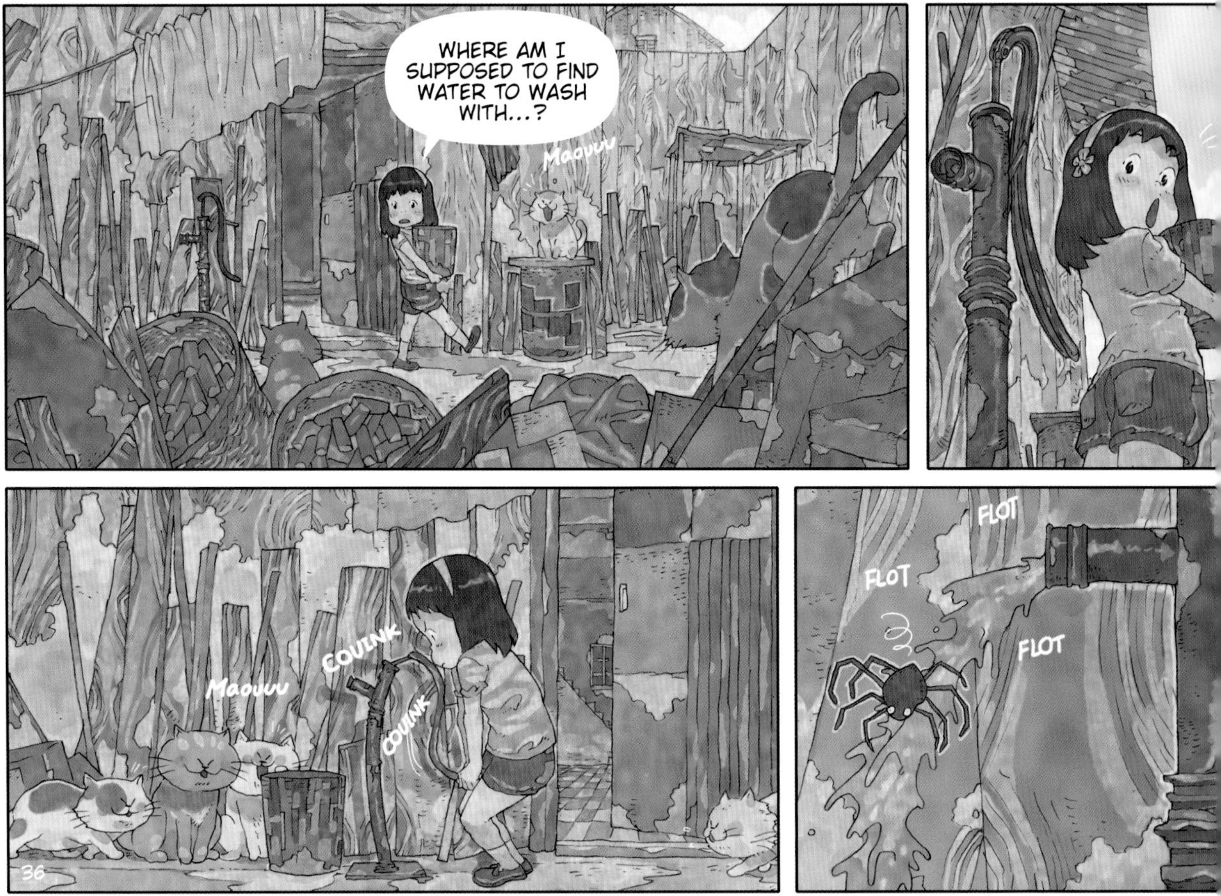
WHERE AM I SUPPOSED TO FIND WATER TO WASH WITH...?
Maouuu
Maouuu
COUINK
COUINK
FLOT
FLOT
FLOT

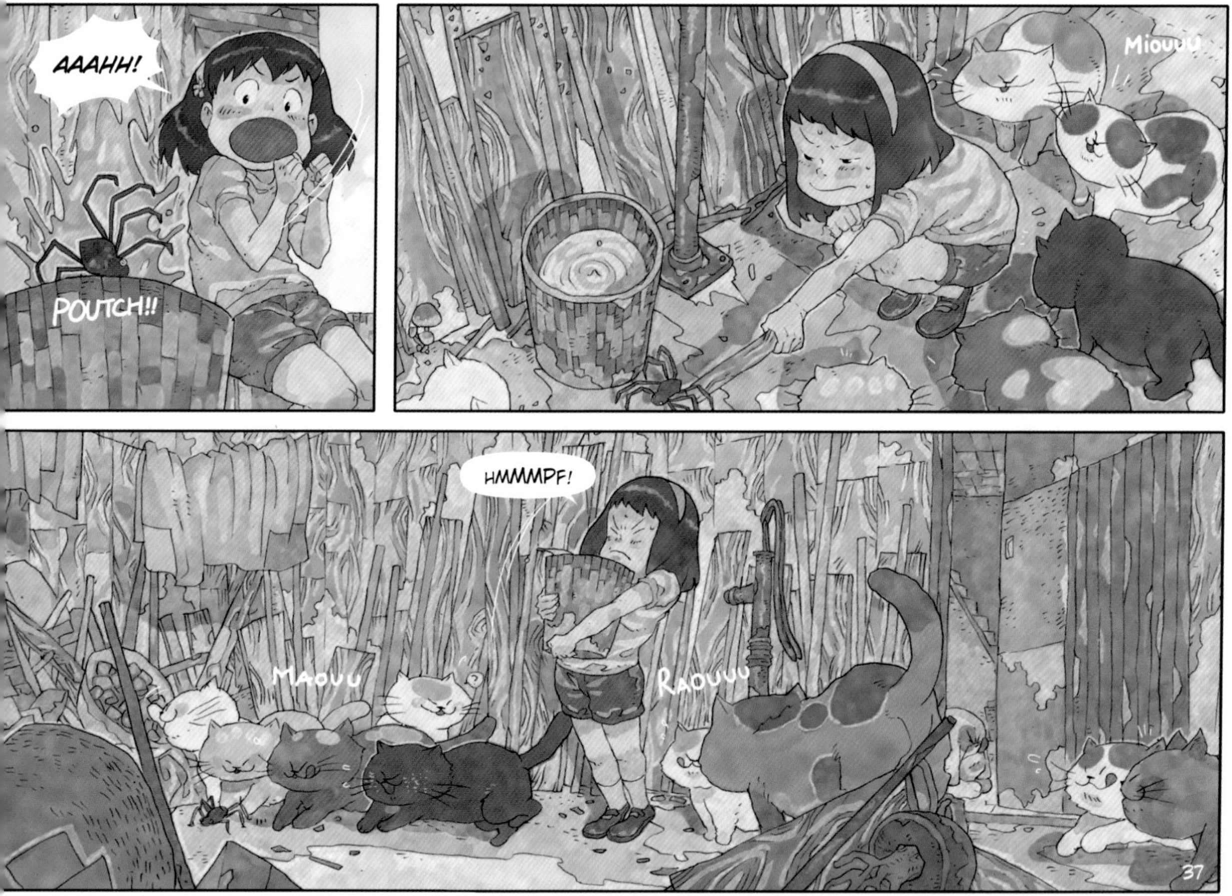
AAAHH!
POUTCH!!
Miouuu
HMMMPF!
Maouu
Raouuu

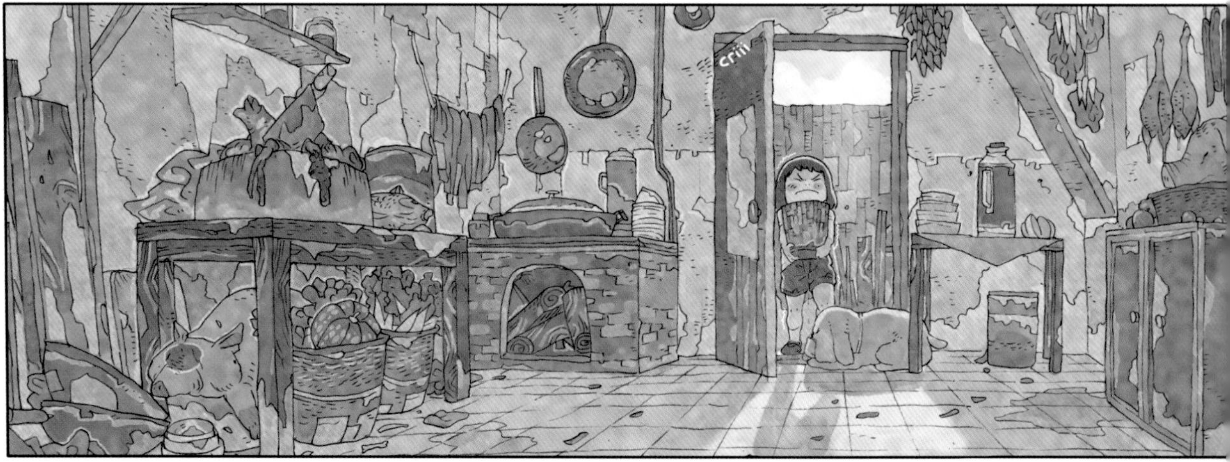
criii

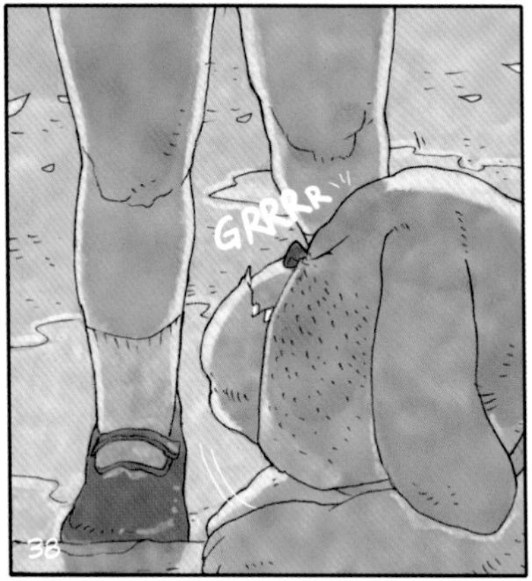
GRRRR

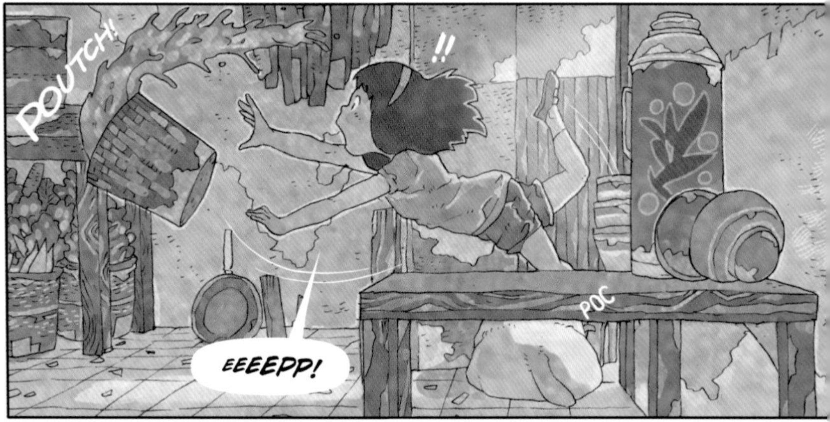
POUTCH!
!!
EEEEPP!
POC

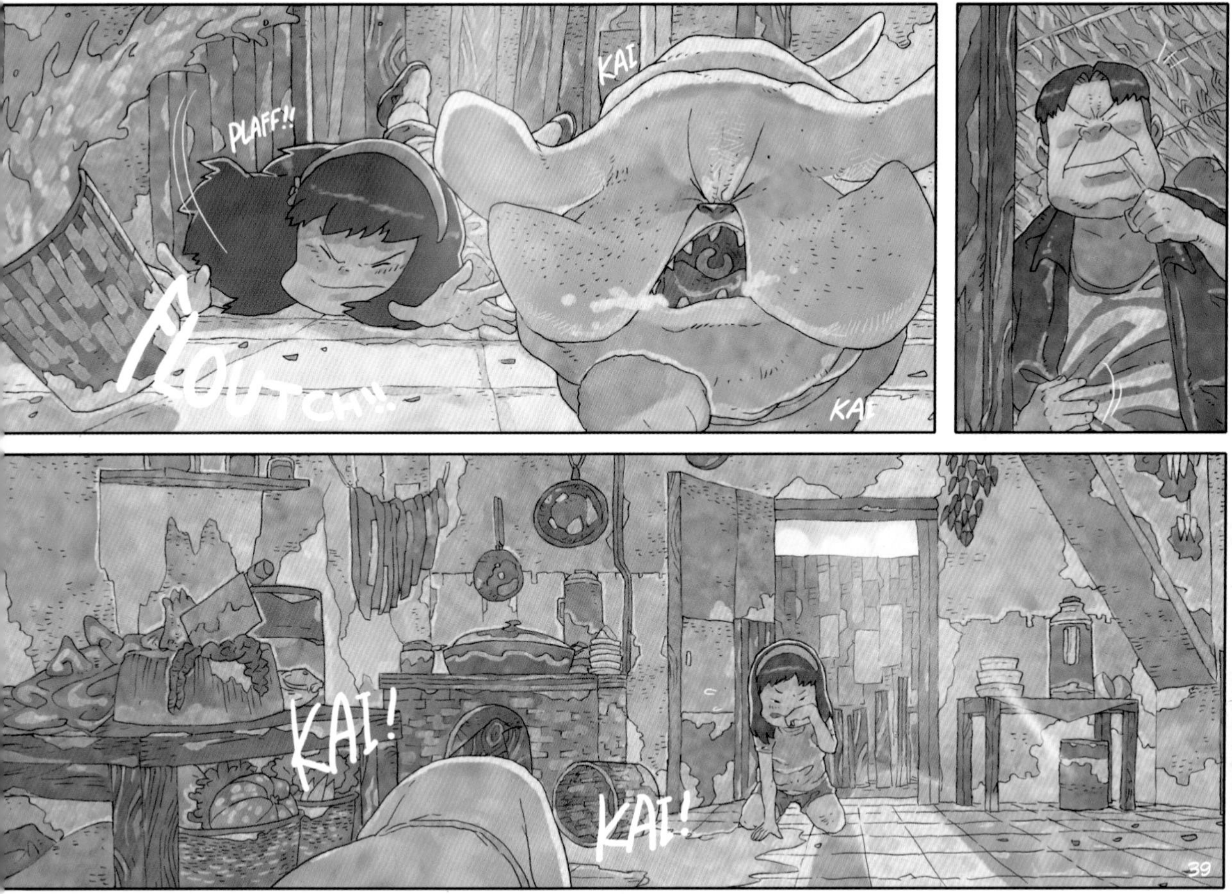
PLAFF!!
KAI
FLOUTCH!!
KAI
KAI!
KAI!

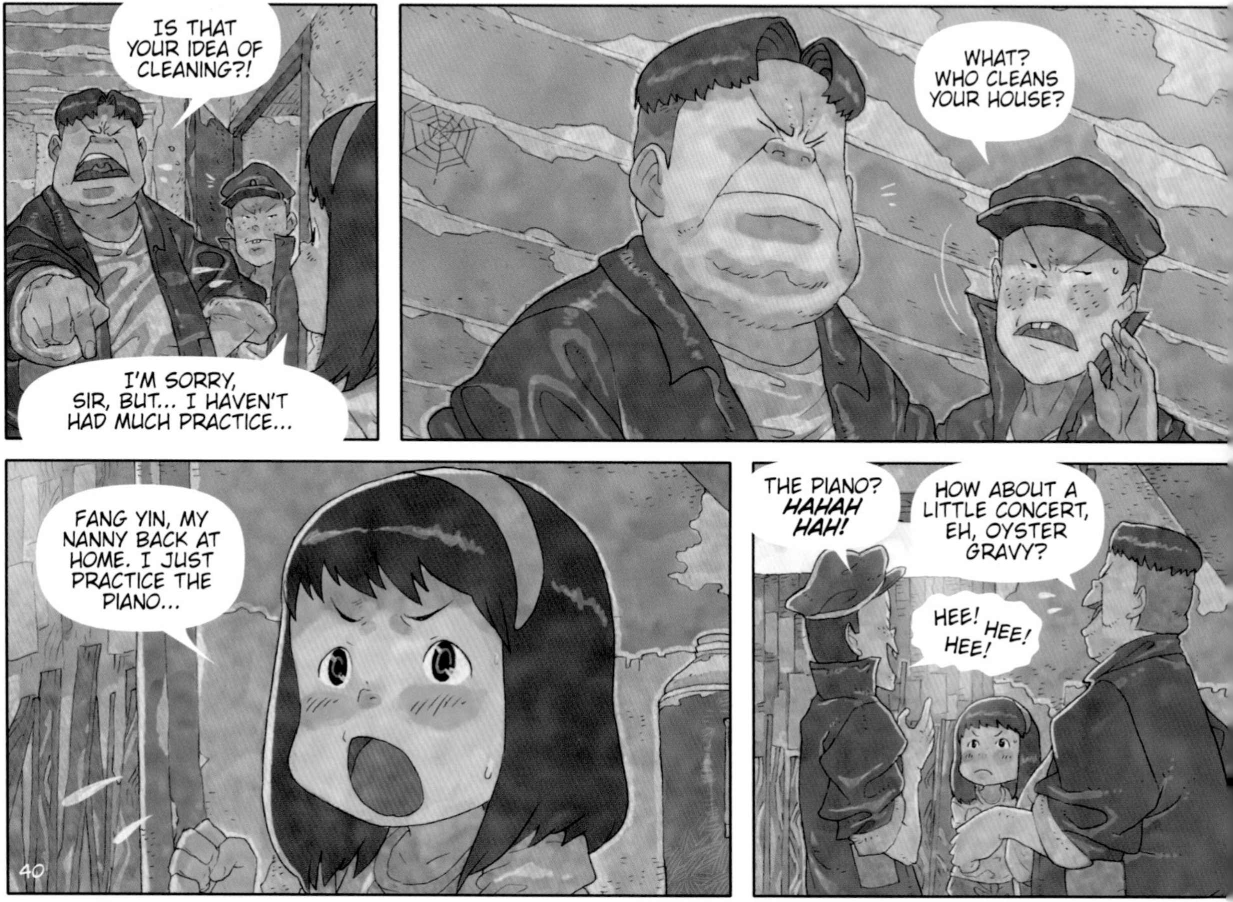
IS THAT YOUR IDEA OF CLEANING?!
I'M SORRY, SIR, BUT... I HAVEN'T HAD MUCH PRACTICE...
WHAT? WHO CLEANS YOUR HOUSE?
FANG YIN, MY NANNY BACK AT HOME. I JUST PRACTICE THE PIANO...
THE PIANO? HAHAH HAH!
HOW ABOUT A LITTLE CONCERT, EH, OYSTER GRAVY?
HEE! HEE! HEE!

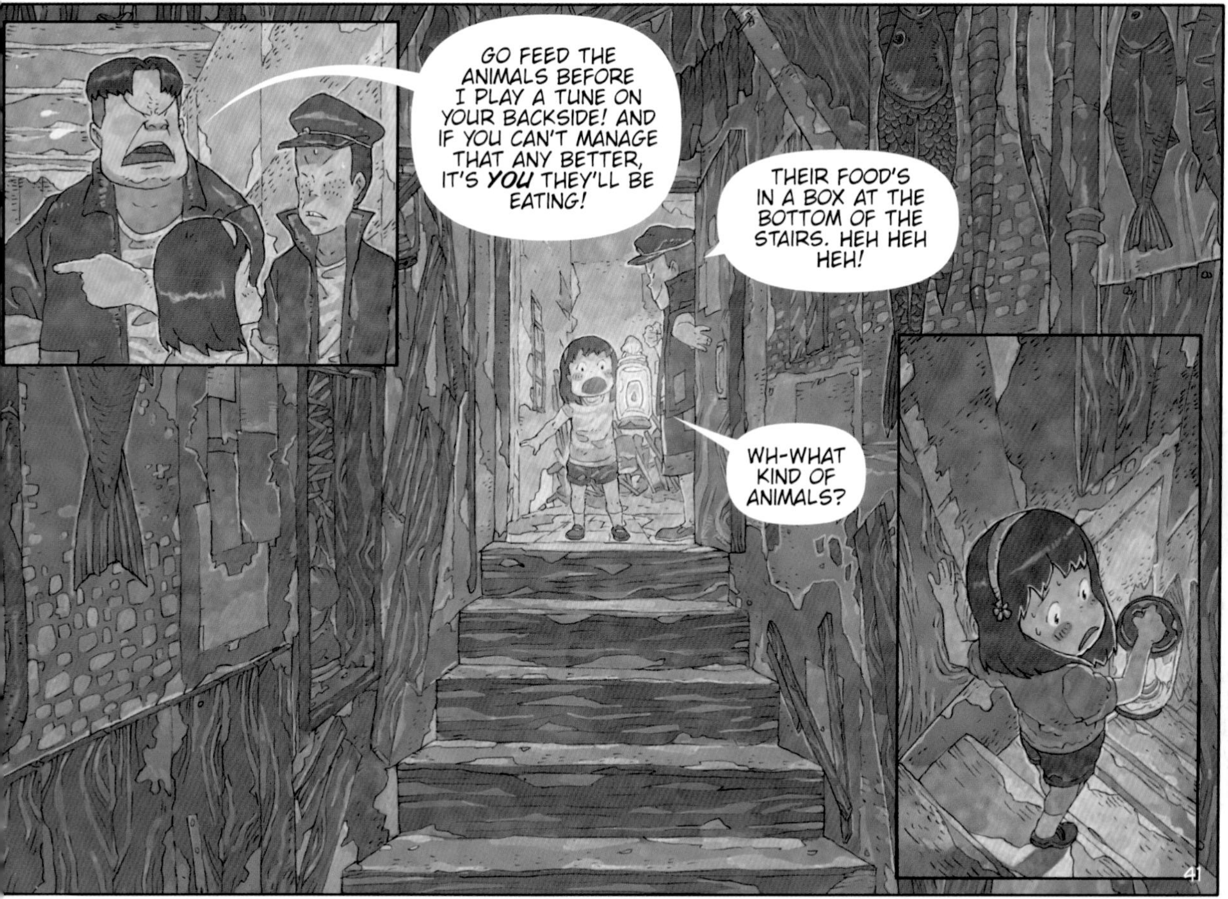
GO FEED THE ANIMALS BEFORE I PLAY A TUNE ON YOUR BACKSIDE! AND IF YOU CAN'T MANAGE THAT ANY BETTER, IT'S ***YOU*** THEY'LL BE EATING!
THEIR FOOD'S IN A BOX AT THE BOTTOM OF THE STAIRS. HEH HEH HEH!
WH-WHAT KIND OF ANIMALS?

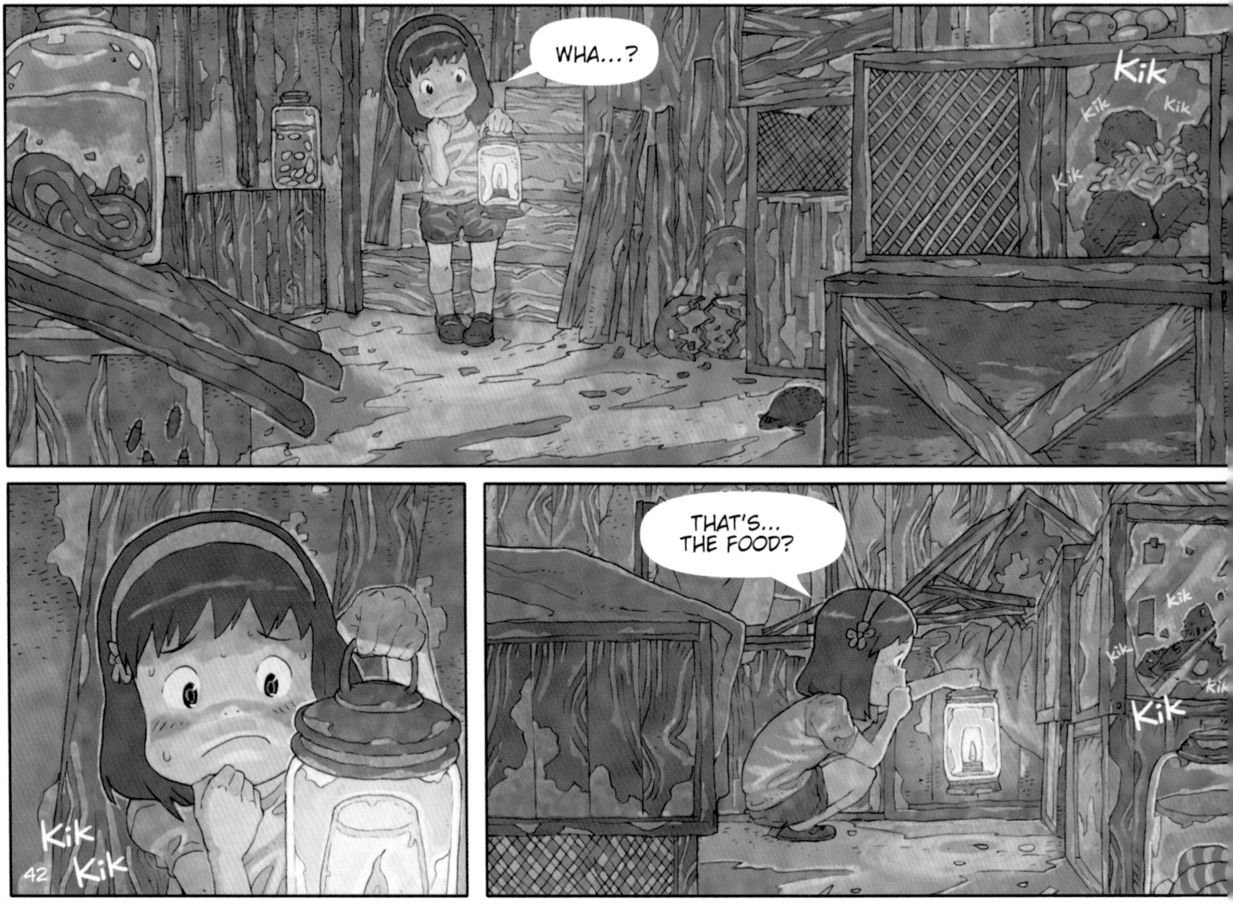
WHA...?
Kik
Kik
Kik
Kik
Kik
Kik
THAT'S... THE FOOD?
kik
kik
Kik

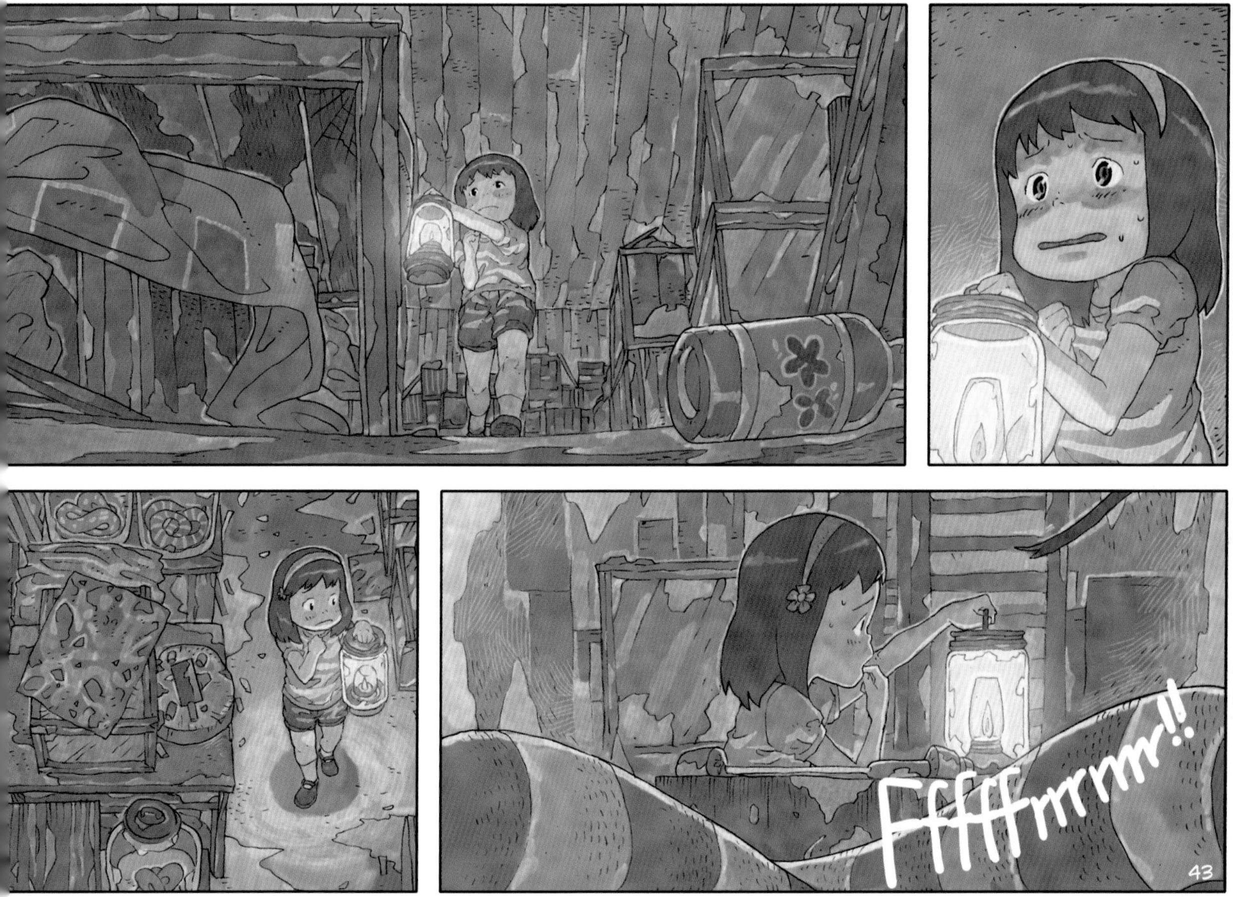
Ffffffrrrrrr!!

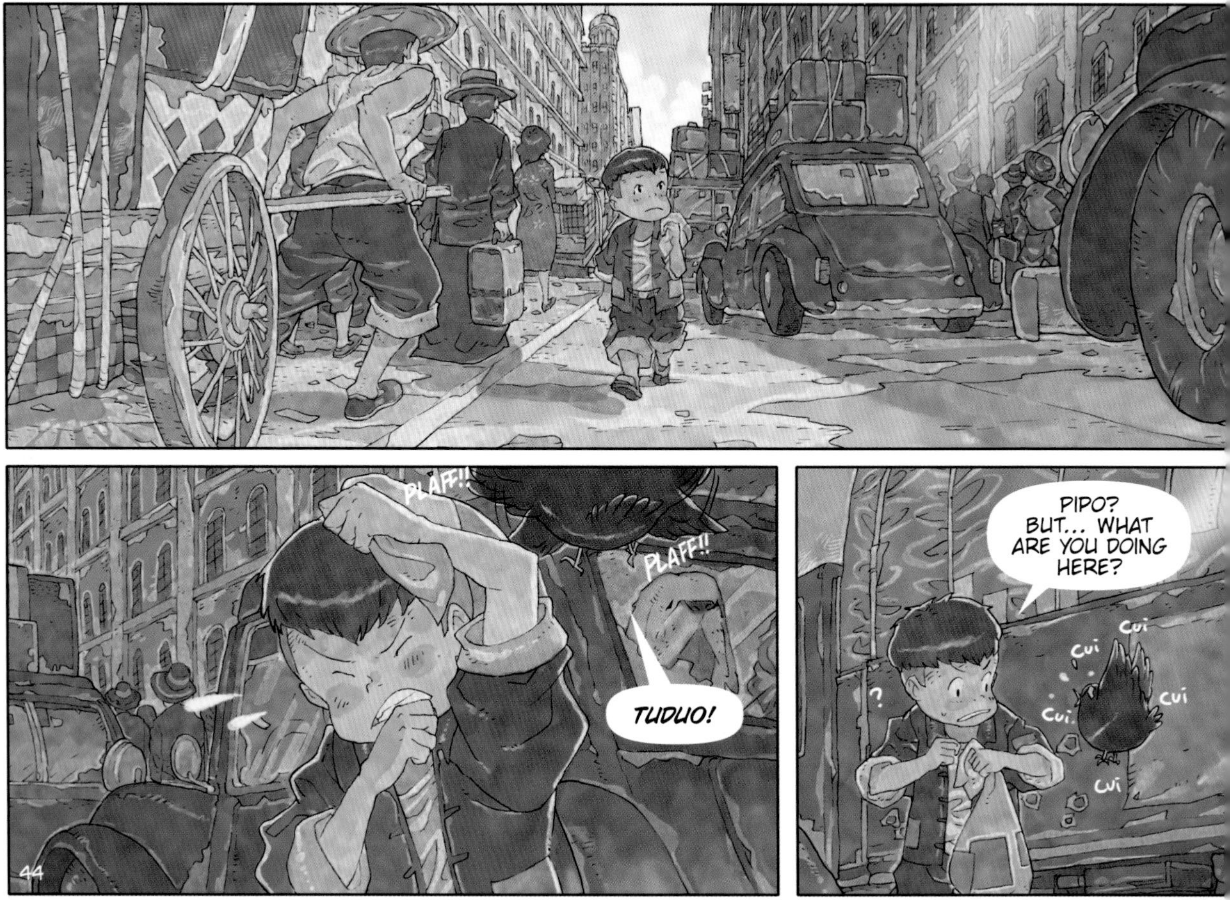
PLAFF!!
PLAFF!!
TUDUO!
PIPO? BUT... WHAT ARE YOU DOING HERE?
?
CUI
CUI
CUI
CUI
CUI

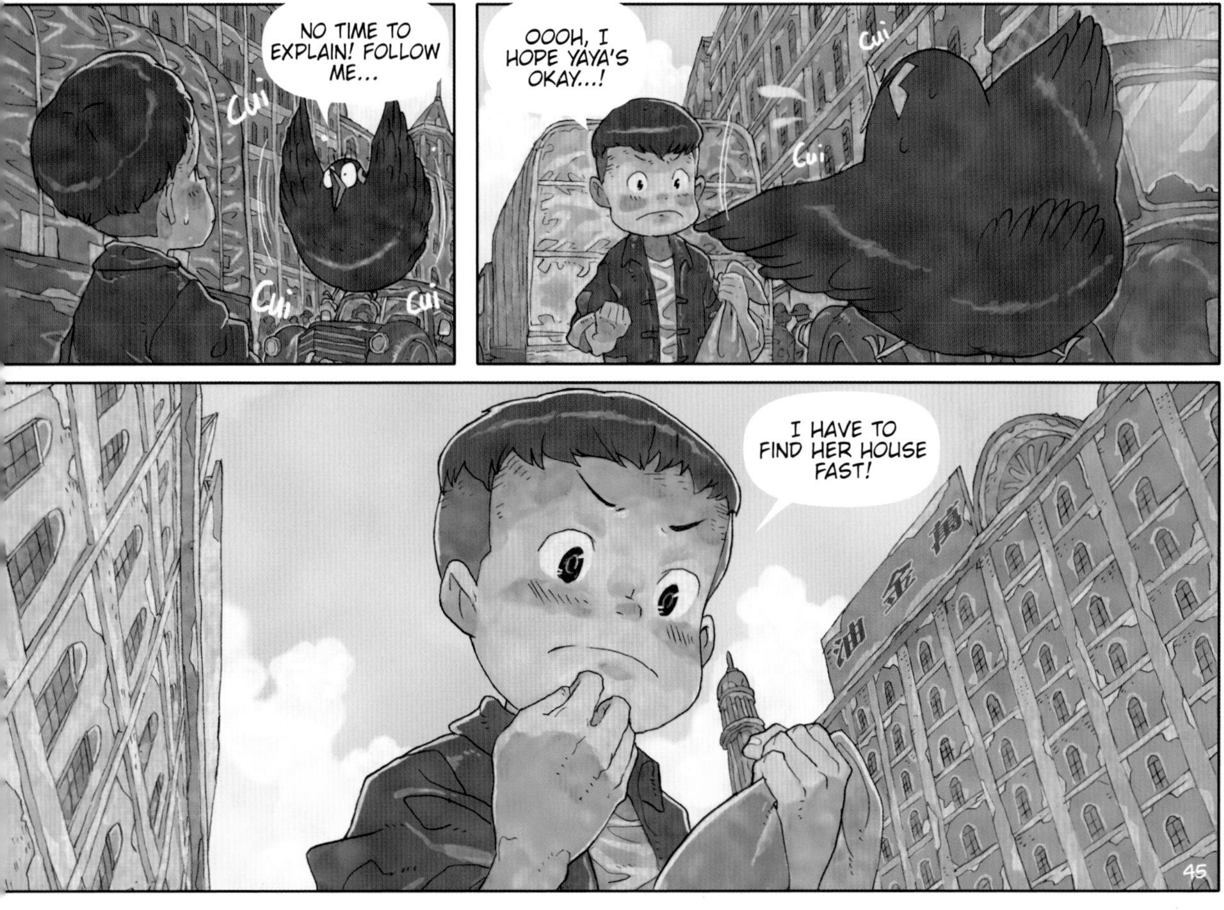
NO TIME TO EXPLAIN! FOLLOW ME...
Cui
Cui
Cui
OOOH, I HOPE YAYA'S OKAY...!
Cui
Cui
I HAVE TO FIND HER HOUSE FAST!

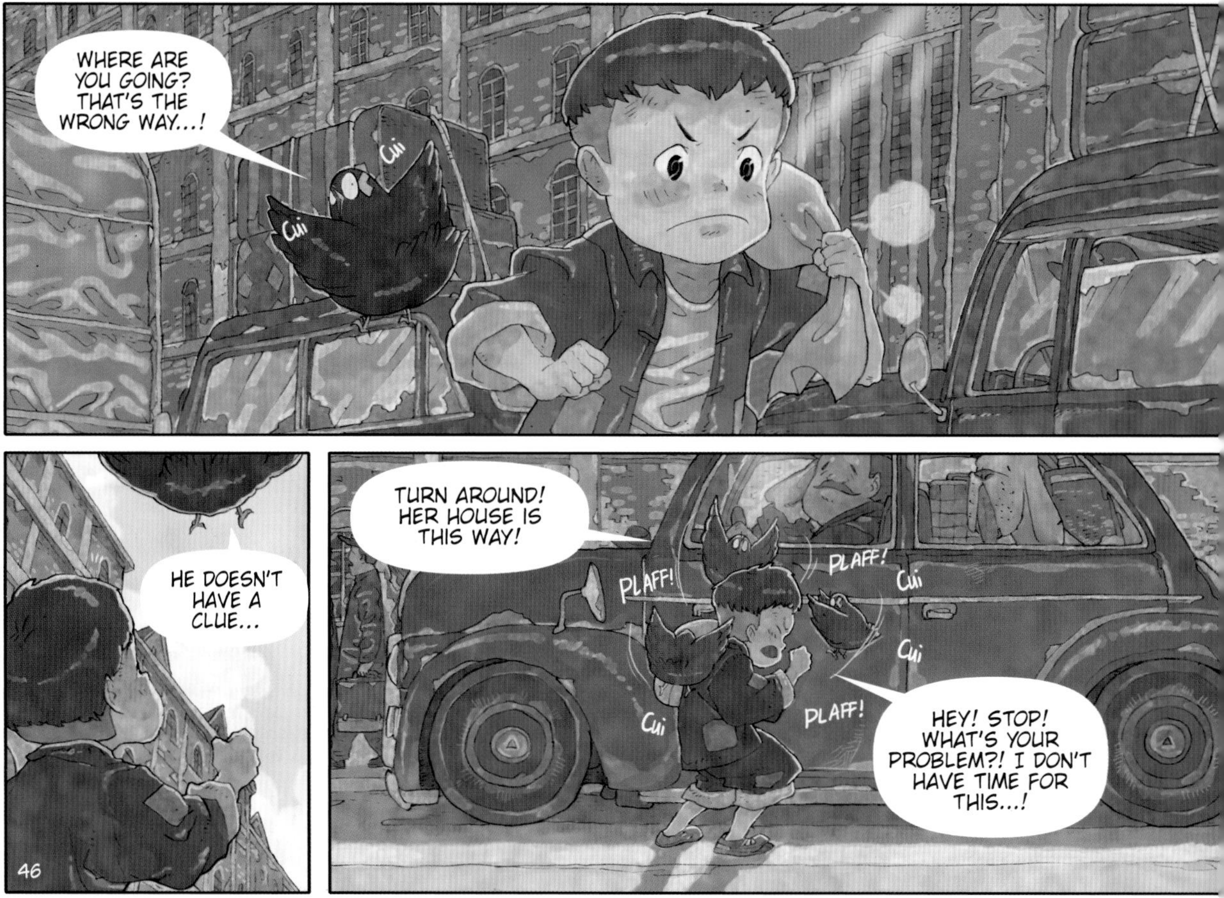
WHERE ARE YOU GOING? THAT'S THE WRONG WAY...!
Cui
Cui
HE DOESN'T HAVE A CLUE...
TURN AROUND! HER HOUSE IS THIS WAY!
PLAFF!
PLAFF!
Cui
Cui
Cui
PLAFF!
HEY! STOP! WHAT'S YOUR PROBLEM?! I DON'T HAVE TIME FOR THIS...!

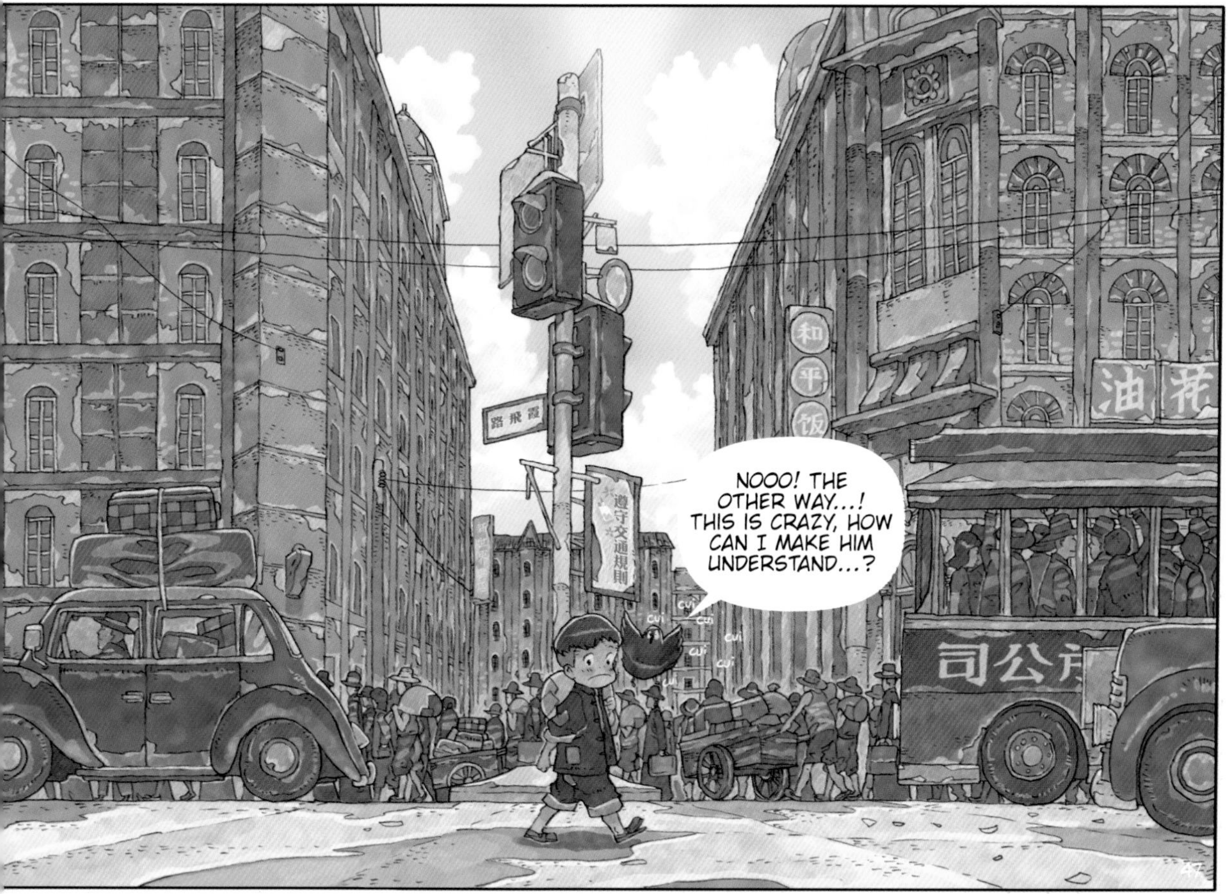
路飛霞
和平饭
遵守交通規則
NOOO! THE OTHER WAY...! THIS IS CRAZY, HOW CAN I MAKE HIM UNDERSTAND...?
cui cui cui cui cui cui cui
司公

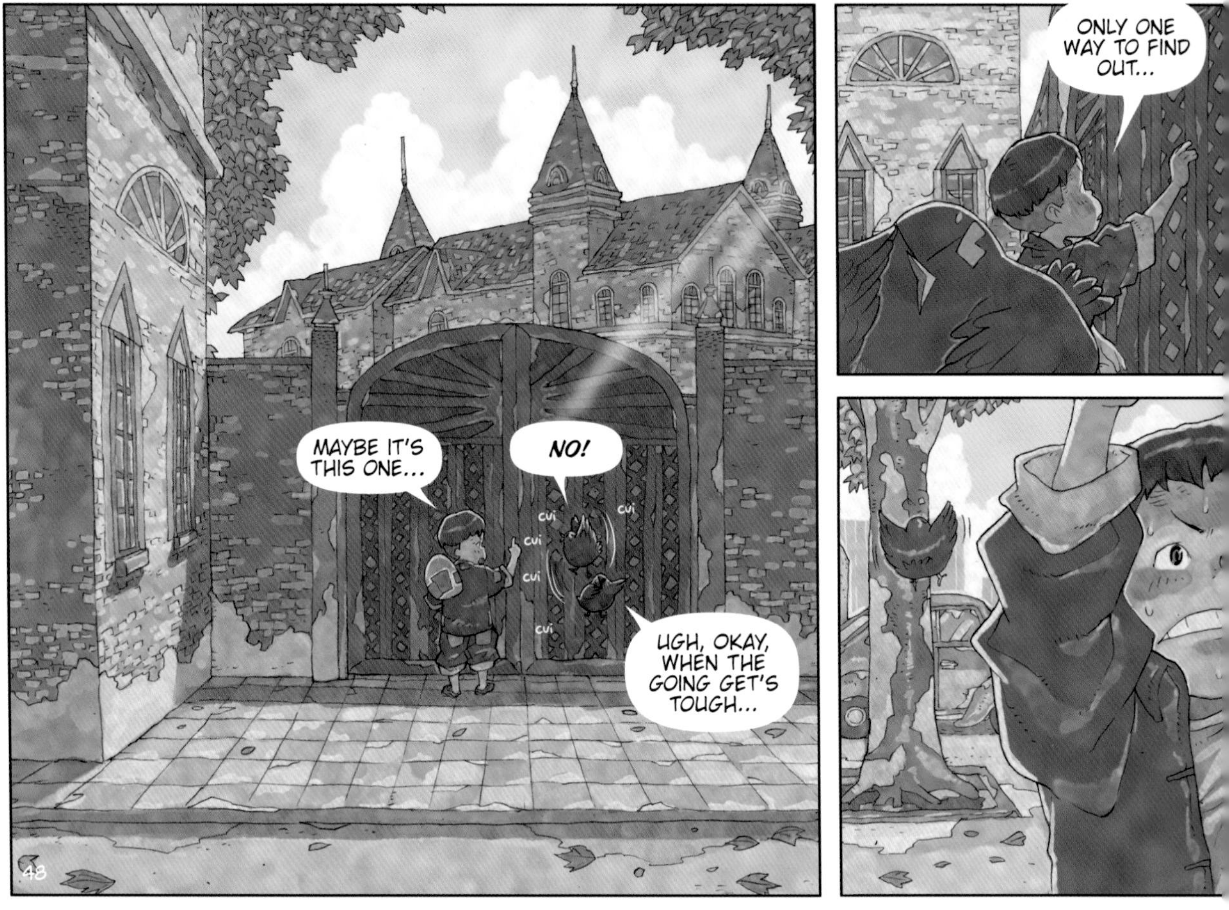
MAYBE IT'S THIS ONE...
NO!
cui
cui
cui
cui
cui
UGH, OKAY, WHEN THE GOING GET'S TOUGH...
ONLY ONE WAY TO FIND OUT...

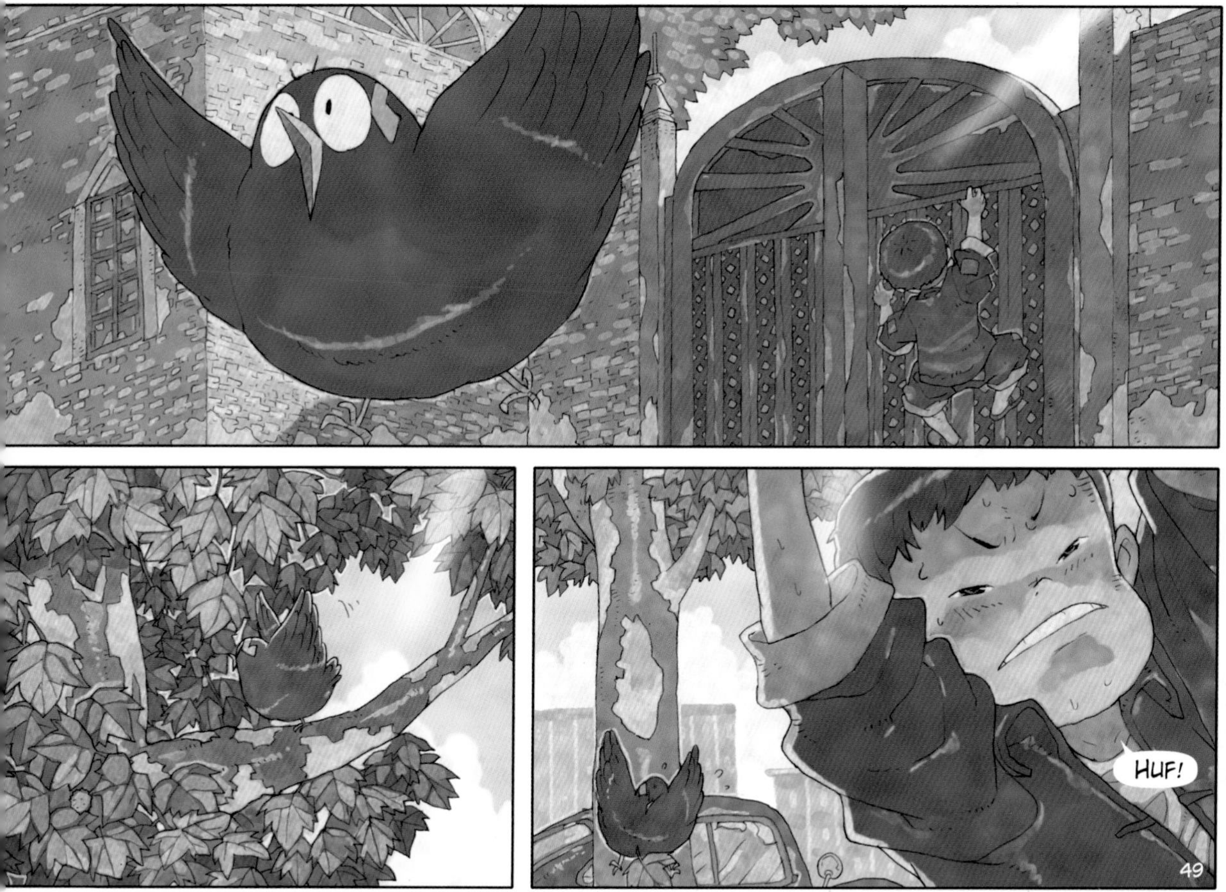
HUF!

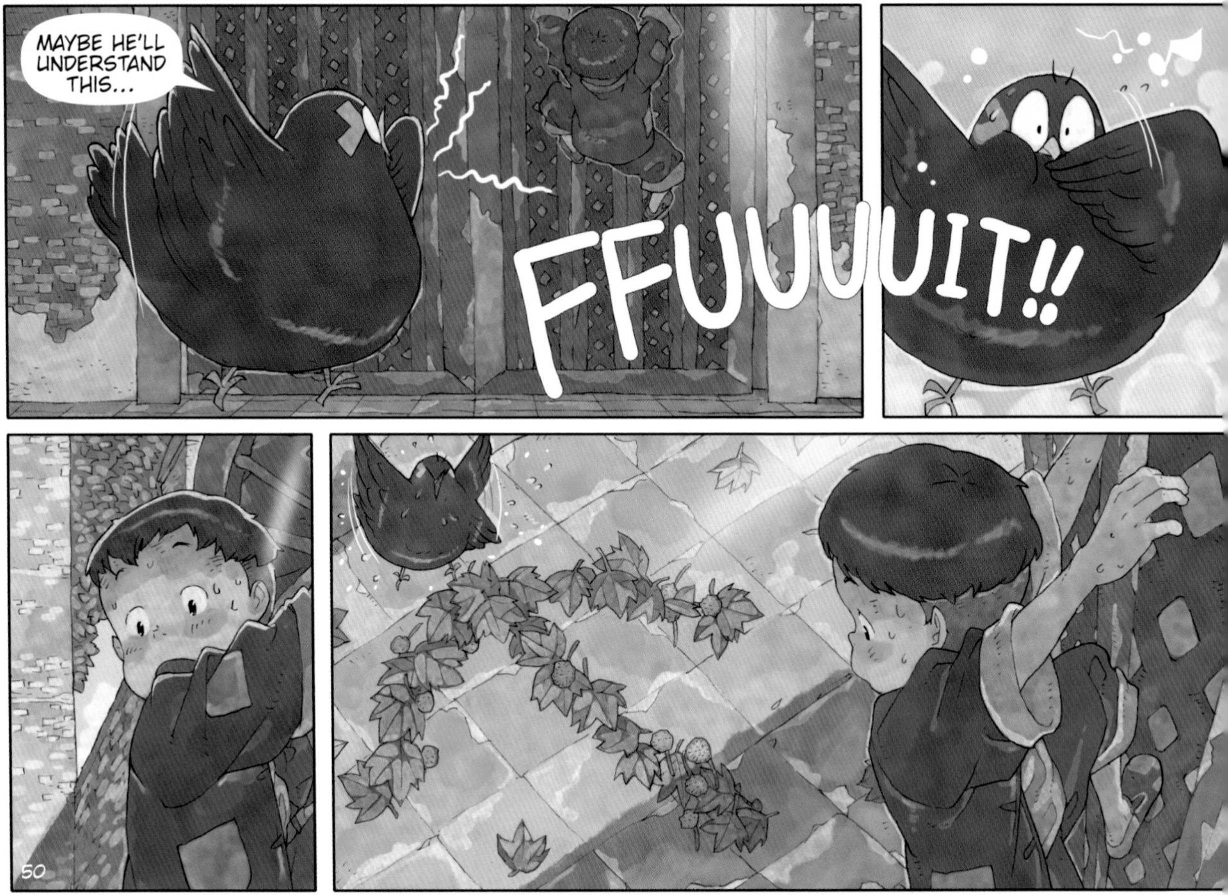
MAYBE HE'LL UNDERSTAND THIS...
FFUUUUUIT!!

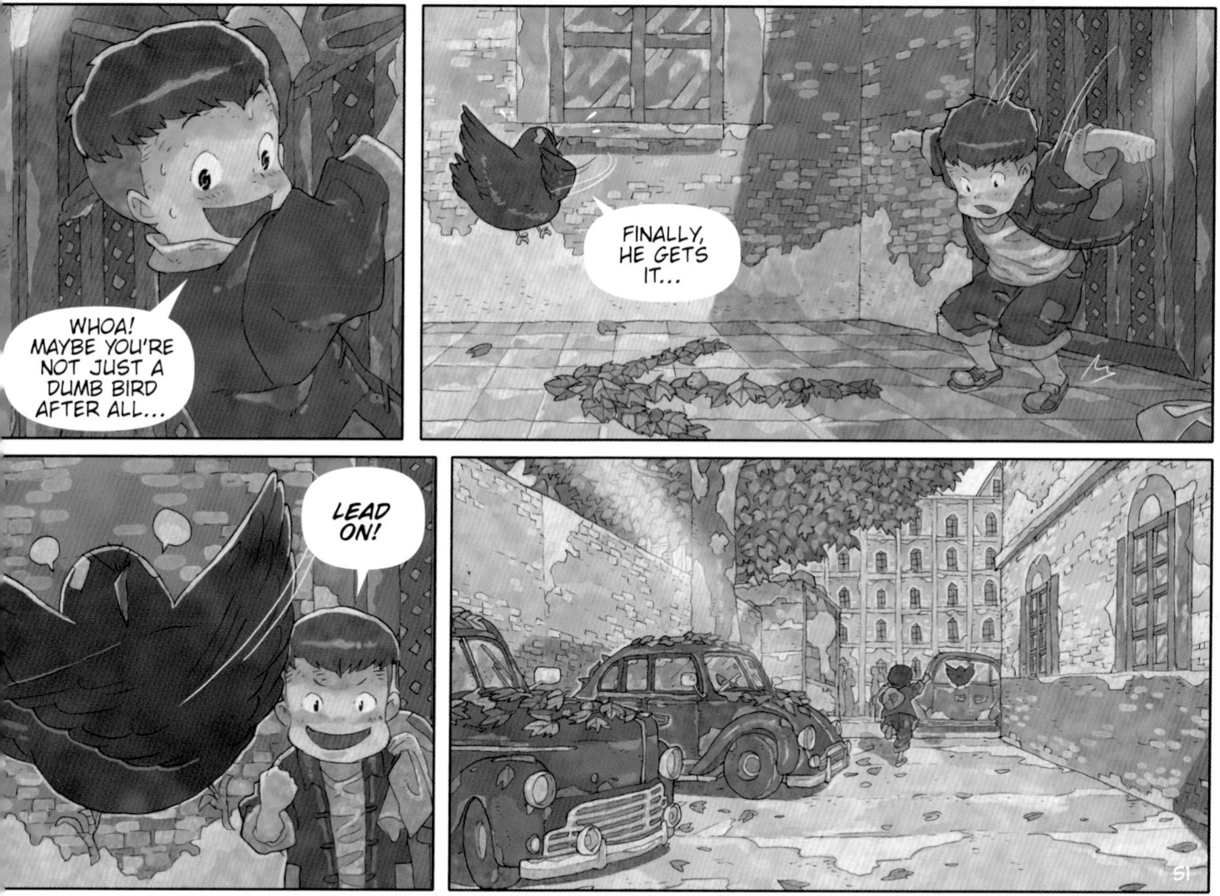
WHOA! MAYBE YOU'RE NOT JUST A DUMB BIRD AFTER ALL...
FINALLY, HE GETS IT...
LEAD ON!

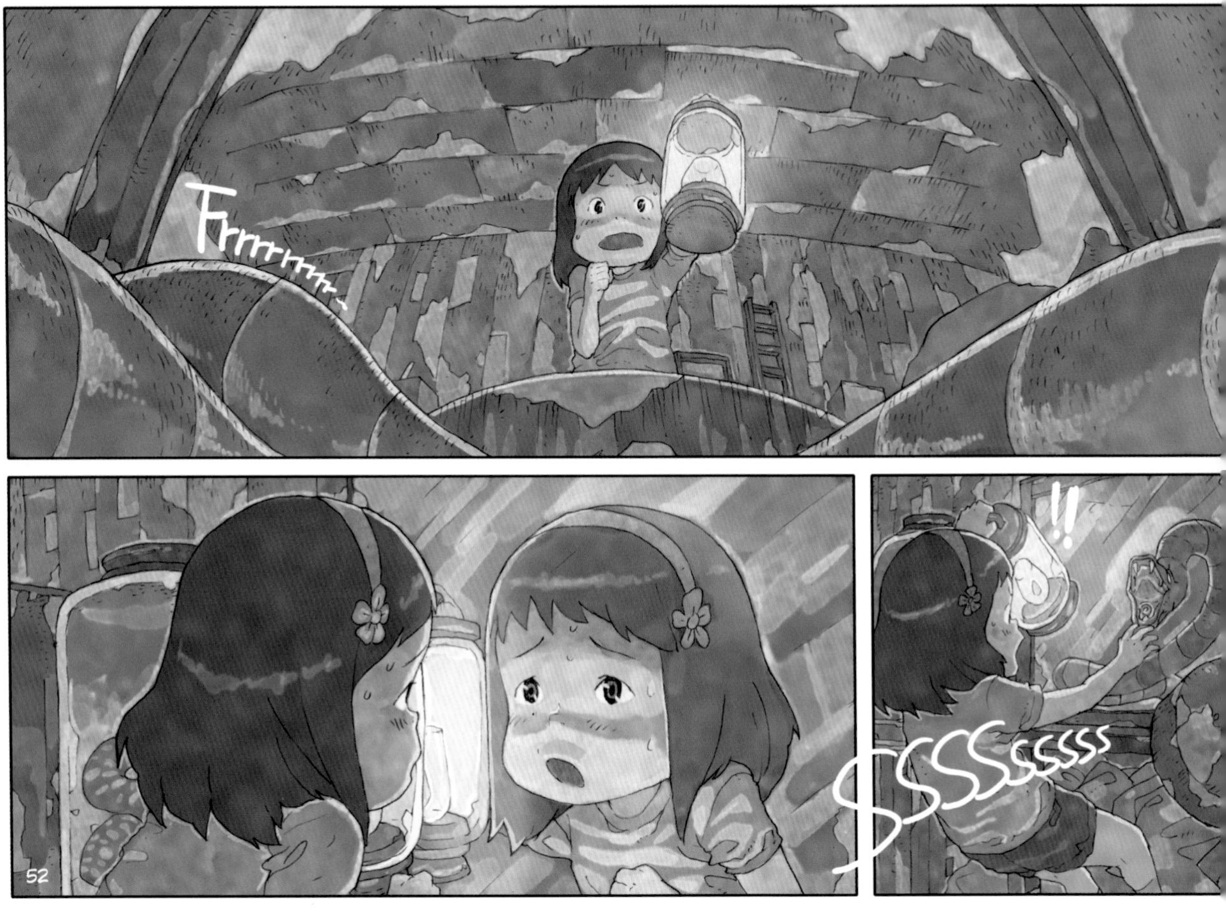
Frrrrrrrr...
!!
SSSSsssss

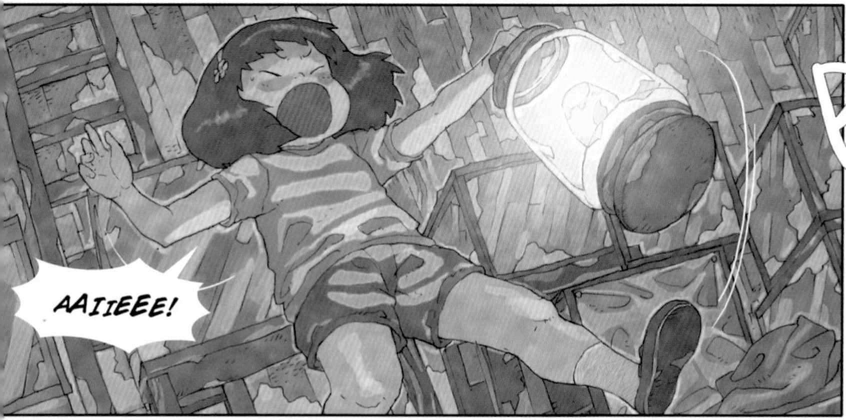
AAIIEEE!

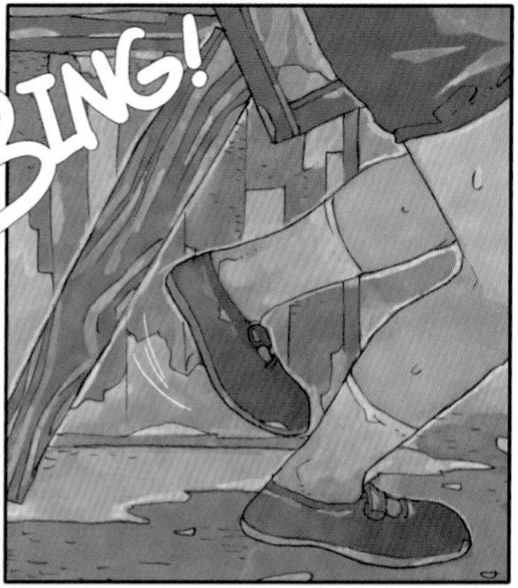
BING!

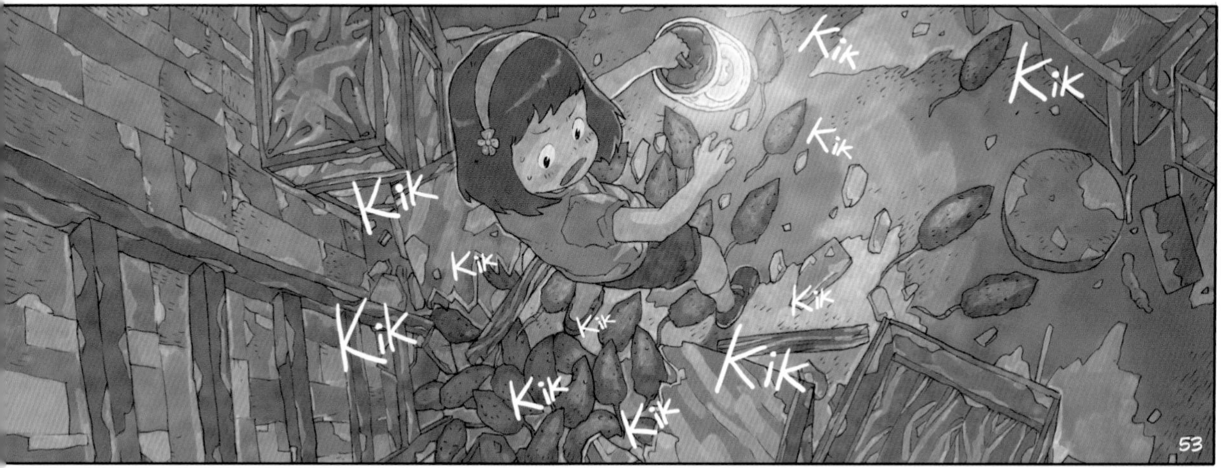
Kik
Kik
Kik
Kik
Kik
Kik
Kik
Kik
Kik
Kik
Kik

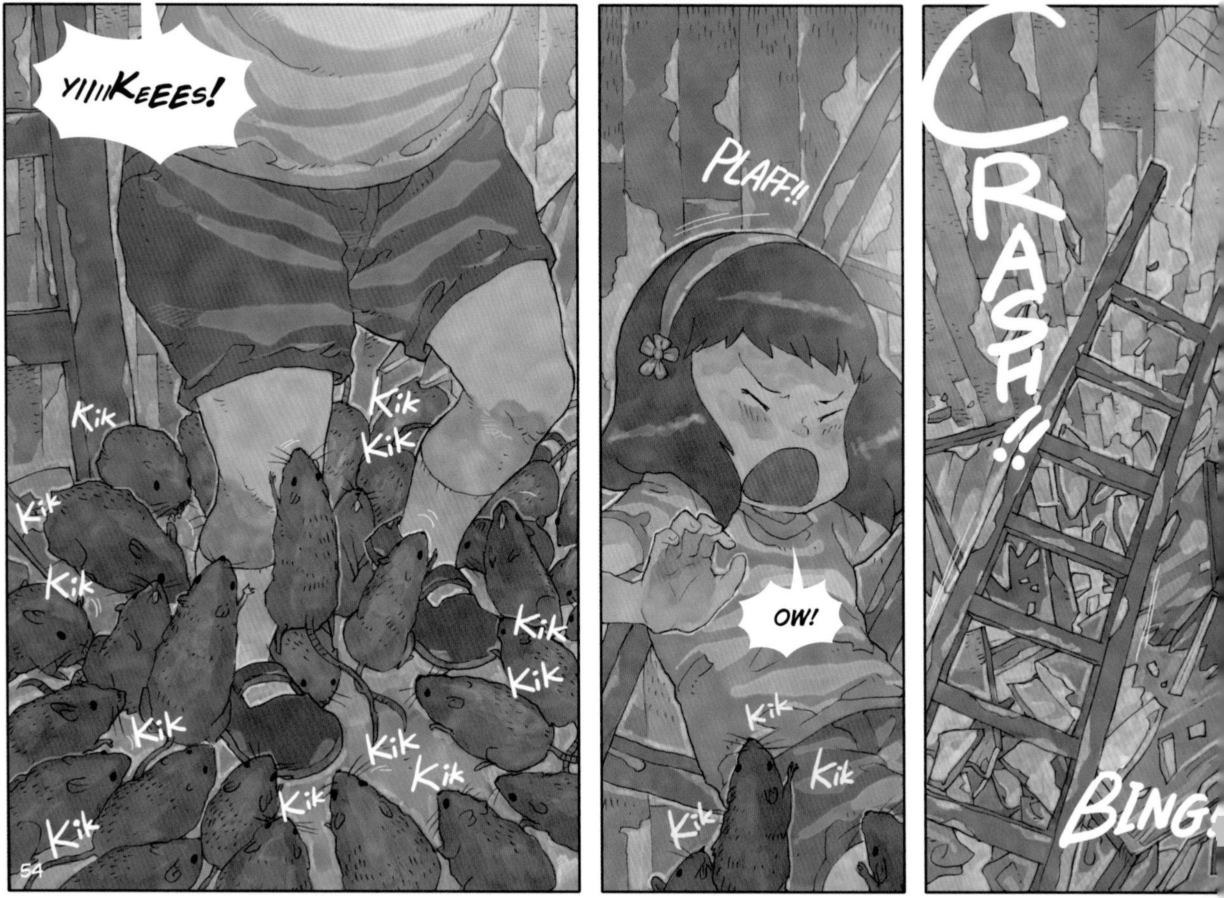
YIIIIKEEEES!
Kik
Kik
Kik
Kik
Kik
Kik
Kik
Kik
Kik
Kik
Kik
Kik
PLAFF!!
OW!
Kik
Kik
Kik
CRASH!!
BING!

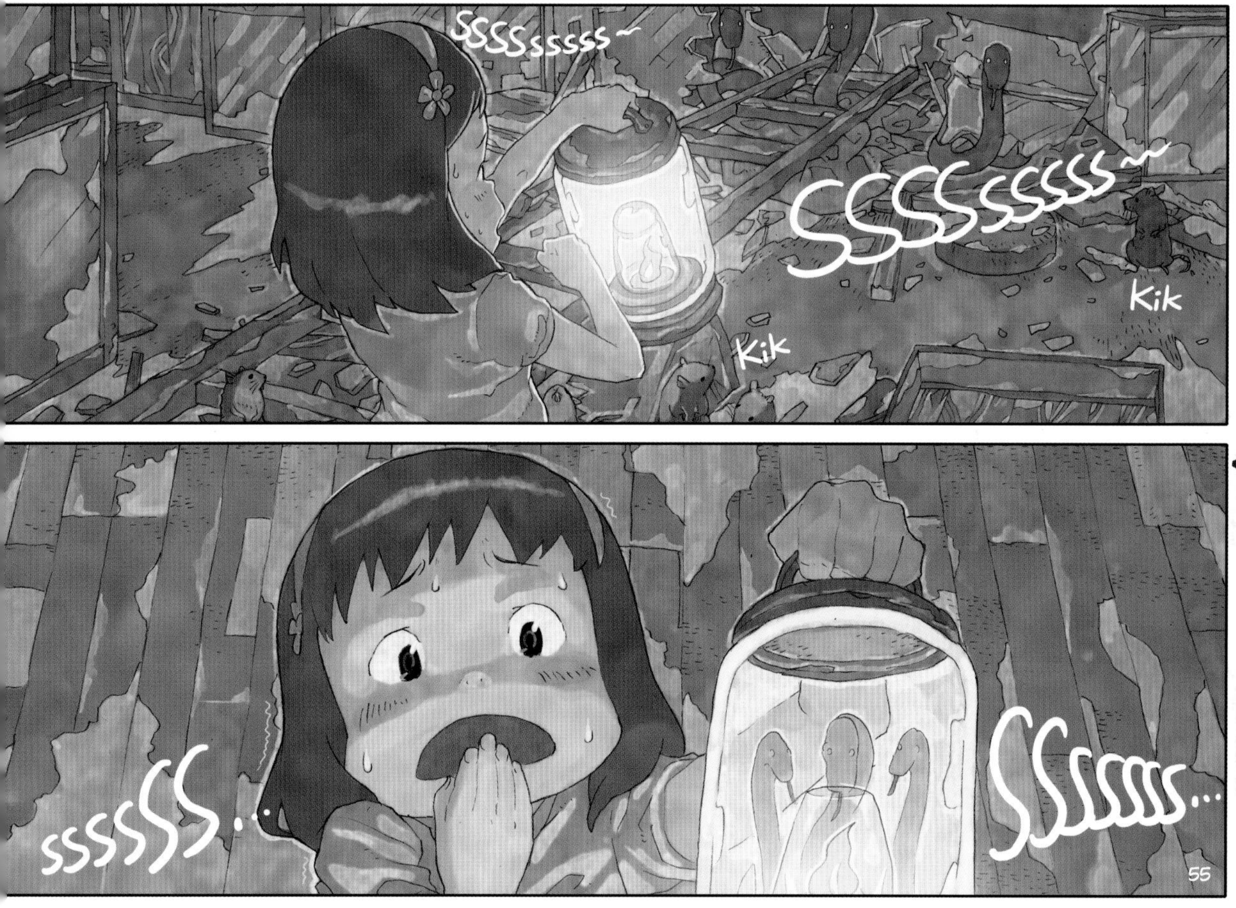

SSSSsssss~
SSSSsssss~
Kik
Kik
ssssSS...
SSssss...

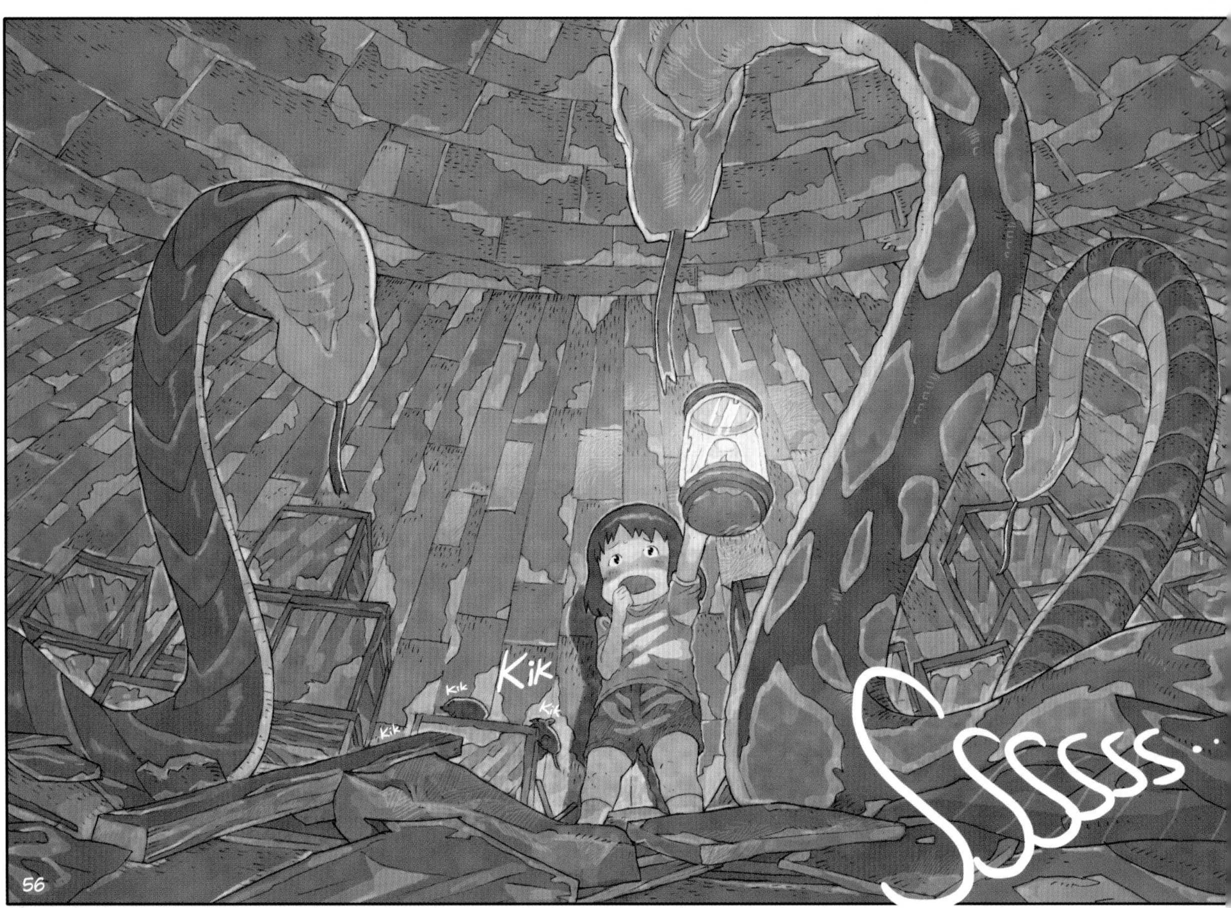
Kik
Kik
Kik
Kik
SSSSSS..

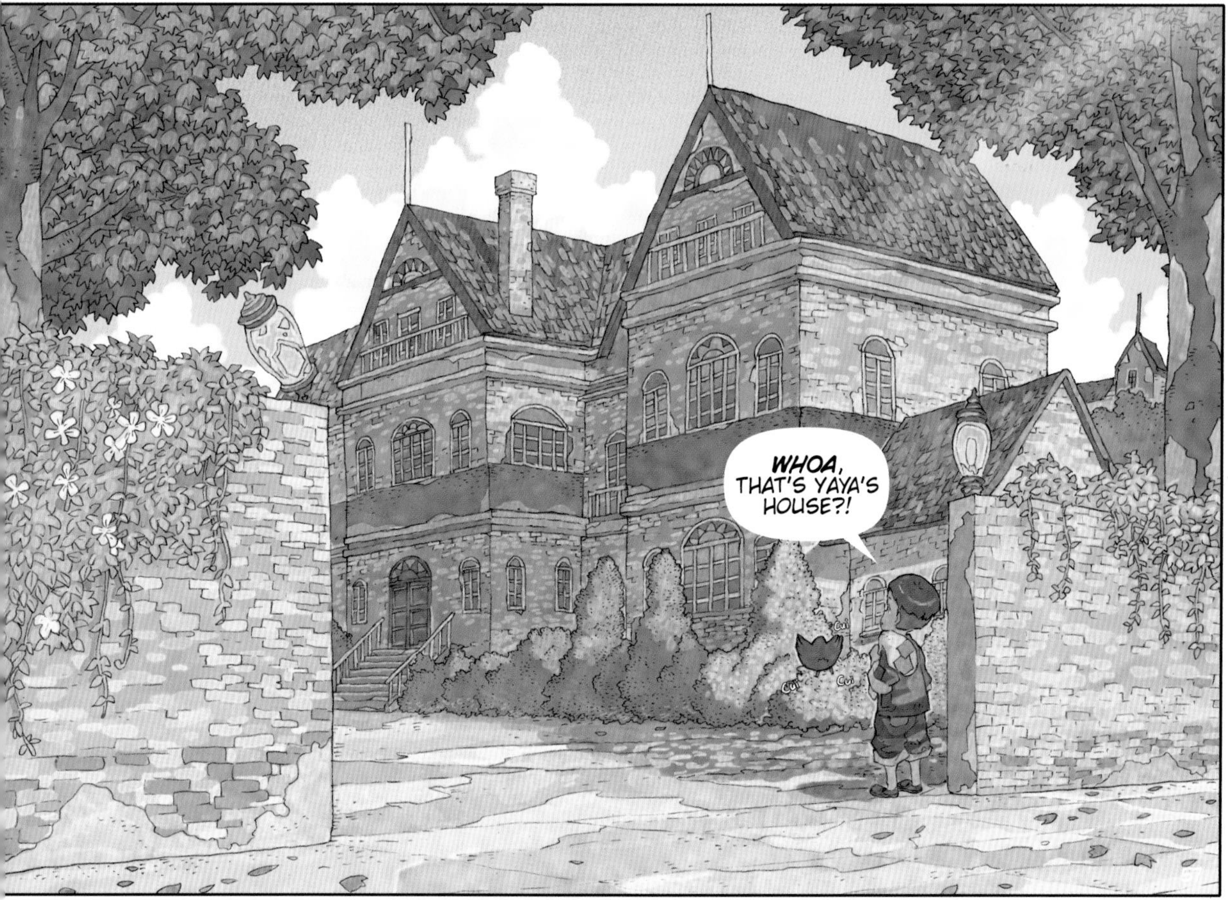
WHOA,
THAT'S YAYA'S
HOUSE?!
Cui
Cui
Cui

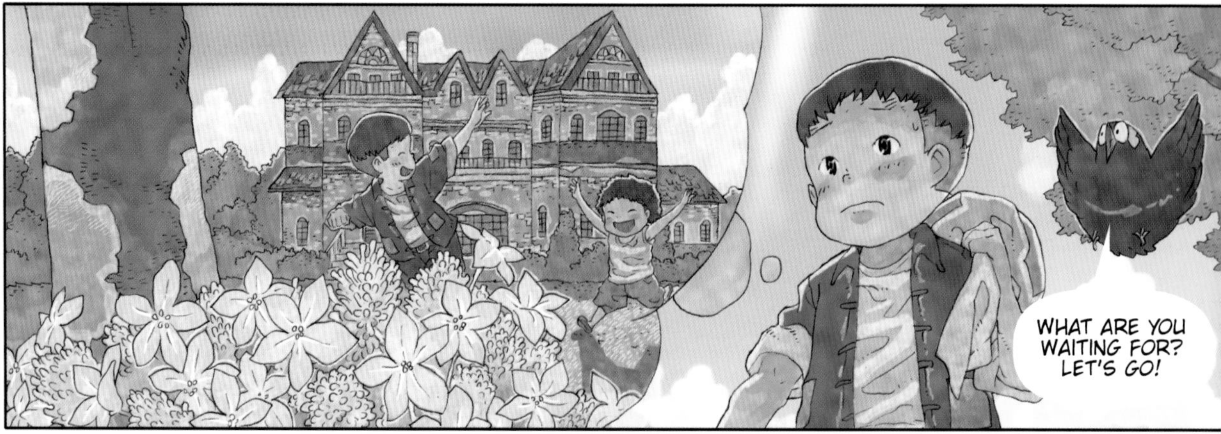
WHAT ARE YOU
WAITING FOR?
LET'S GO!

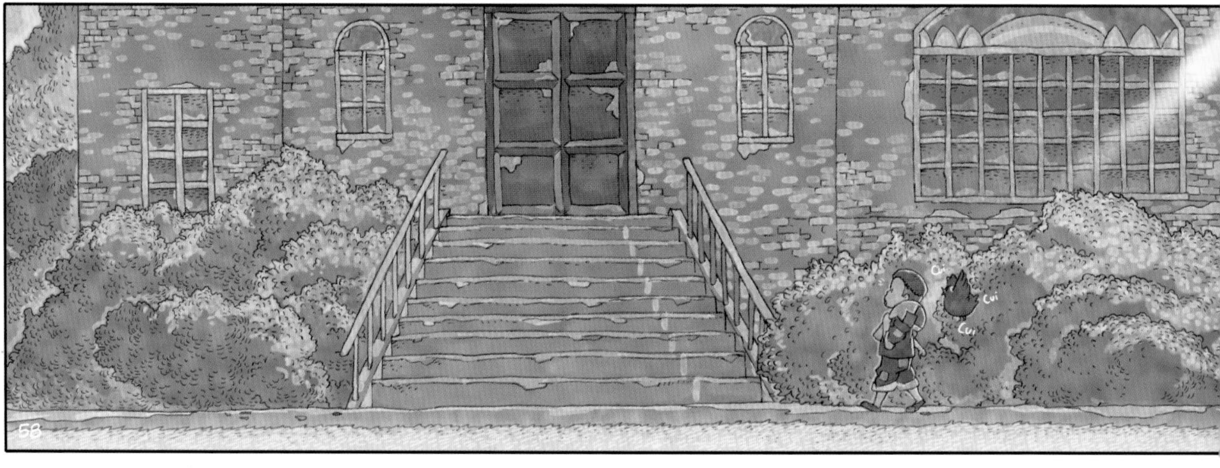
Cui
Cui
Cui

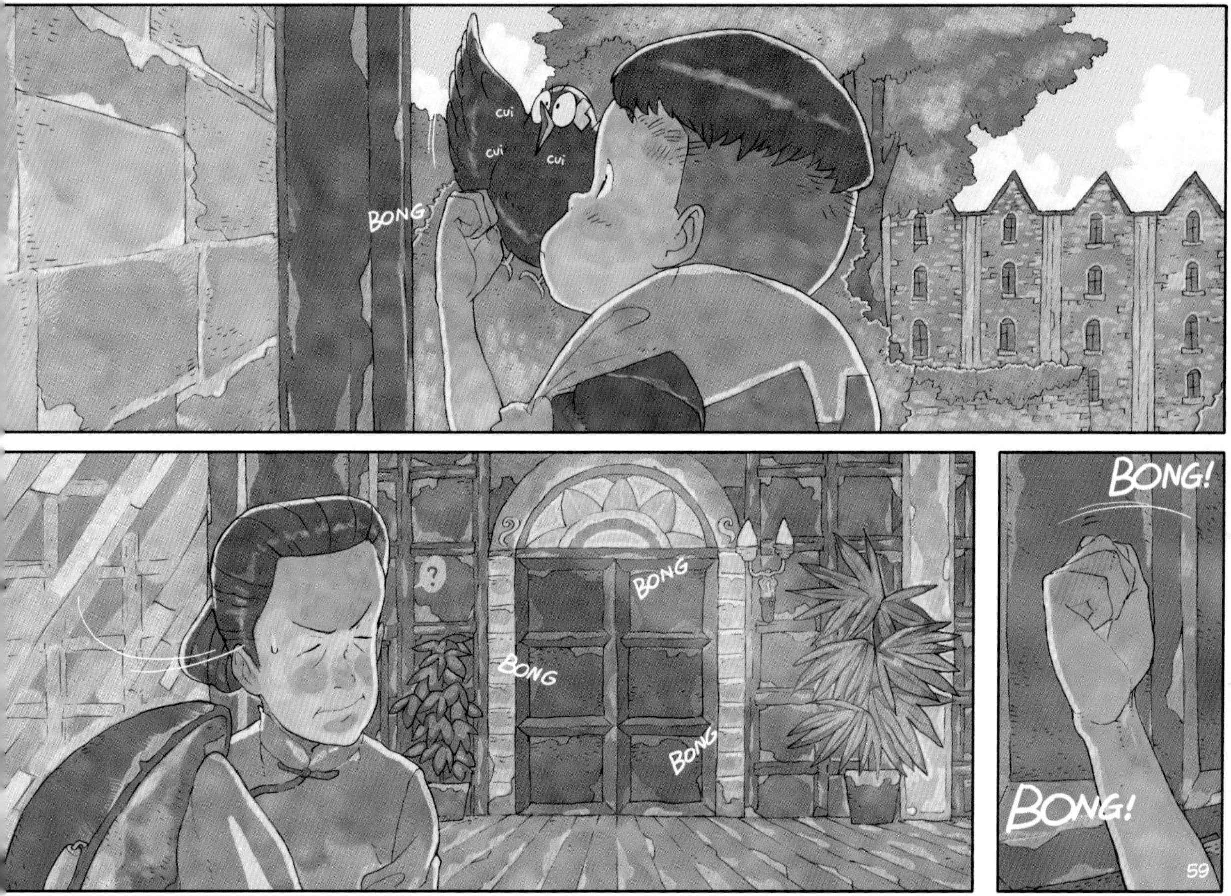
cui
cui
cui
BONG
?
BONG
BONG
BONG
BONG!
BONG!

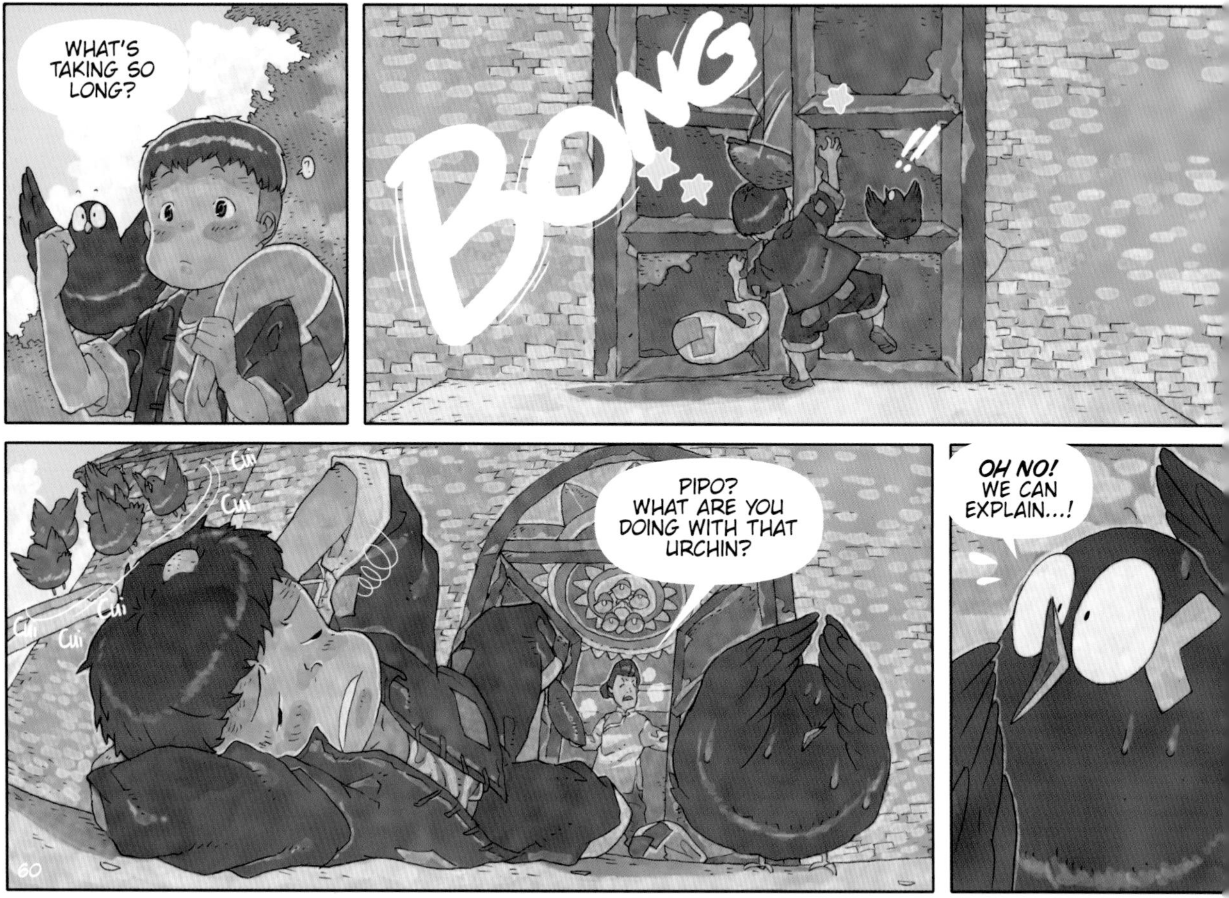
WHAT'S TAKING SO LONG?
?
BONG
!!
Cui
Cui
Cui
Cui
Cui
PIPO? WHAT ARE YOU DOING WITH THAT URCHIN?
OH NO! WE CAN EXPLAIN...!

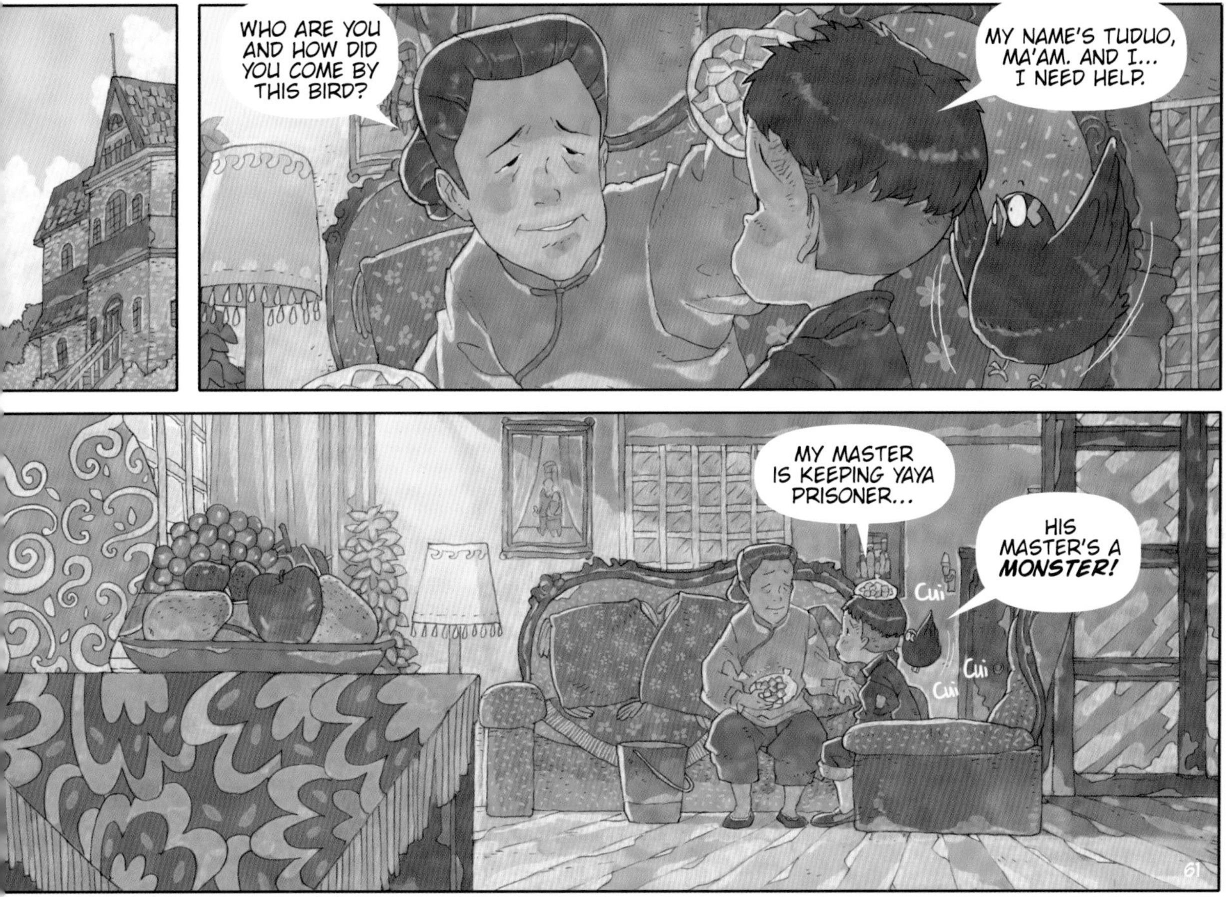
WHO ARE YOU AND HOW DID YOU COME BY THIS BIRD?
MY NAME'S TUDUO, MA'AM. AND I... I NEED HELP.
MY MASTER IS KEEPING YAYA PRISONER...
Cui
HIS MASTER'S A *MONSTER!*
Cui
Cui

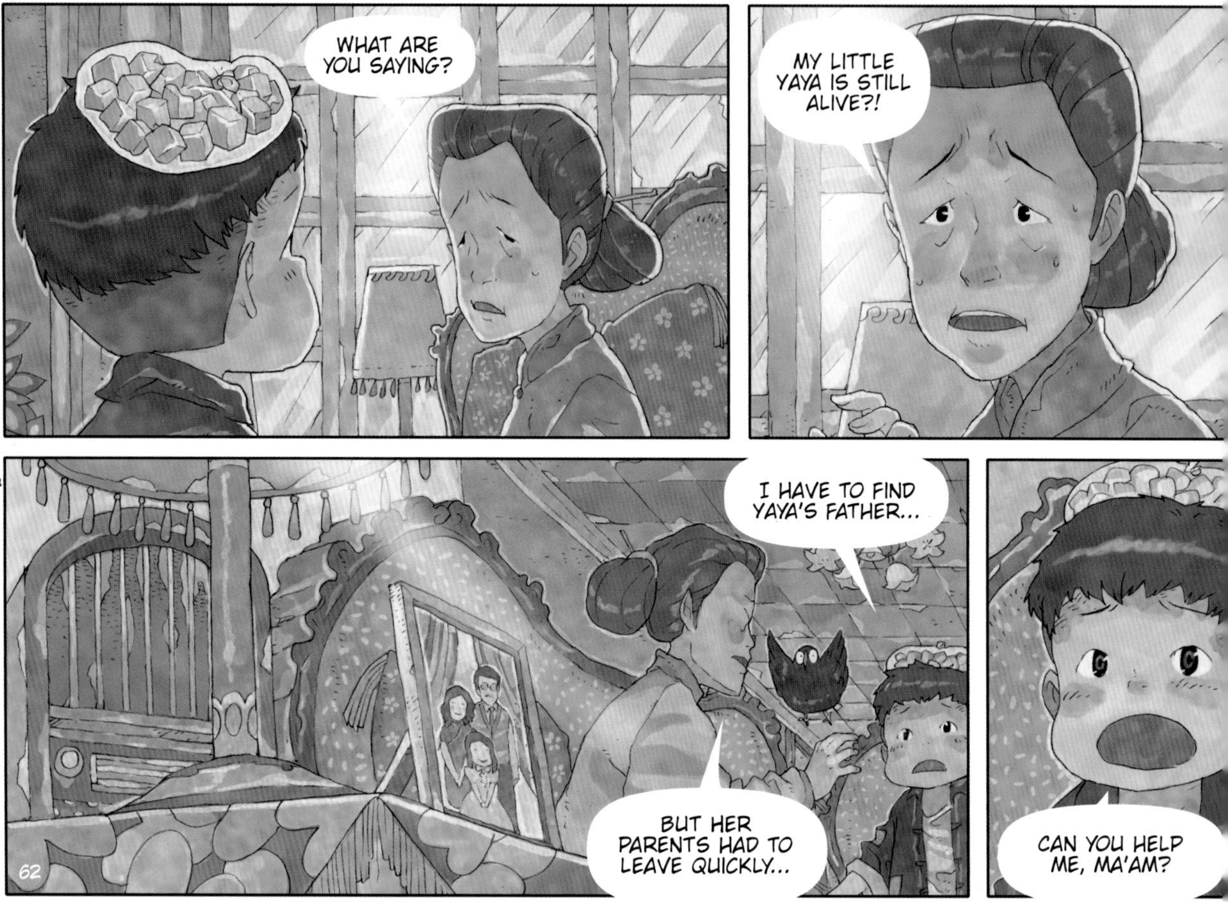
WHAT ARE YOU SAYING?
MY LITTLE YAYA IS STILL ALIVE?!
I HAVE TO FIND YAYA'S FATHER...
BUT HER PARENTS HAD TO LEAVE QUICKLY...
CAN YOU HELP ME, MA'AM?

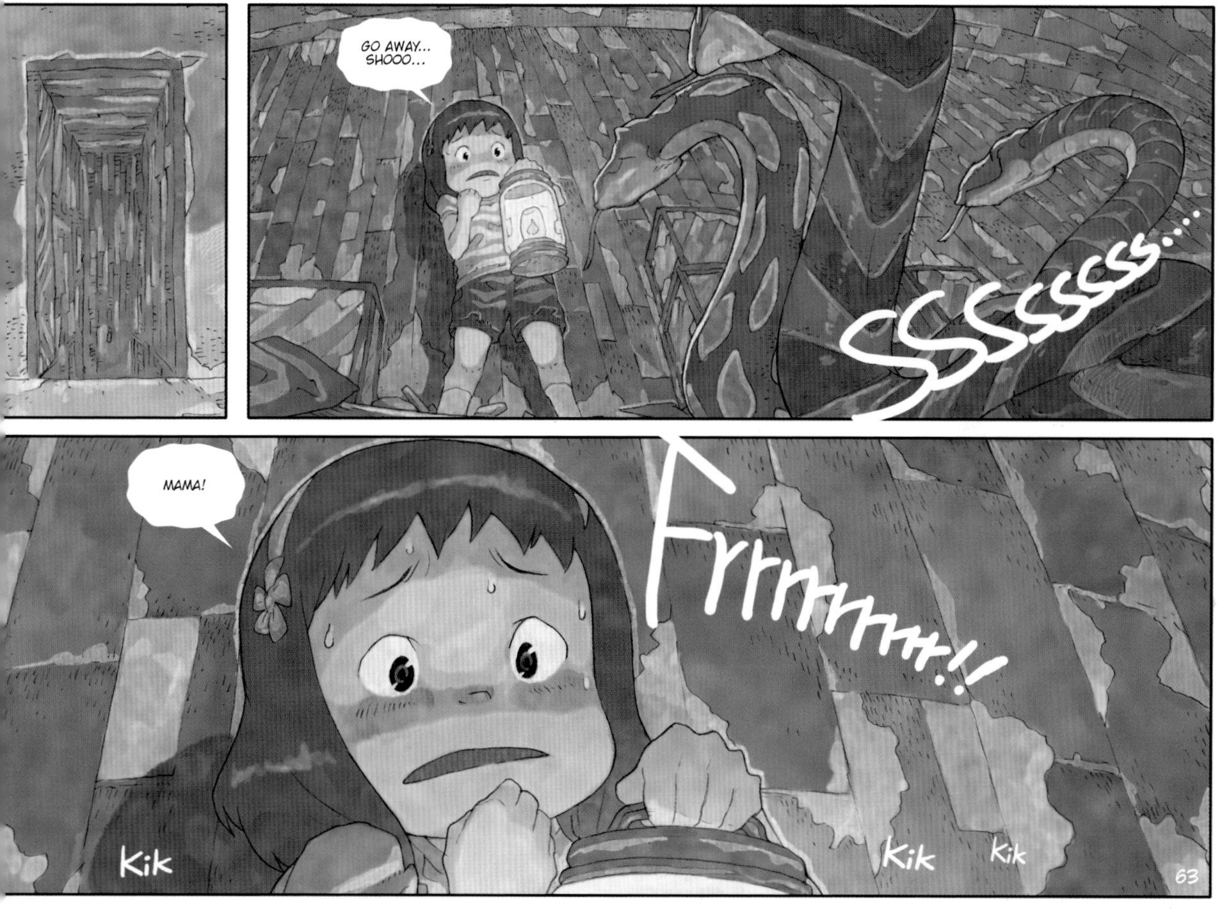
GO AWAY... SHOOO...
SSSSSSS...
MAMA!
Frrrrrrrr!!
Kik
Kik
Kik

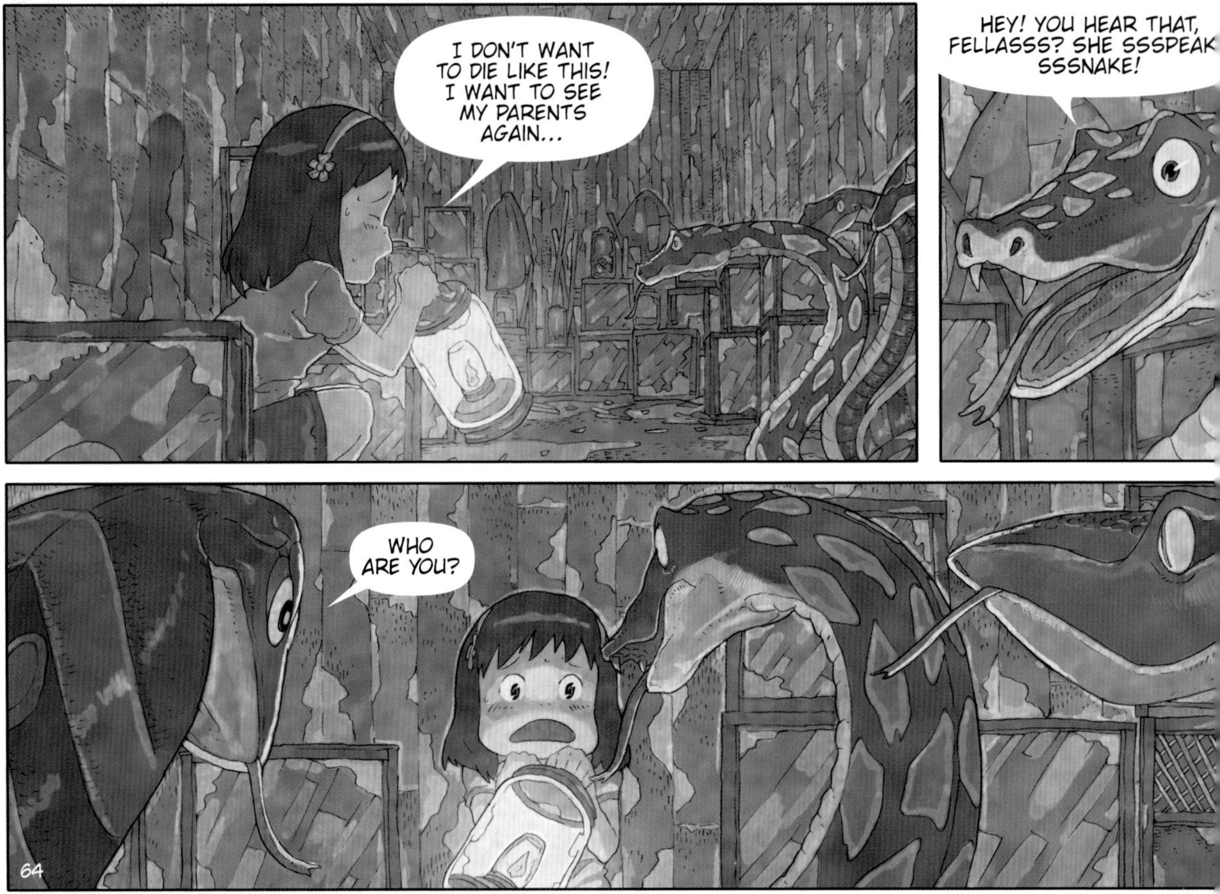
I DON'T WANT TO DIE LIKE THIS! I WANT TO SEE MY PARENTS AGAIN...
HEY! YOU HEAR THAT, FELLASSS? SHE SSSPEAK SSSNAKE!
WHO ARE YOU?
64

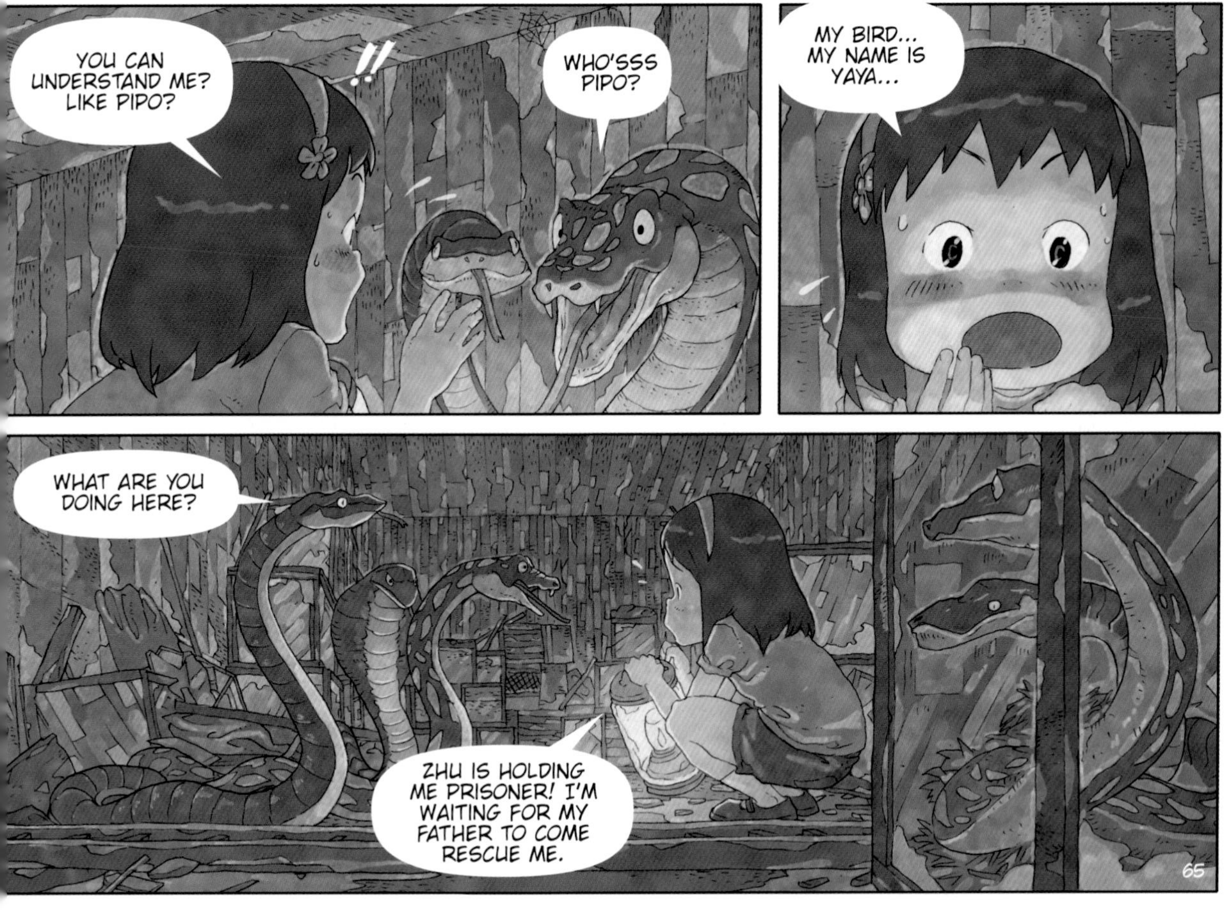
YOU CAN UNDERSTAND ME? LIKE PIPO?
!!
WHO'SSS PIPO?
MY BIRD... MY NAME IS YAYA...
WHAT ARE YOU DOING HERE?
ZHU IS HOLDING ME PRISONER! I'M WAITING FOR MY FATHER TO COME RESCUE ME.

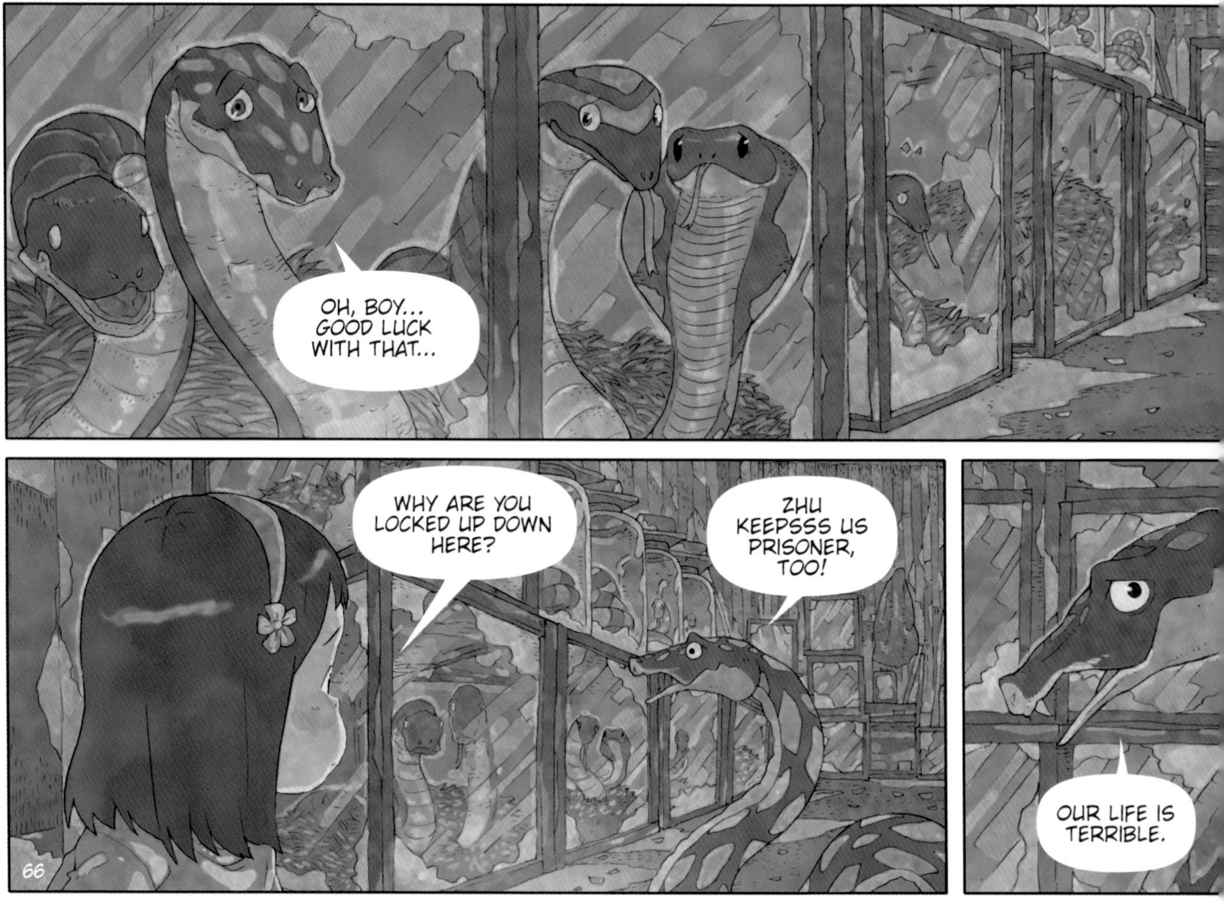
OH, BOY... GOOD LUCK WITH THAT...
WHY ARE YOU LOCKED UP DOWN HERE?
ZHU KEEPSSS US PRISONER, TOO!
OUR LIFE IS TERRIBLE.

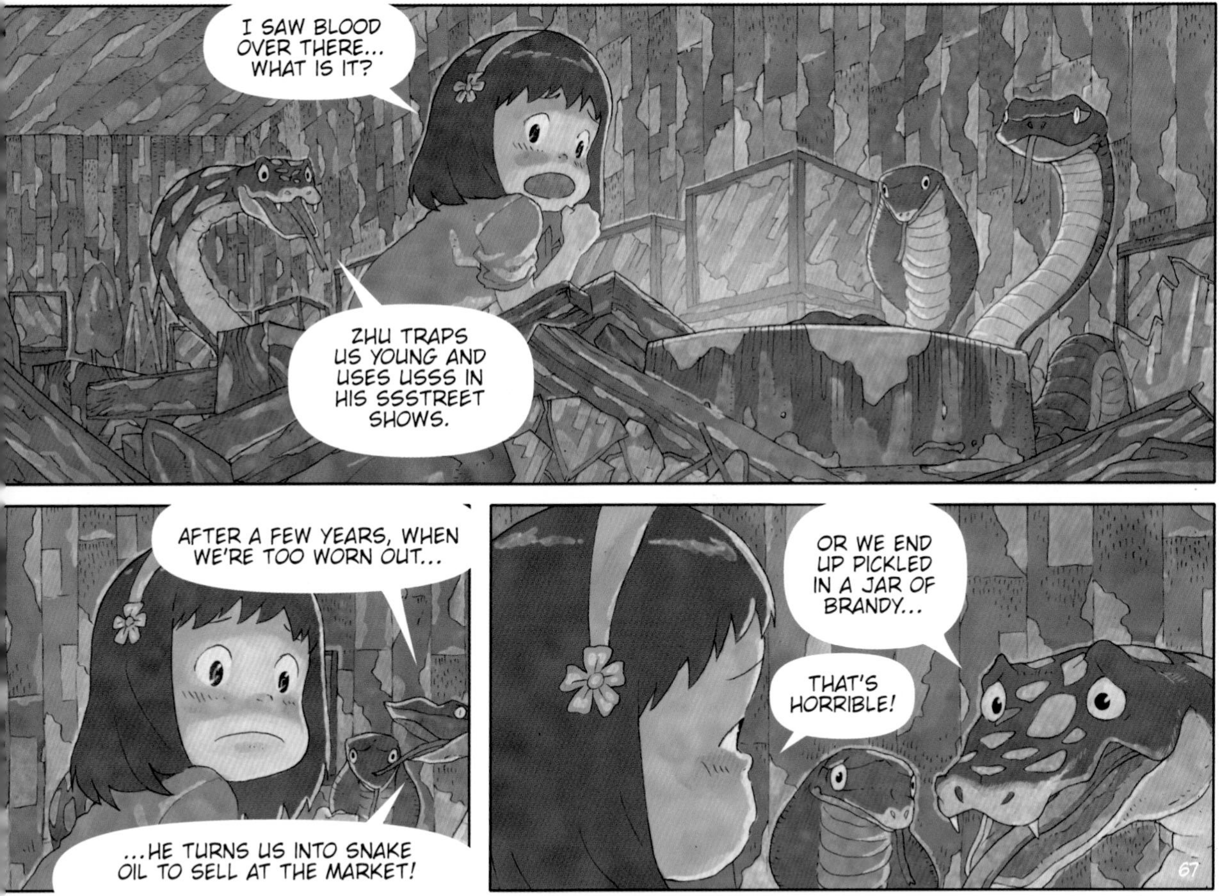
I SAW BLOOD OVER THERE... WHAT IS IT?
ZHU TRAPS US YOUNG AND USES USSS IN HIS SSSTREET SHOWS.
AFTER A FEW YEARS, WHEN WE'RE TOO WORN OUT...
...HE TURNS US INTO SNAKE OIL TO SELL AT THE MARKET!
OR WE END UP PICKLED IN A JAR OF BRANDY...
THAT'S HORRIBLE!

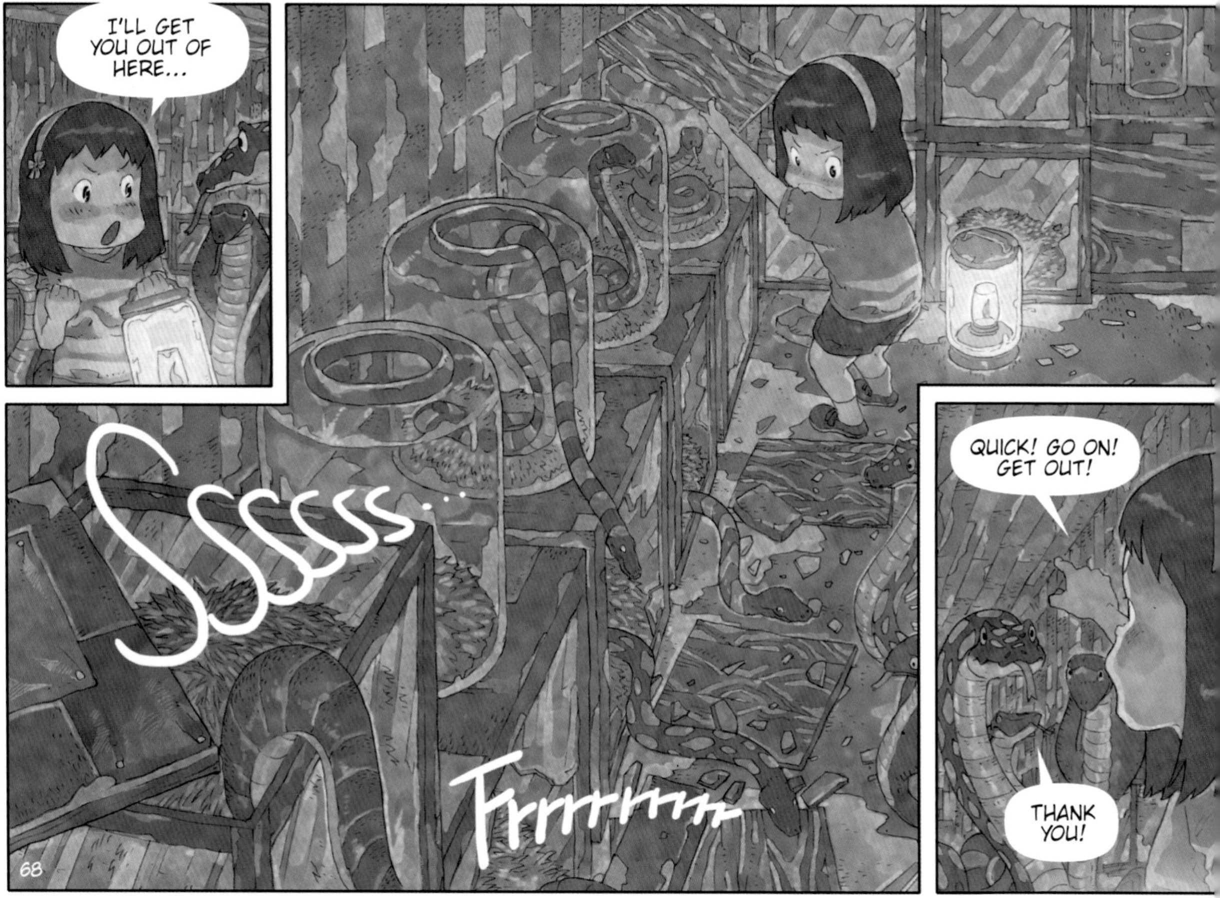
I'LL GET YOU OUT OF HERE...
Ssssss...
Frrrrrrrr
QUICK! GO ON! GET OUT!
THANK YOU!

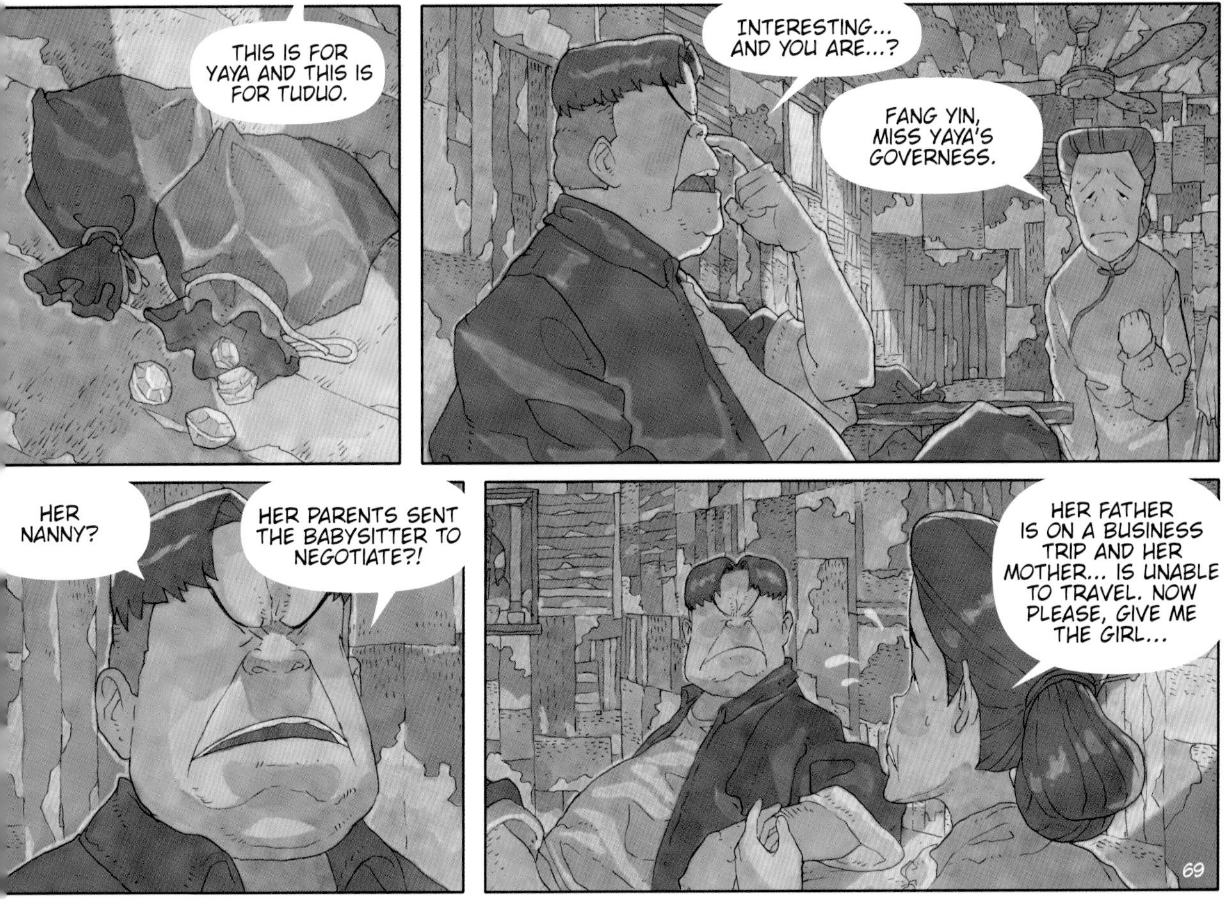
THIS IS FOR YAYA AND THIS IS FOR TUDUO.
INTERESTING... AND YOU ARE...?
FANG YIN, MISS YAYA'S GOVERNESS.
HER NANNY?
HER PARENTS SENT THE BABYSITTER TO NEGOTIATE?!
HER FATHER IS ON A BUSINESS TRIP AND HER MOTHER... IS UNABLE TO TRAVEL. NOW PLEASE, GIVE ME THE GIRL...

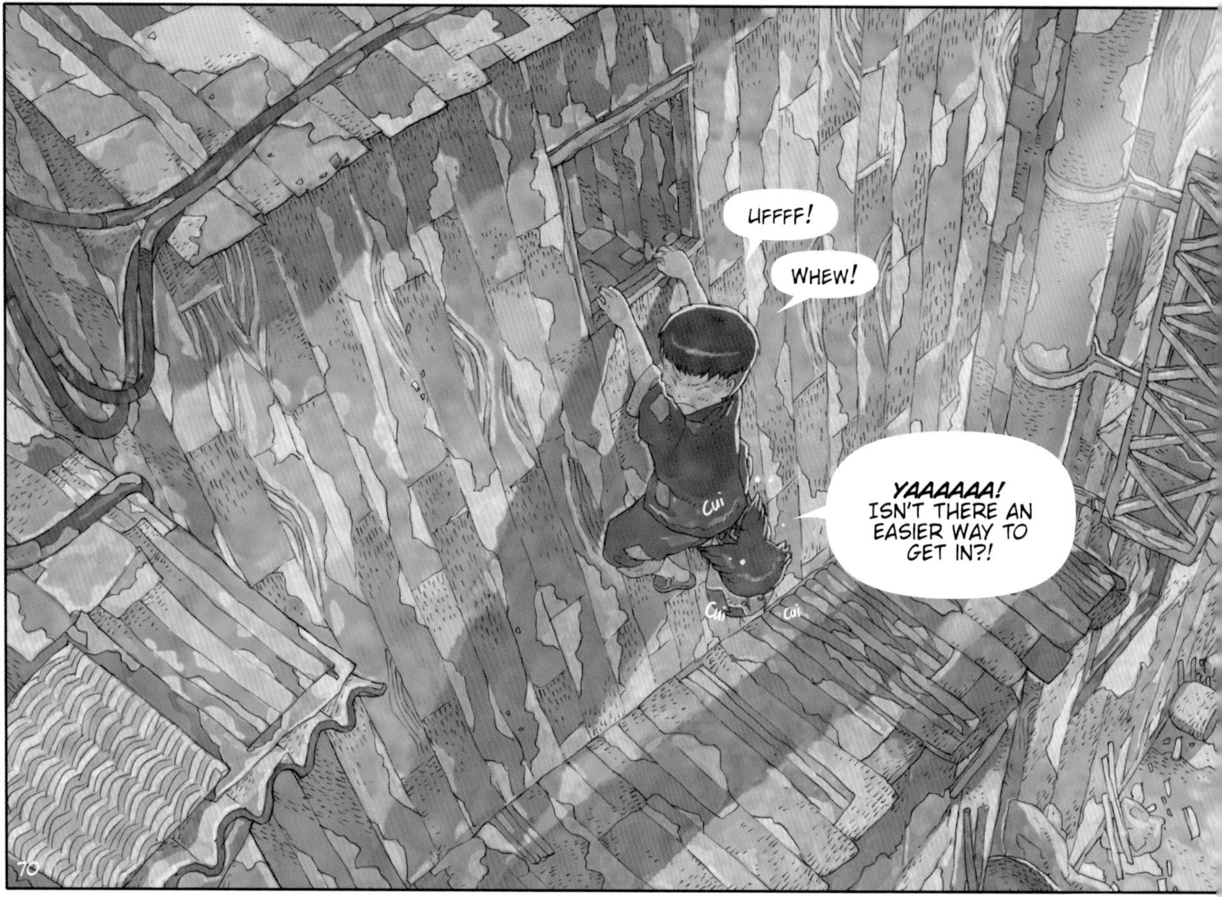
UFFFF!
WHEW!
Cui
YAAAAAA! ISN'T THERE AN EASIER WAY TO GET IN?!
Cui
Cui

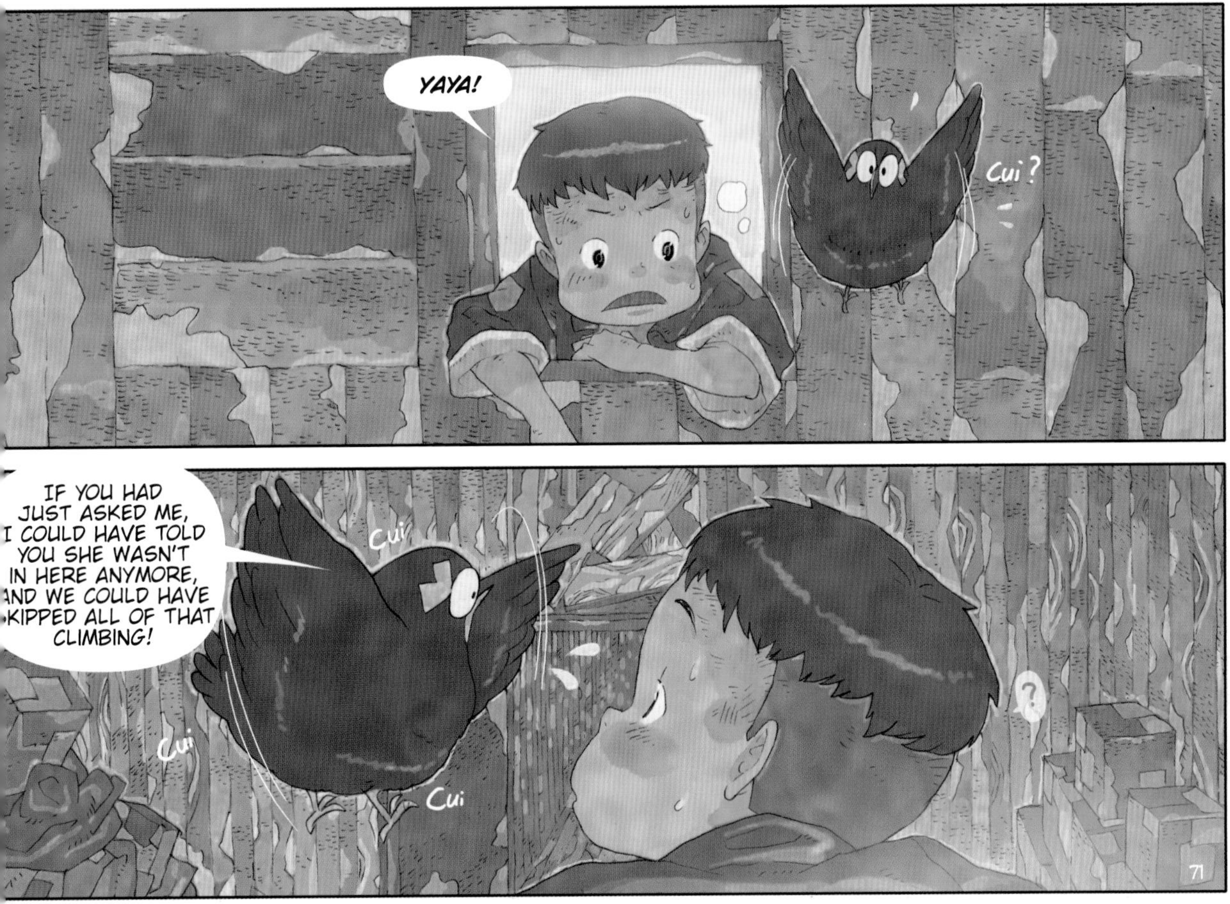
YAYA!
Cui ?
IF YOU HAD JUST ASKED ME, I COULD HAVE TOLD YOU SHE WASN'T IN HERE ANYMORE, AND WE COULD HAVE SKIPPED ALL OF THAT CLIMBING!
Cui
Cui
Cui
?

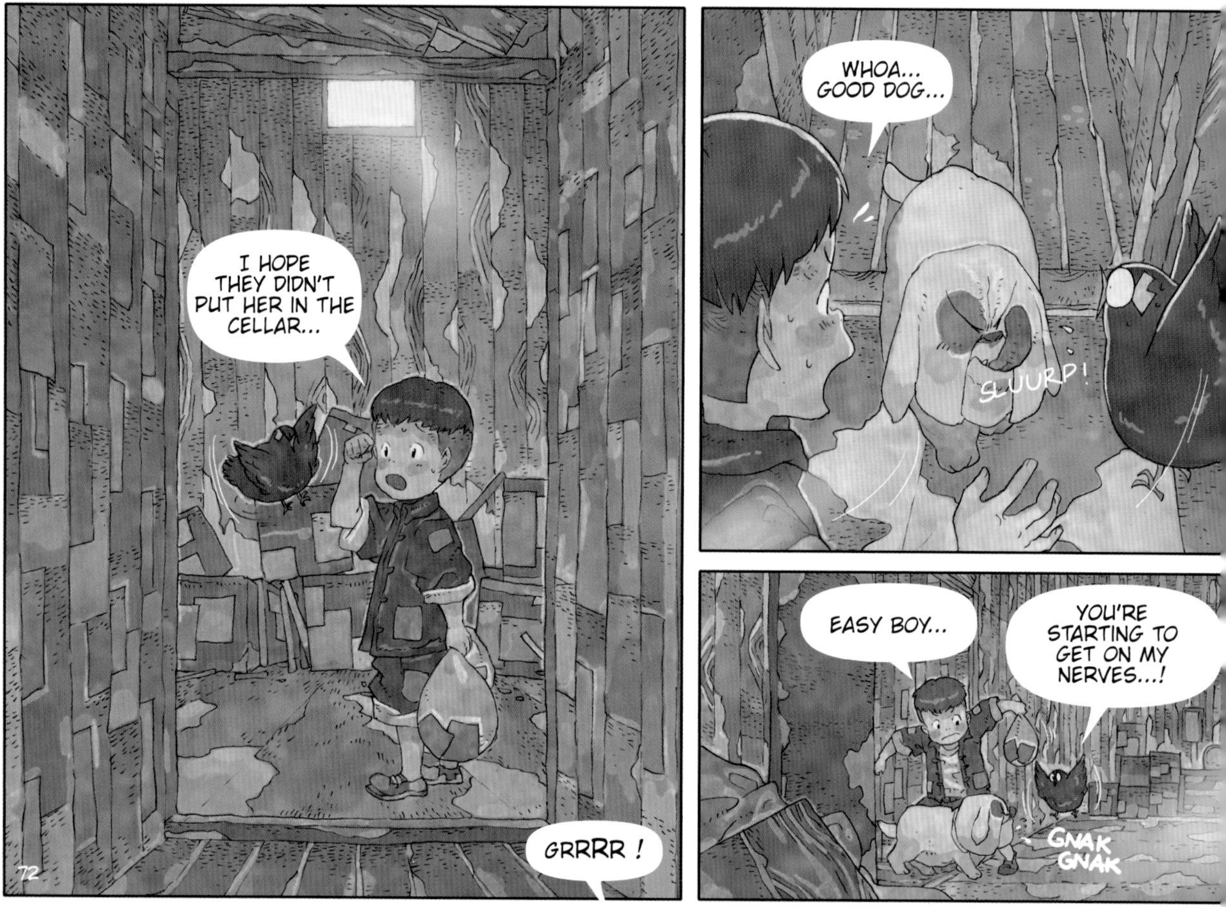
I HOPE THEY DIDN'T PUT HER IN THE CELLAR...
GRRRR !
WHOA... GOOD DOG...
SLUURP!
EASY BOY...
YOU'RE STARTING TO GET ON MY NERVES...!
GNAK GNAK

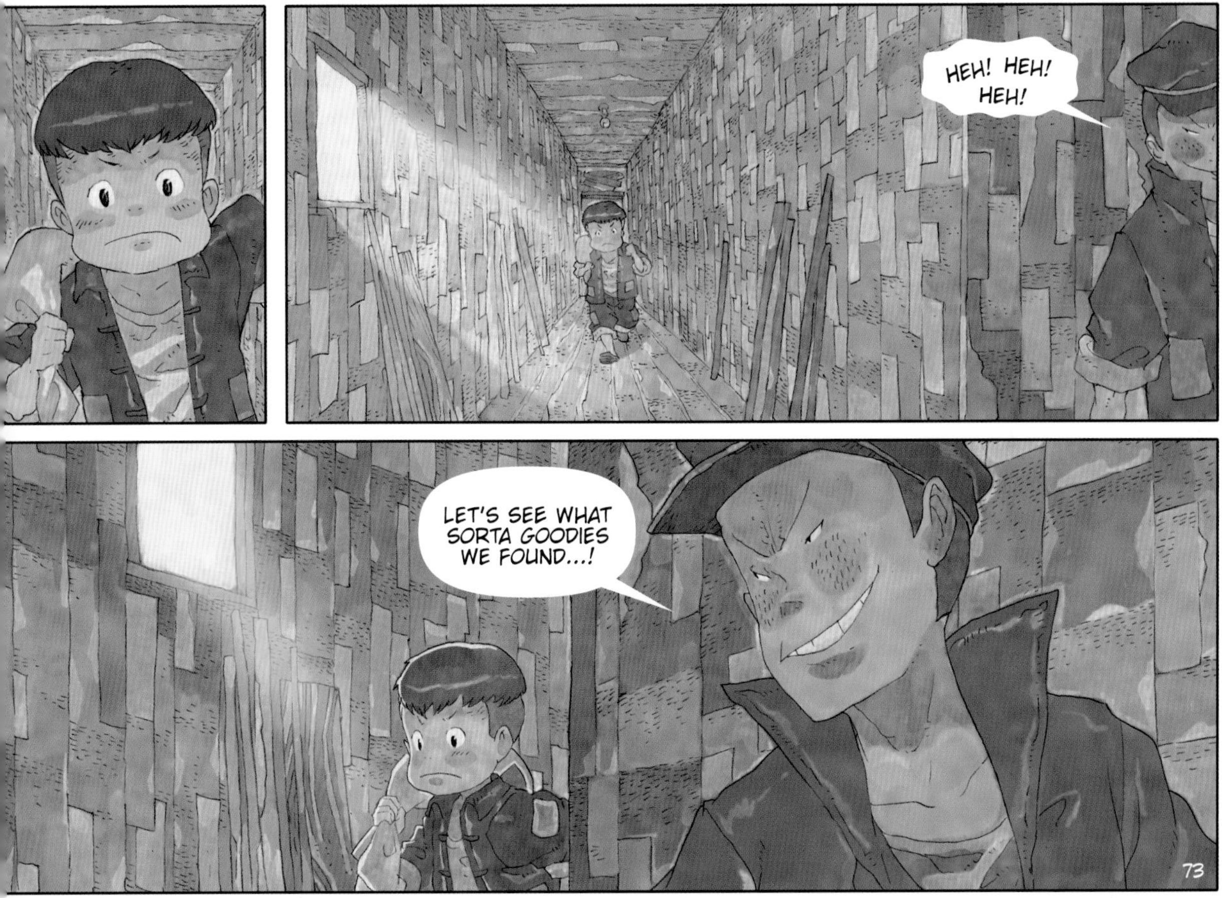
HEH! HEH! HEH!
LET'S SEE WHAT SORTA GOODIES WE FOUND...!

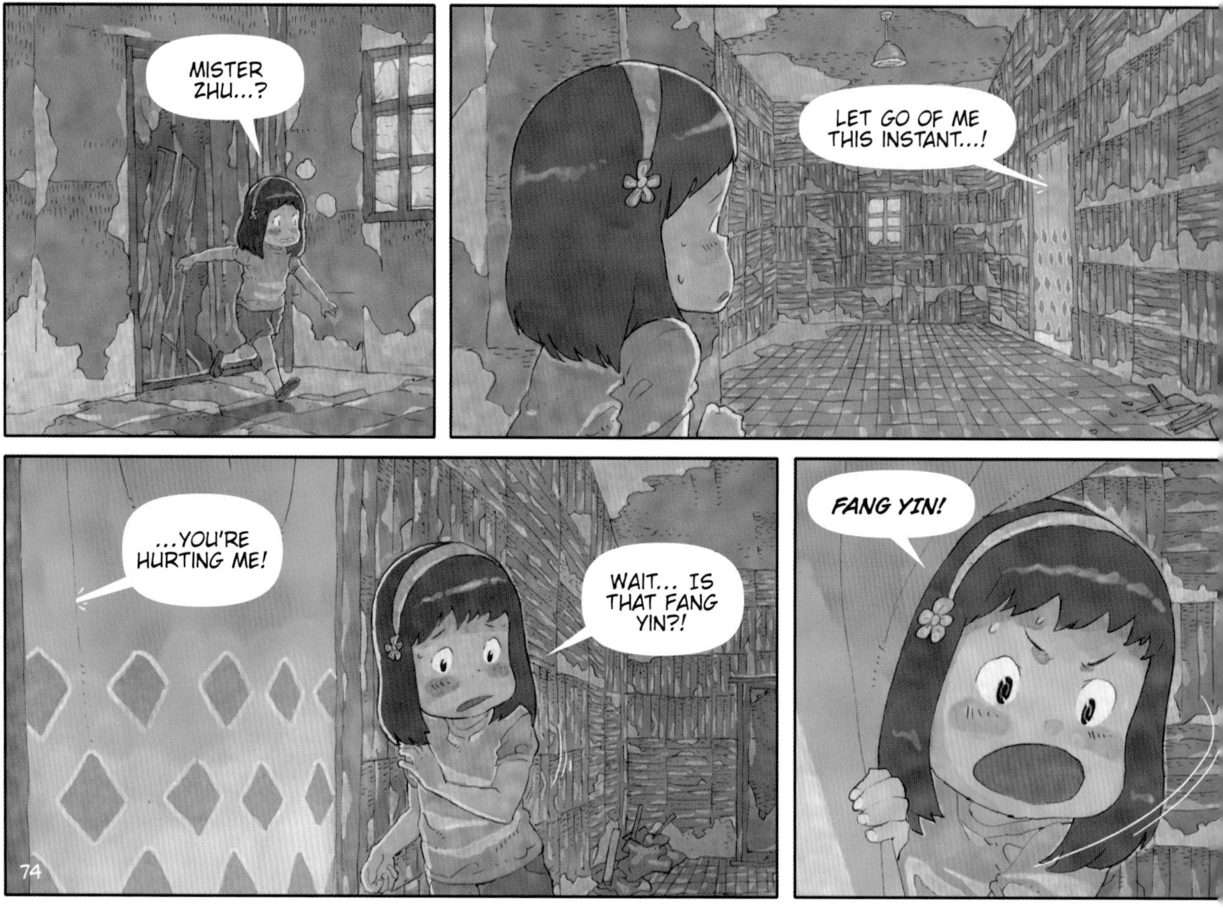
MISTER ZHU...?
LET GO OF ME THIS INSTANT...!
...YOU'RE HURTING ME!
WAIT... IS THAT FANG YIN?!
FANG YIN!

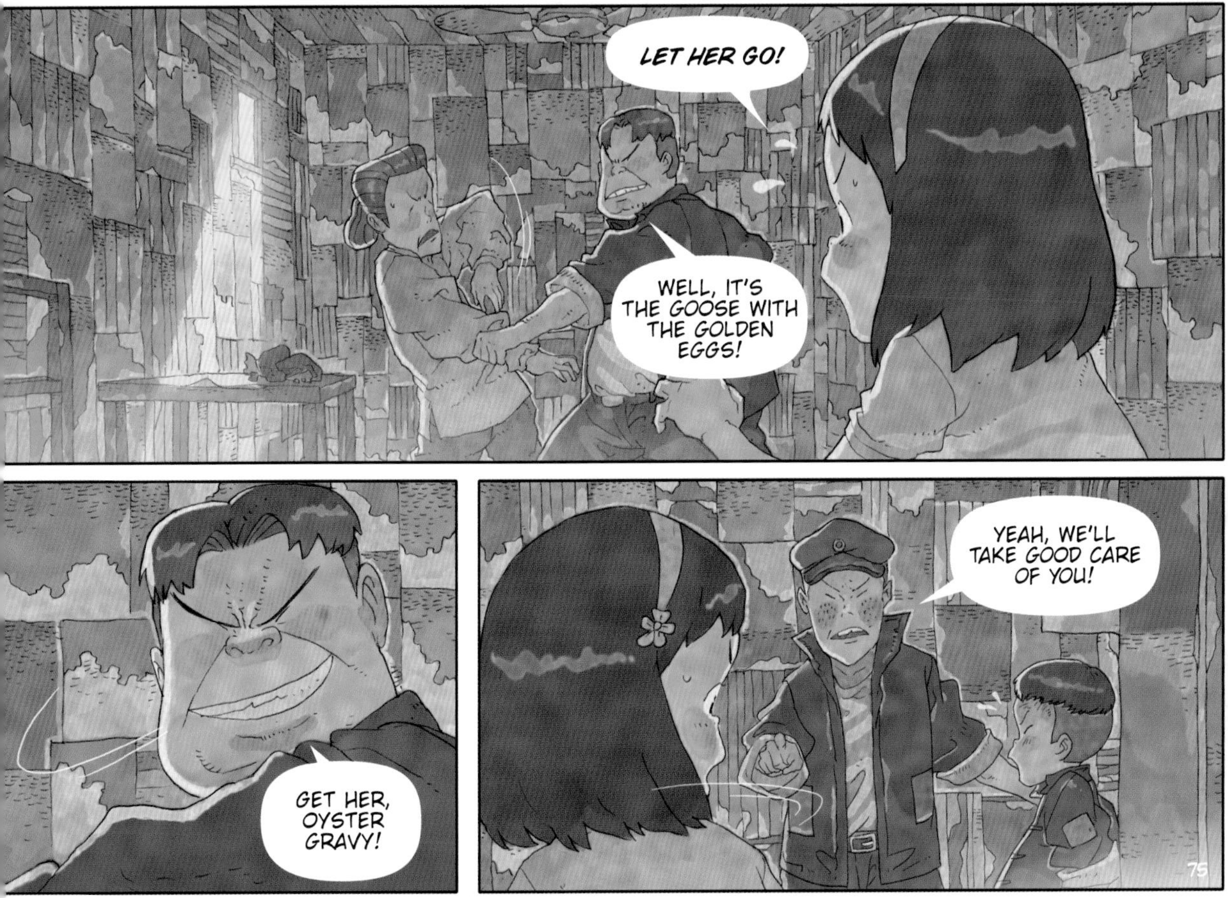
LET HER GO!
WELL, IT'S THE GOOSE WITH THE GOLDEN EGGS!
GET HER, OYSTER GRAVY!
YEAH, WE'LL TAKE GOOD CARE OF YOU!

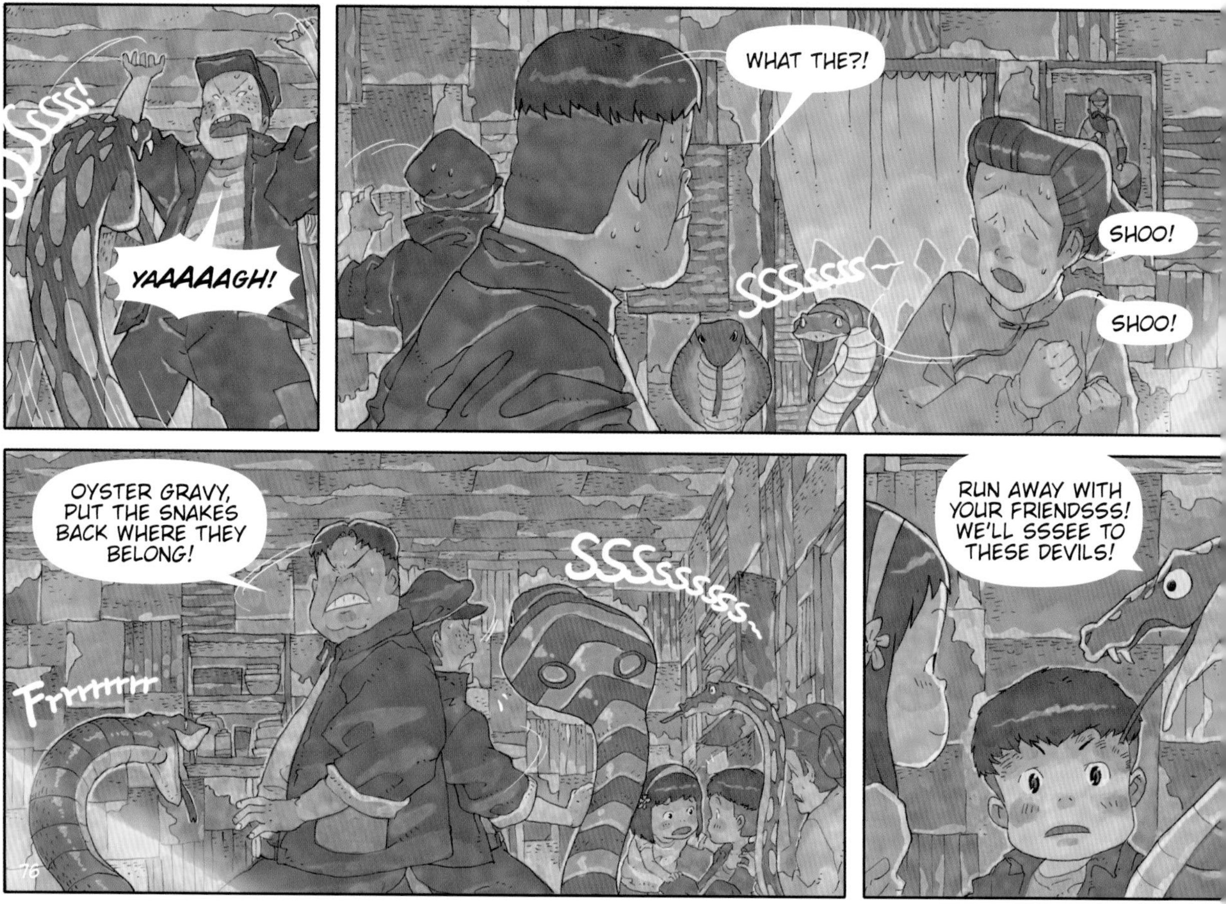
SSSSSS!
YAAAAAGH!
WHAT THE?!
SSSSSSS~
SHOO!
SHOO!
OYSTER GRAVY, PUT THE SNAKES BACK WHERE THEY BELONG!
Frrrrrrrr
SSSSSSSSS~
RUN AWAY WITH YOUR FRIENDSSS! WE'LL SSSEE TO THESE DEVILS!

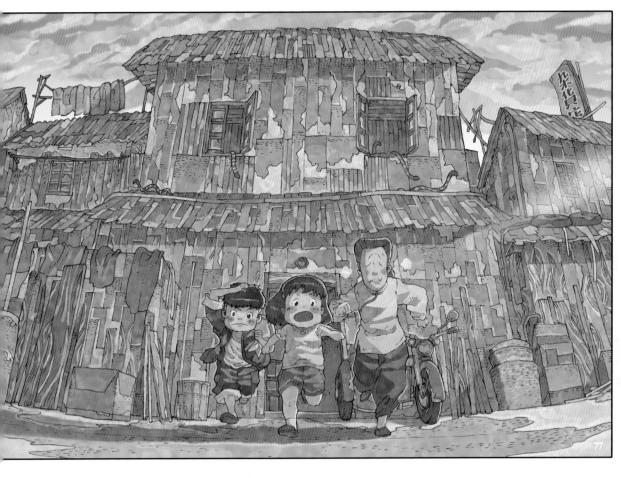

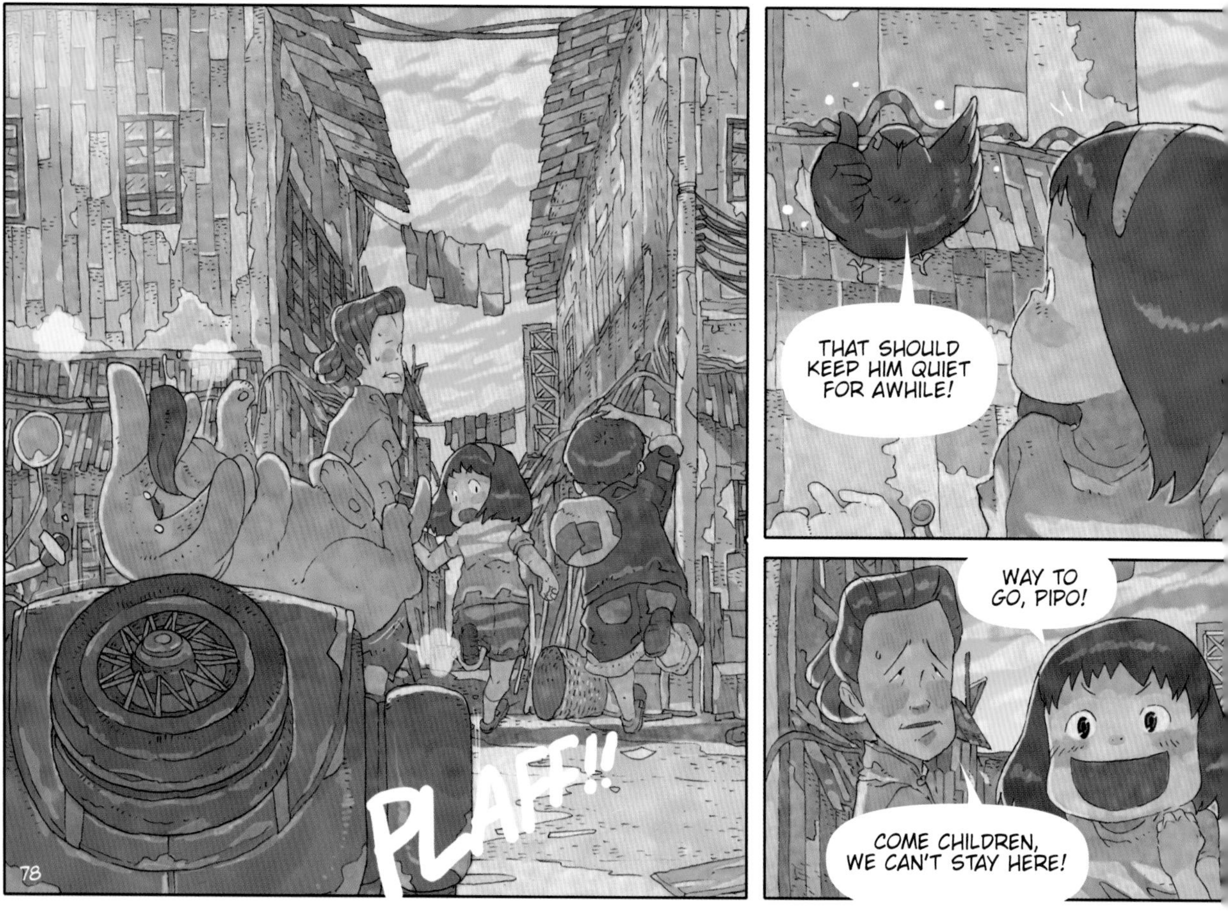
PLAFF!!
THAT SHOULD KEEP HIM QUIET FOR AWHILE!
WAY TO GO, PIPO!
COME CHILDREN, WE CAN'T STAY HERE!

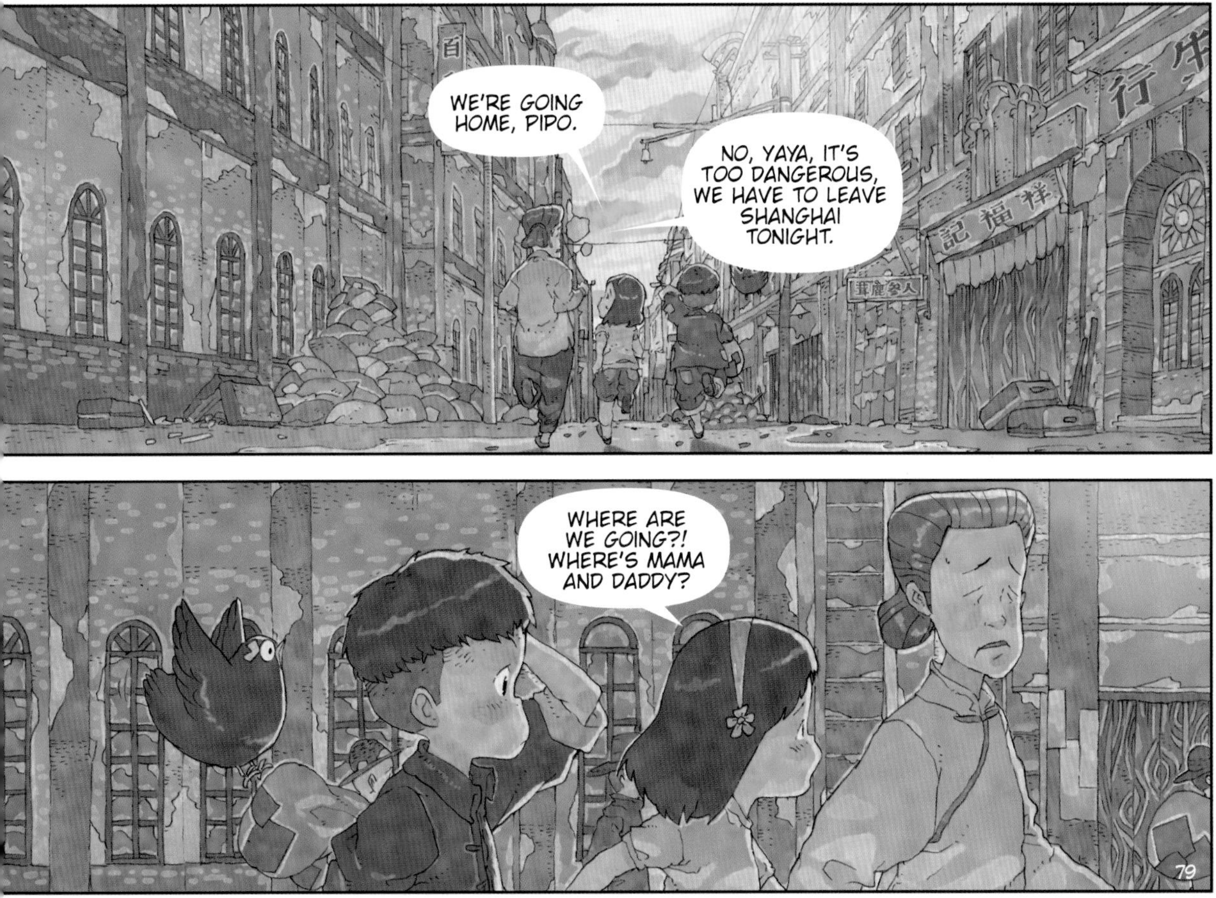
WE'RE GOING HOME, PIPO.
NO, YAYA, IT'S TOO DANGEROUS, WE HAVE TO LEAVE SHANGHAI TONIGHT.
WHERE ARE WE GOING?! WHERE'S MAMA AND DADDY?

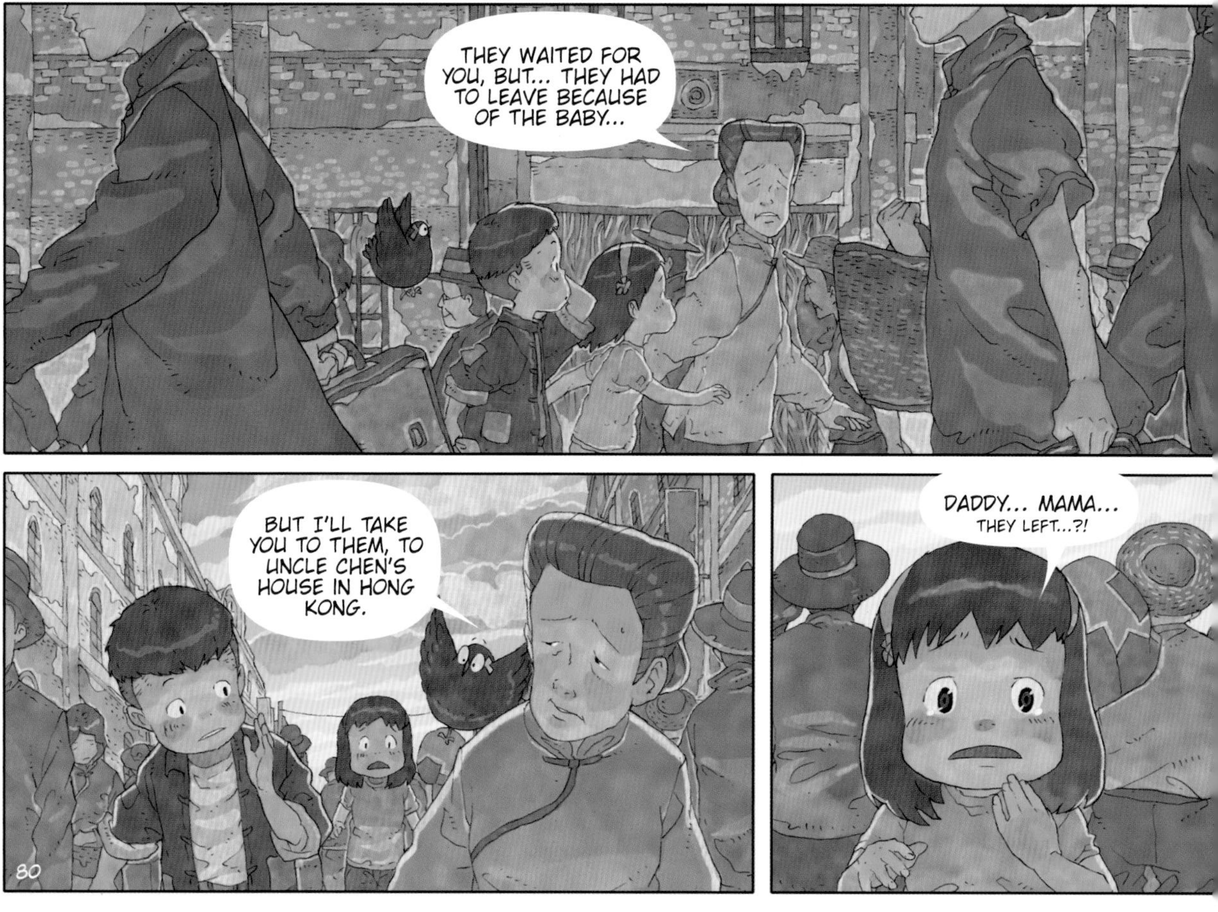
THEY WAITED FOR YOU, BUT... THEY HAD TO LEAVE BECAUSE OF THE BABY...
BUT I'LL TAKE YOU TO THEM, TO UNCLE CHEN'S HOUSE IN HONG KONG.
DADDY... MAMA... THEY LEFT...?!

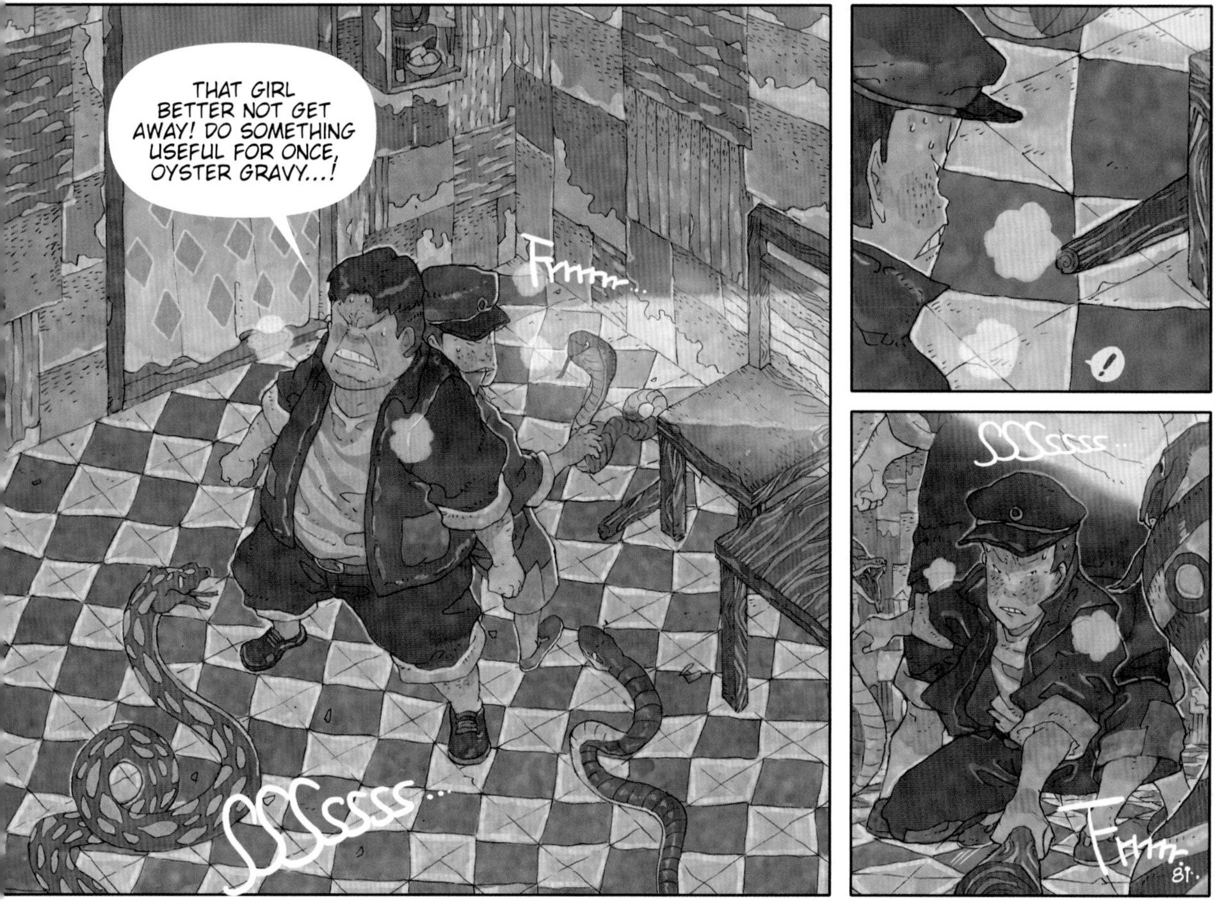
THAT GIRL BETTER NOT GET AWAY! DO SOMETHING USEFUL FOR ONCE, OYSTER GRAVY...!
Frrrrr...
SSSssss...
!
SSSssss...
Frrrr.

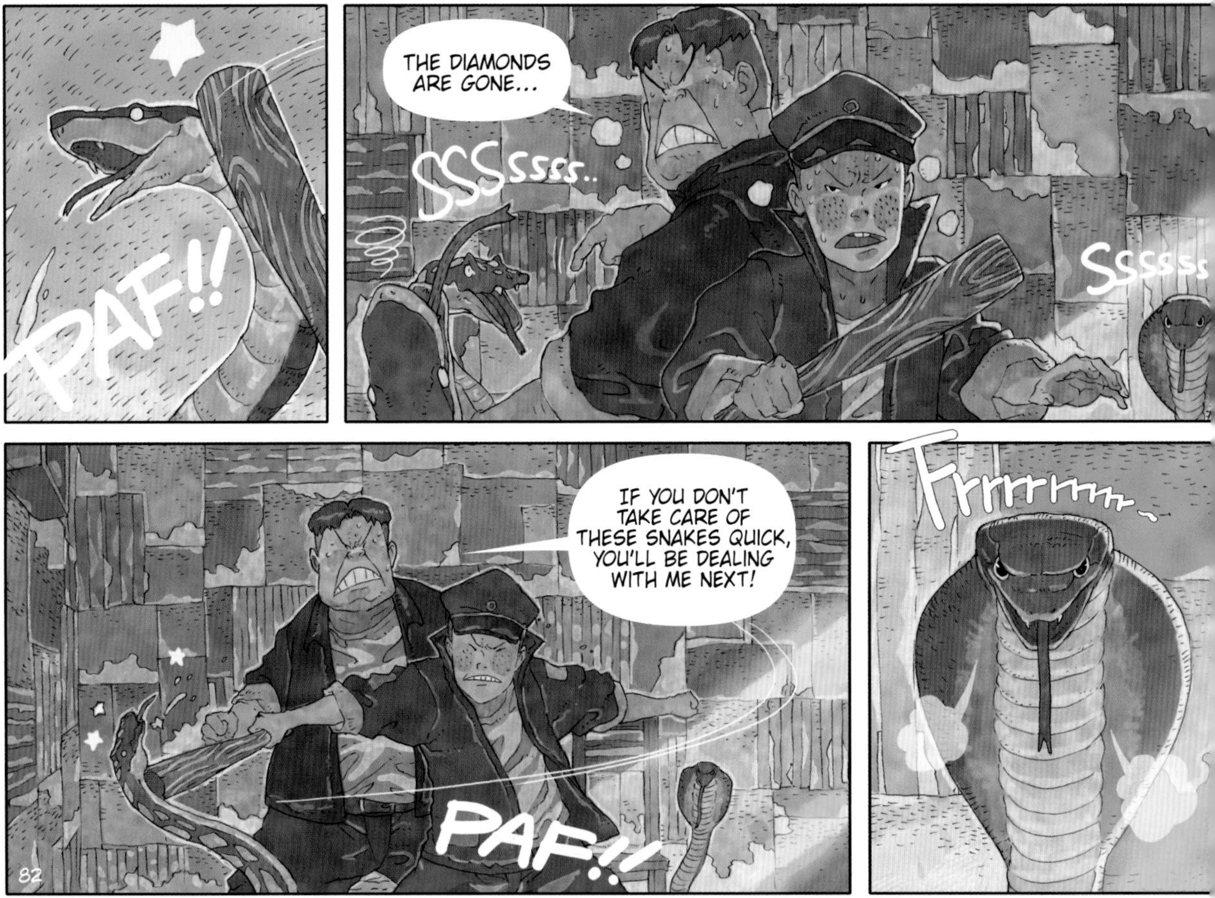
PAF!!
THE DIAMONDS ARE GONE...
SSSssss..
Ssssss
IF YOU DON'T TAKE CARE OF THESE SNAKES QUICK, YOU'LL BE DEALING WITH ME NEXT!
PAF!!
Frrrrrrrr

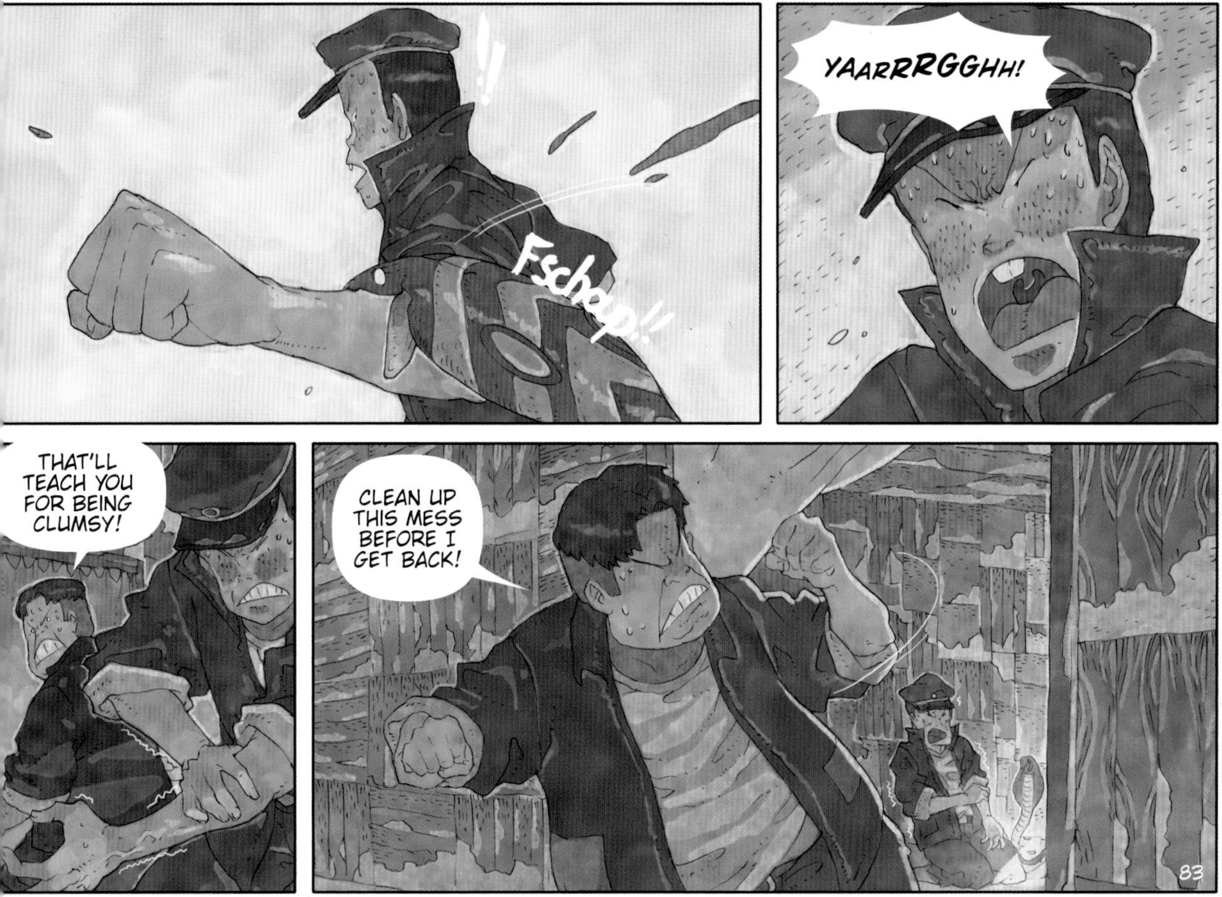
!!
Fschap!!
YAARRRGGHH!
THAT'LL TEACH YOU FOR BEING CLUMSY!
CLEAN UP THIS MESS BEFORE I GET BACK!

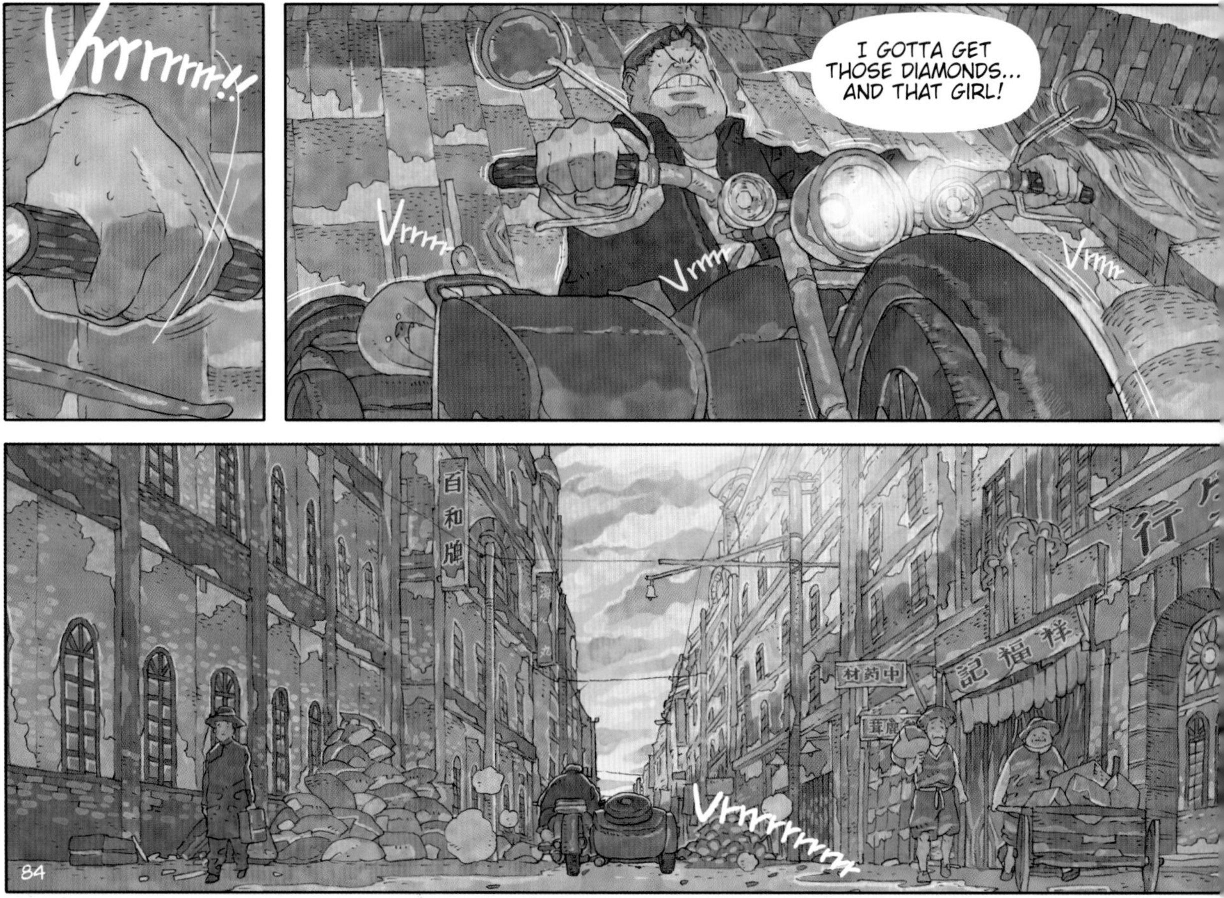
Vrrrrrrr!!
Vrrrrr
Vrrrr
I GOTTA GET THOSE DIAMONDS... AND THAT GIRL!
Vrrrr
百和牌
中葯材
祥福記
Vrrrrrrrrrr

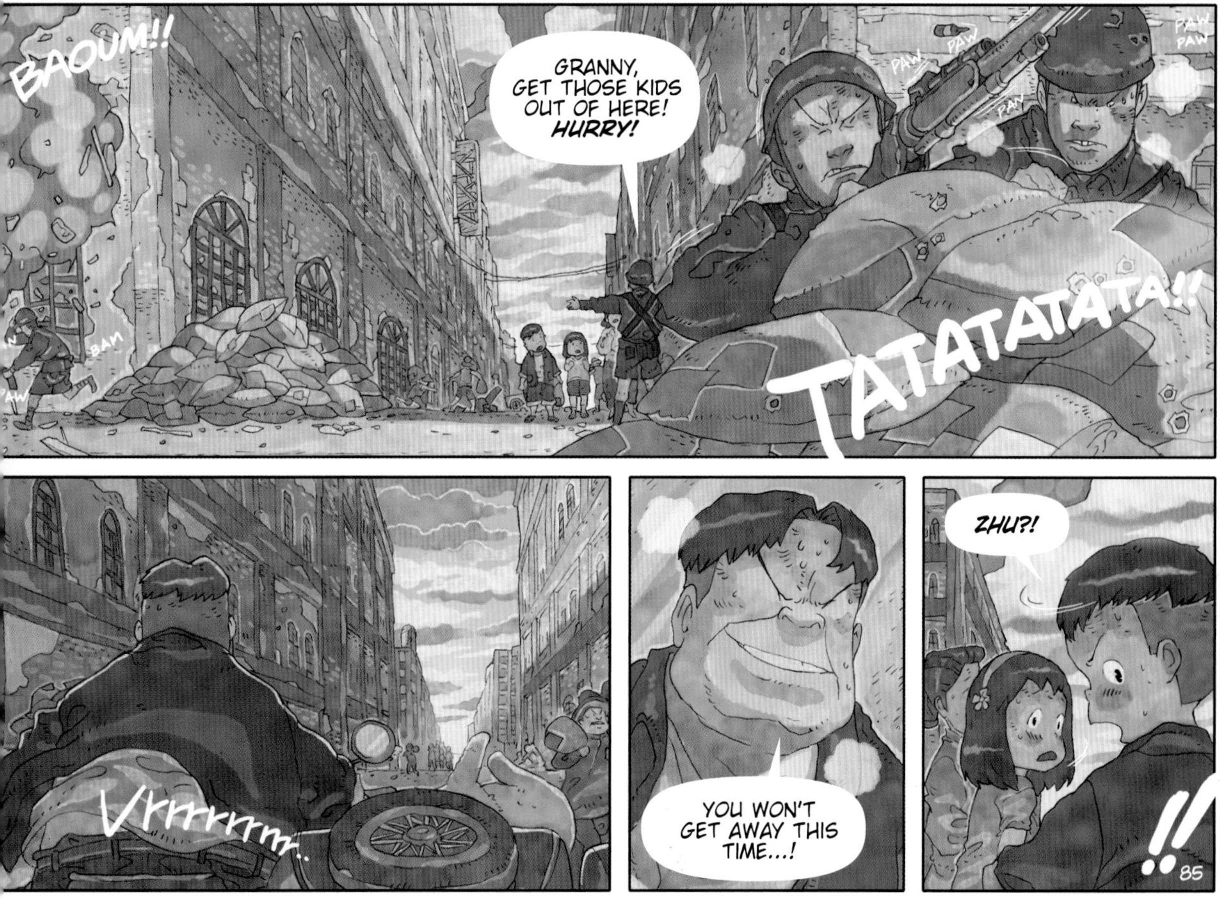
BAOUM!!
GRANNY, GET THOSE KIDS OUT OF HERE! *HURRY!*
PAW PAW
PAW
PAW
PAW PAW
BAM
TATATATATA!!
Vrrrrrrrm..
YOU WON'T GET AWAY THIS TIME...!
ZHU?!
!!

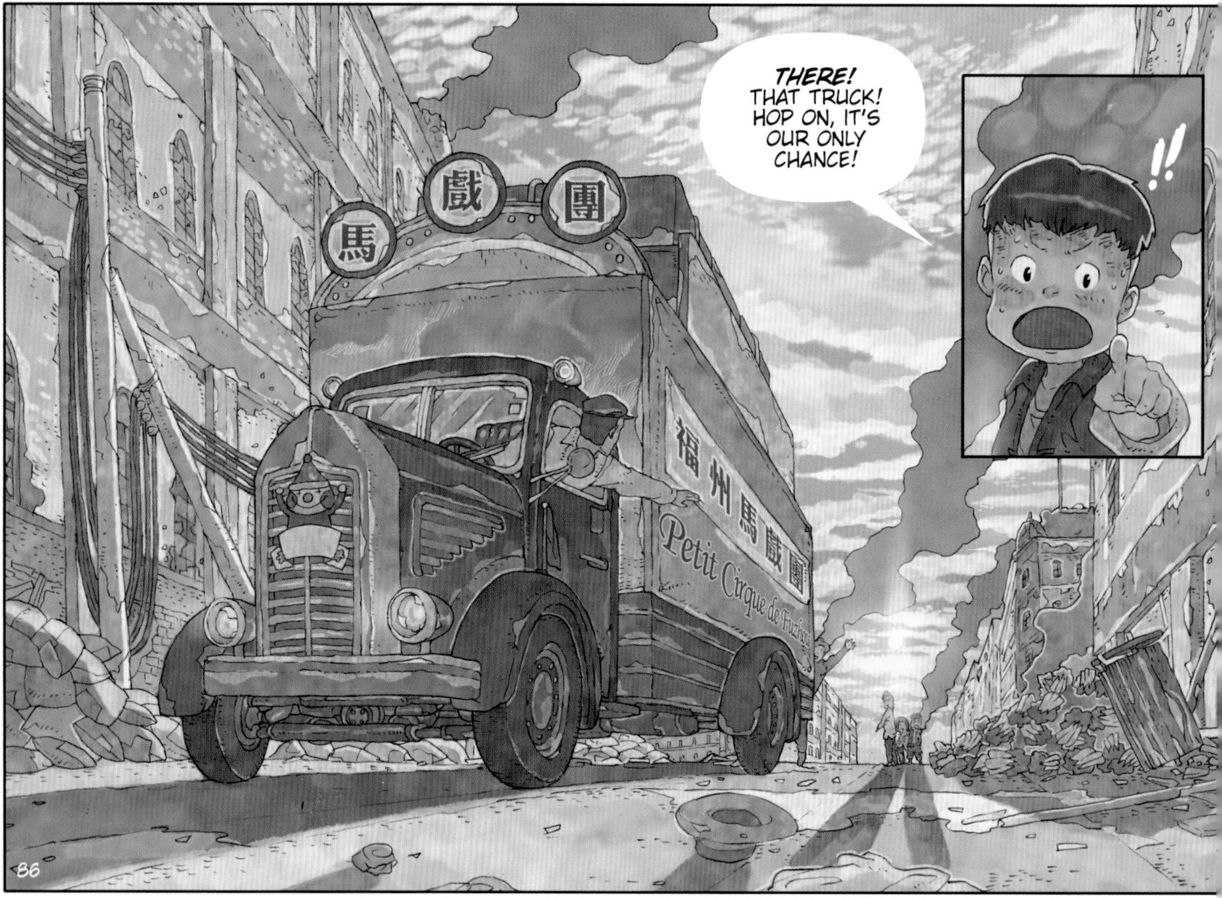
馬戲團
THERE! THAT TRUCK! HOP ON, IT'S OUR ONLY CHANCE!
!!
福州馬戲團
Petit Cirque de

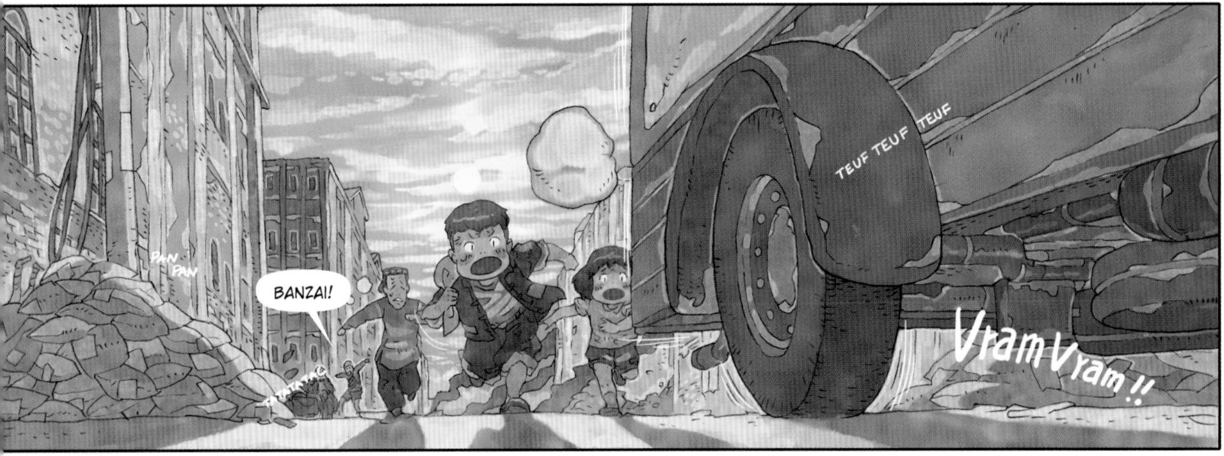
PAN
PAN
BANZAI!
TEUF TEUF TEUF
VramVram!!

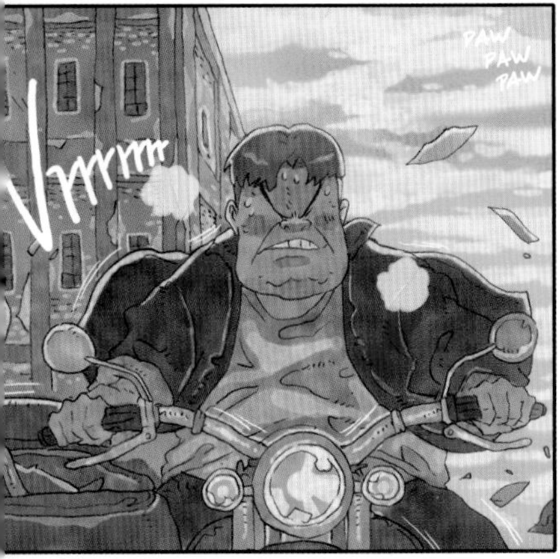
PAW
PAW
PAW
Vrrrrrr

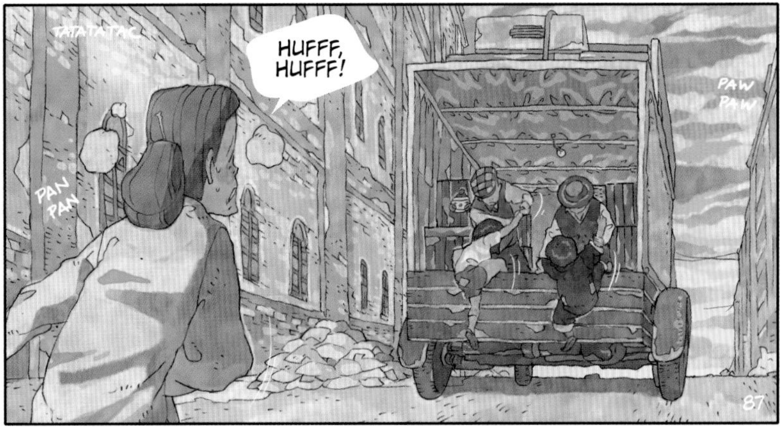
TATATATAC
HUFFF, HUFFF!
PAN
PAN
PAW
PAW

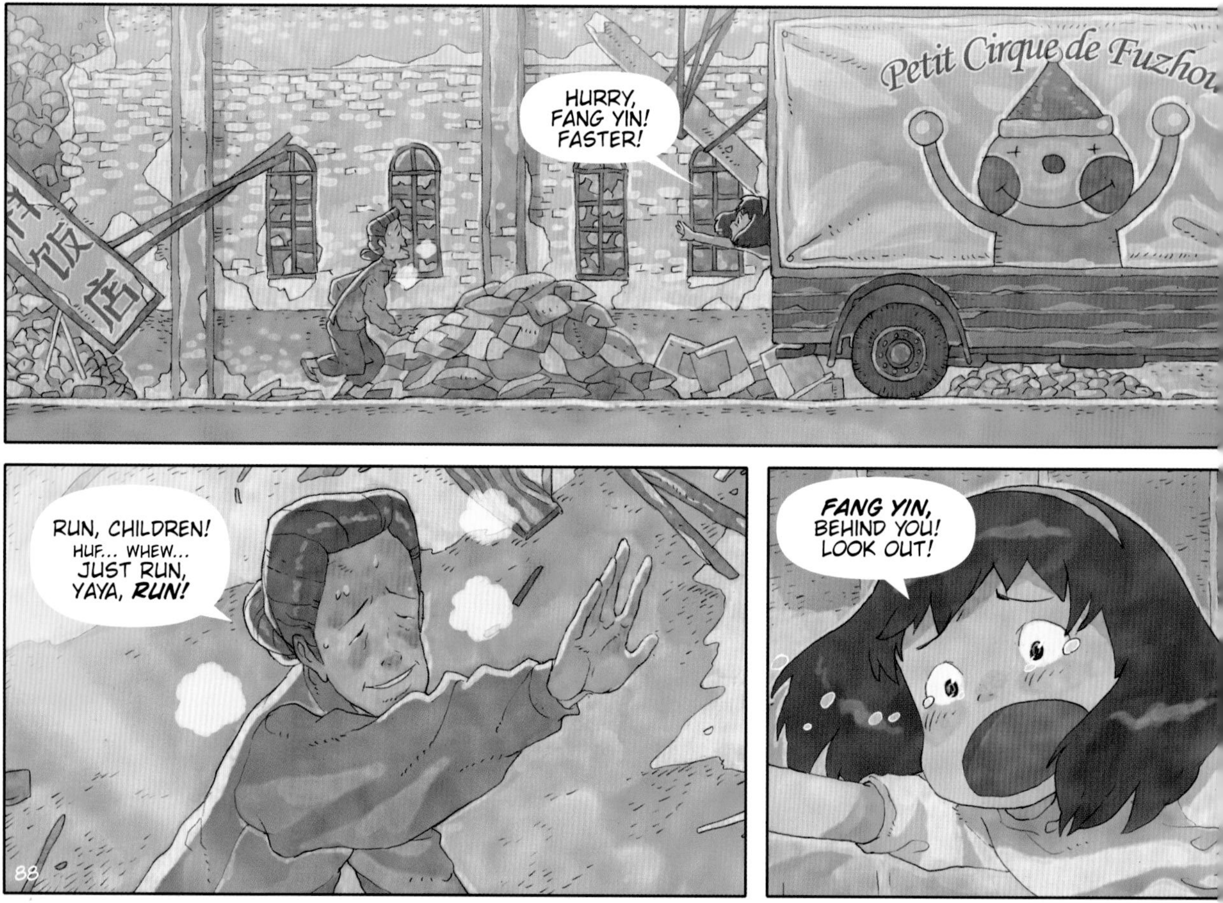
Petit Cirque de Fuzhou
HURRY, FANG YIN! FASTER!
RUN, CHILDREN! HUF... WHEW... JUST RUN, YAYA, RUN!
FANG YIN, BEHIND YOU! LOOK OUT!

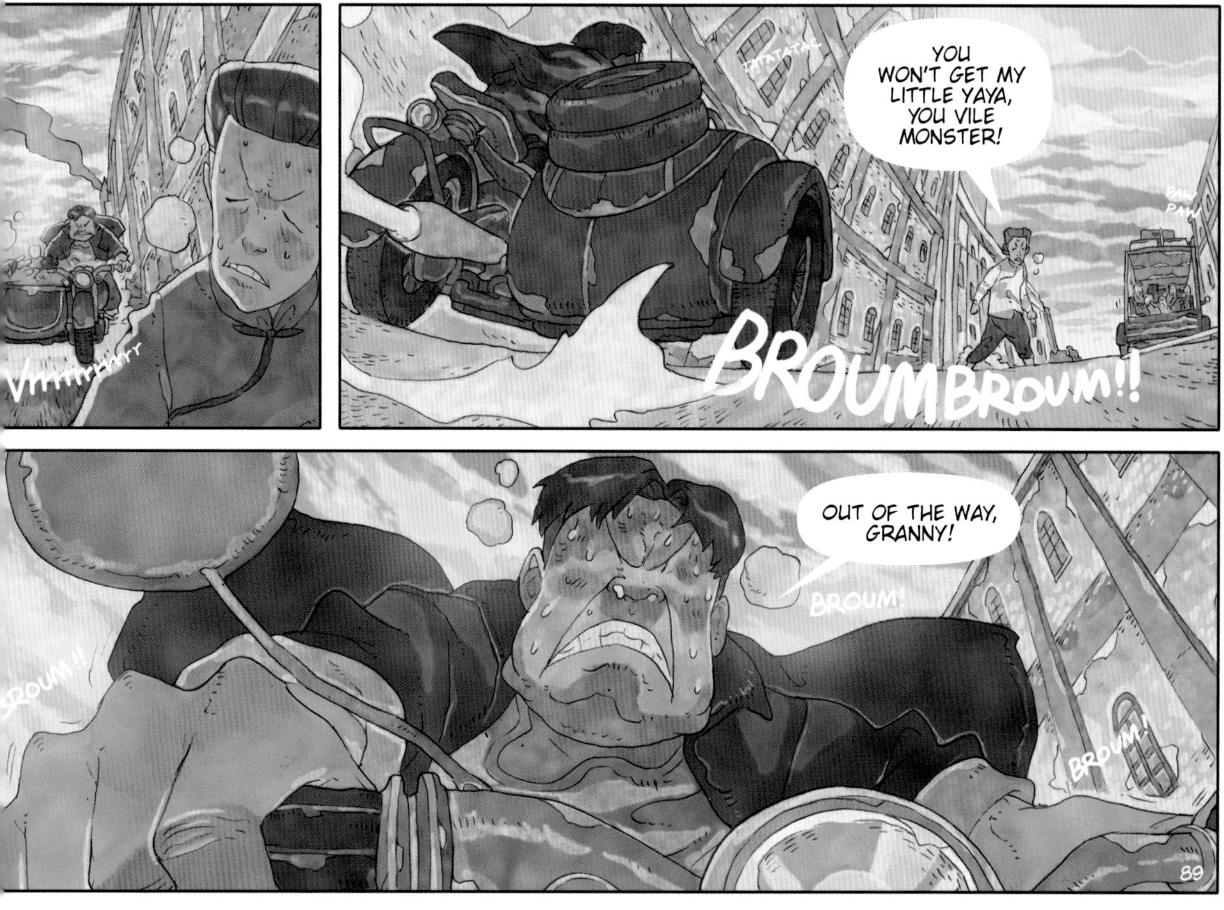
Vrrrrrrrr
TATATATAC
YOU WON'T GET MY LITTLE YAYA, YOU VILE MONSTER!
PAW PAW
BROUMBROUM!!
OUT OF THE WAY, GRANNY!
BROUM!
BROUM!!
BROUM!

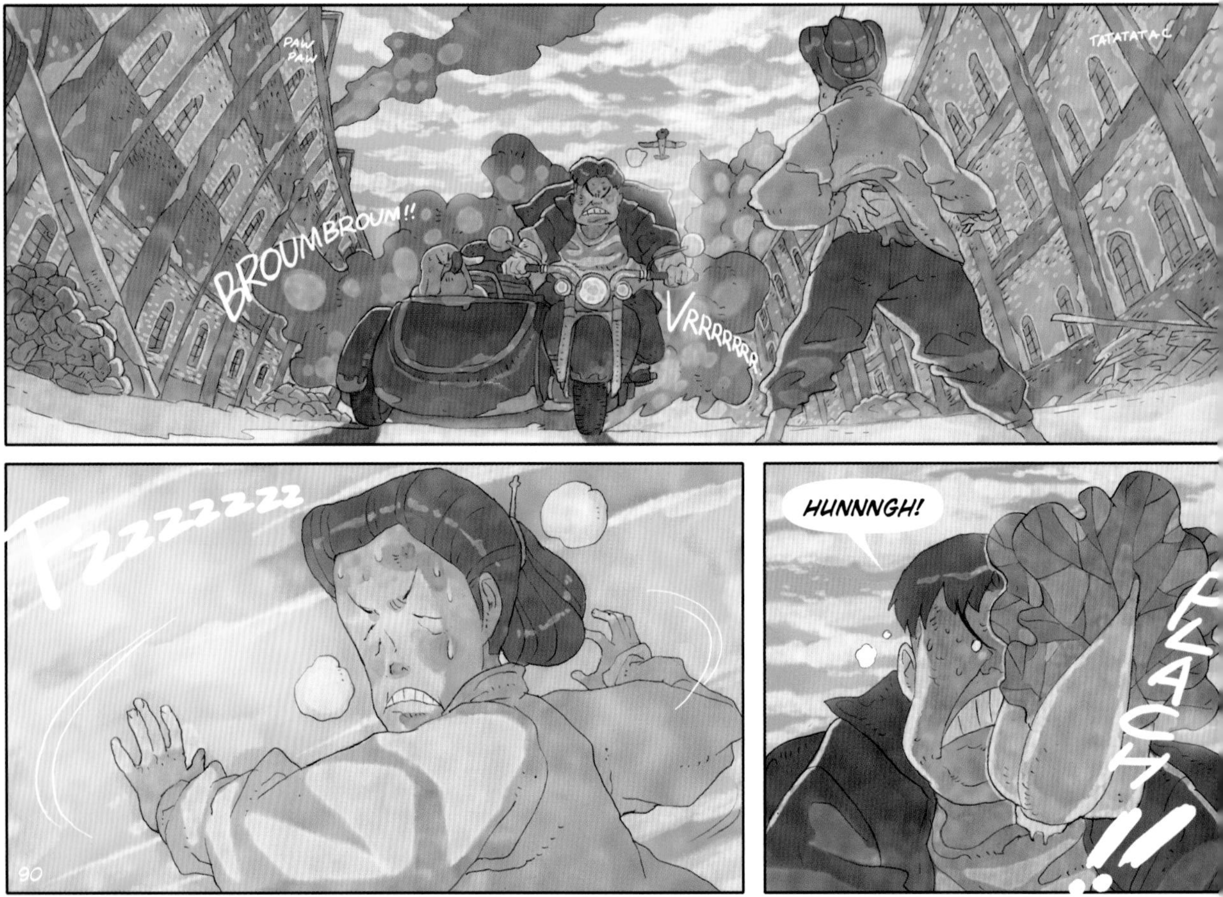
PAW
PAW
TATATATAC
BROUMBROUM!!
VRRRRRRRR.
FZZZZZZZ
HUNNNGH!
FLACH!!

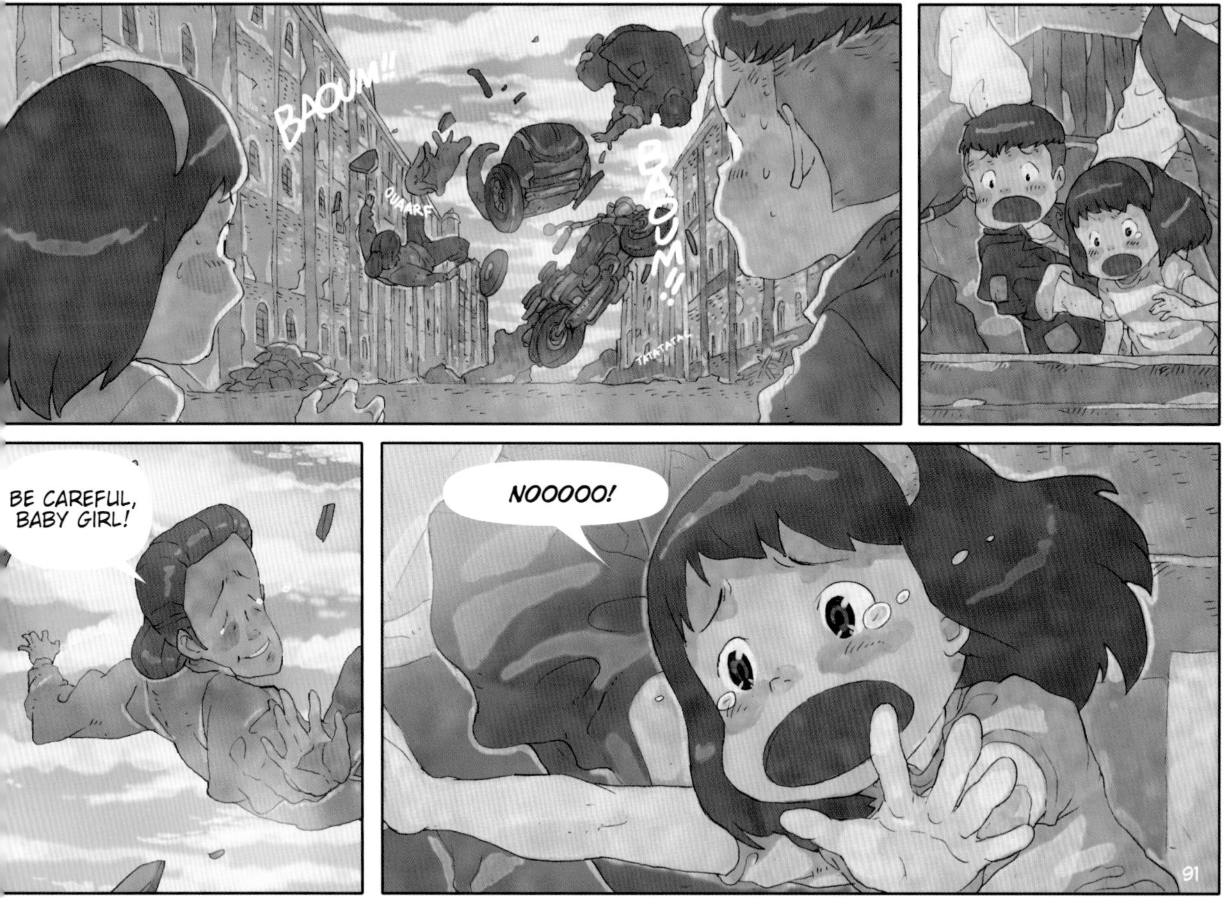
BAOUM!!
QUAARF
BAOUM!!
BE CAREFUL, BABY GIRL!
NOOOOO!

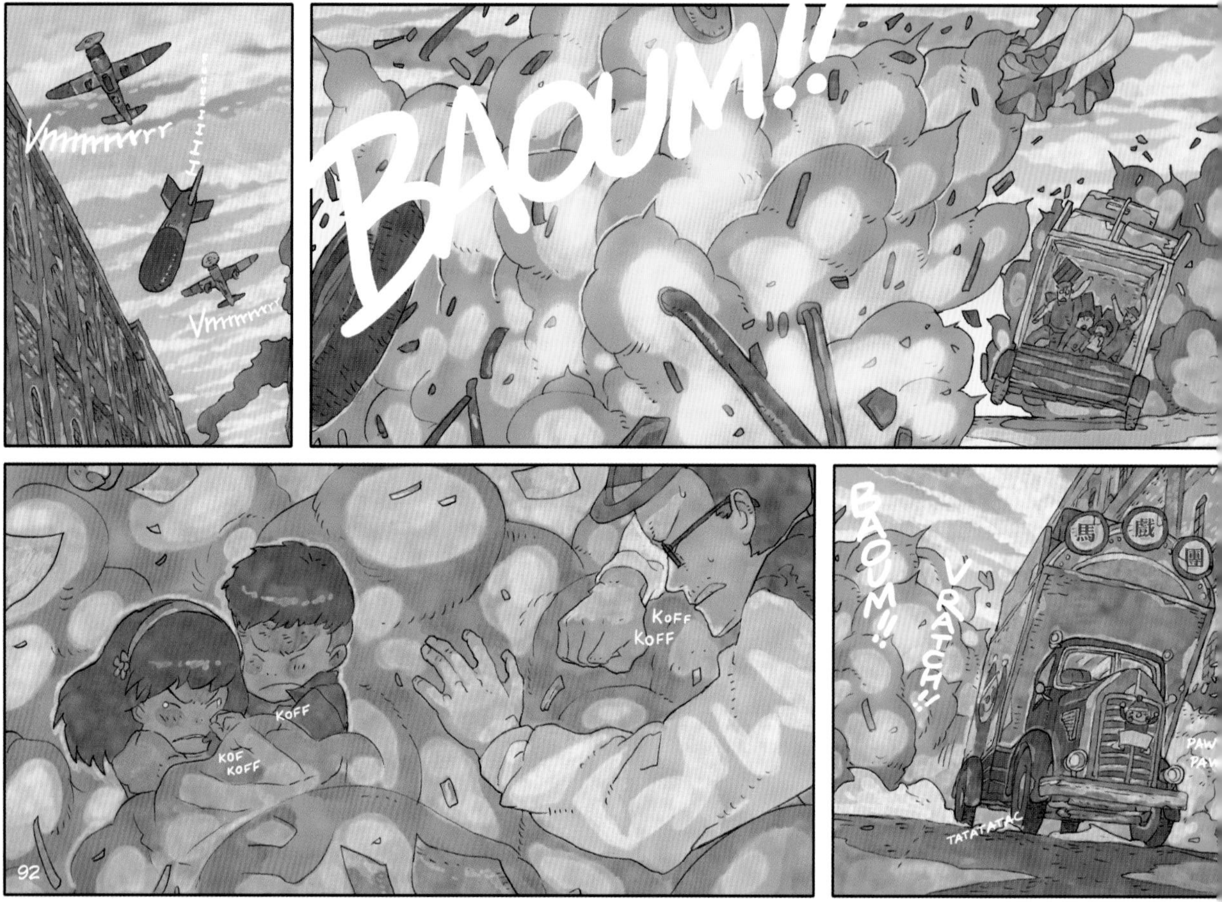
Vmmmrrrrr
Vmmmrrrrr
BAOUM!!
KOFF
KOFF
KOFF
KOF
KOFF
BAOUM!!
VRATCH!!
PAW
TATATATAC

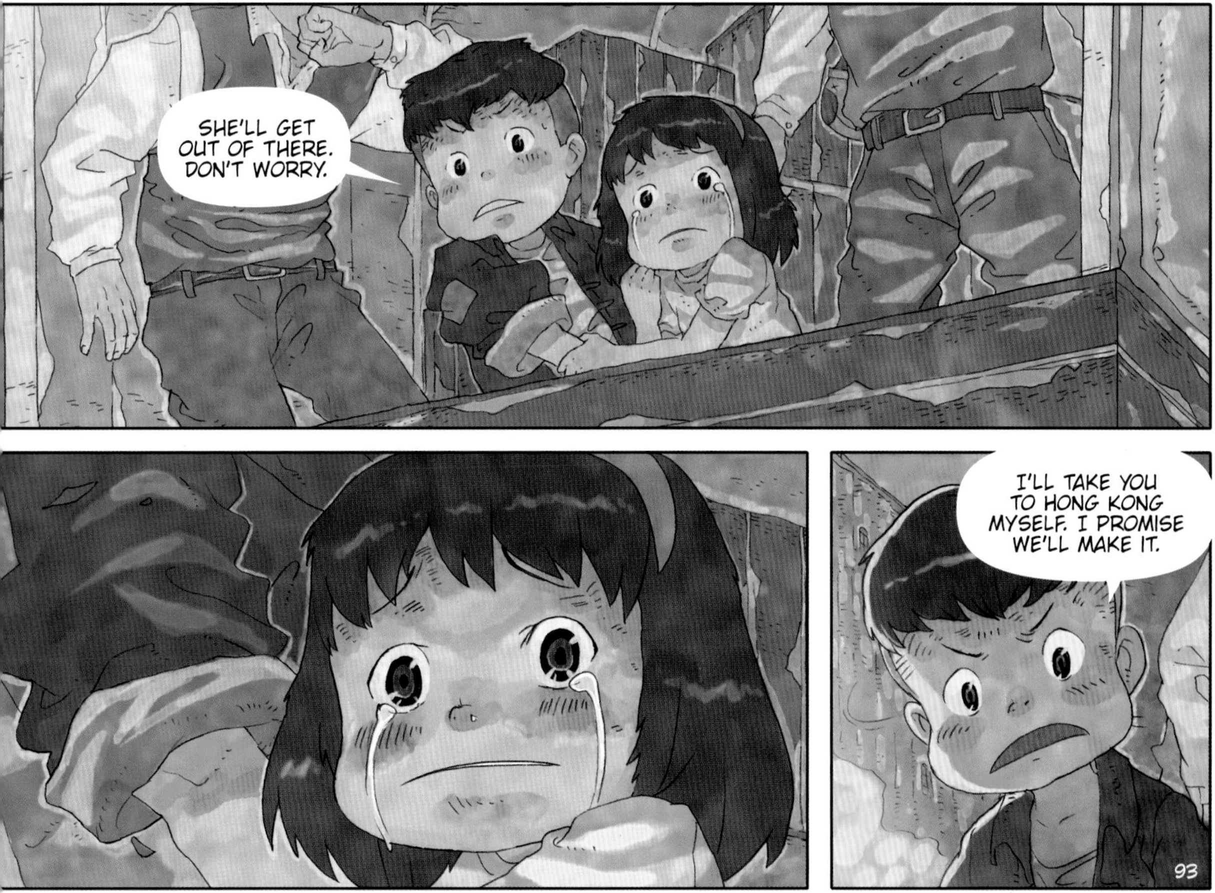
SHE'LL GET OUT OF THERE. DON'T WORRY.
I'LL TAKE YOU TO HONG KONG MYSELF. I PROMISE WE'LL MAKE IT.

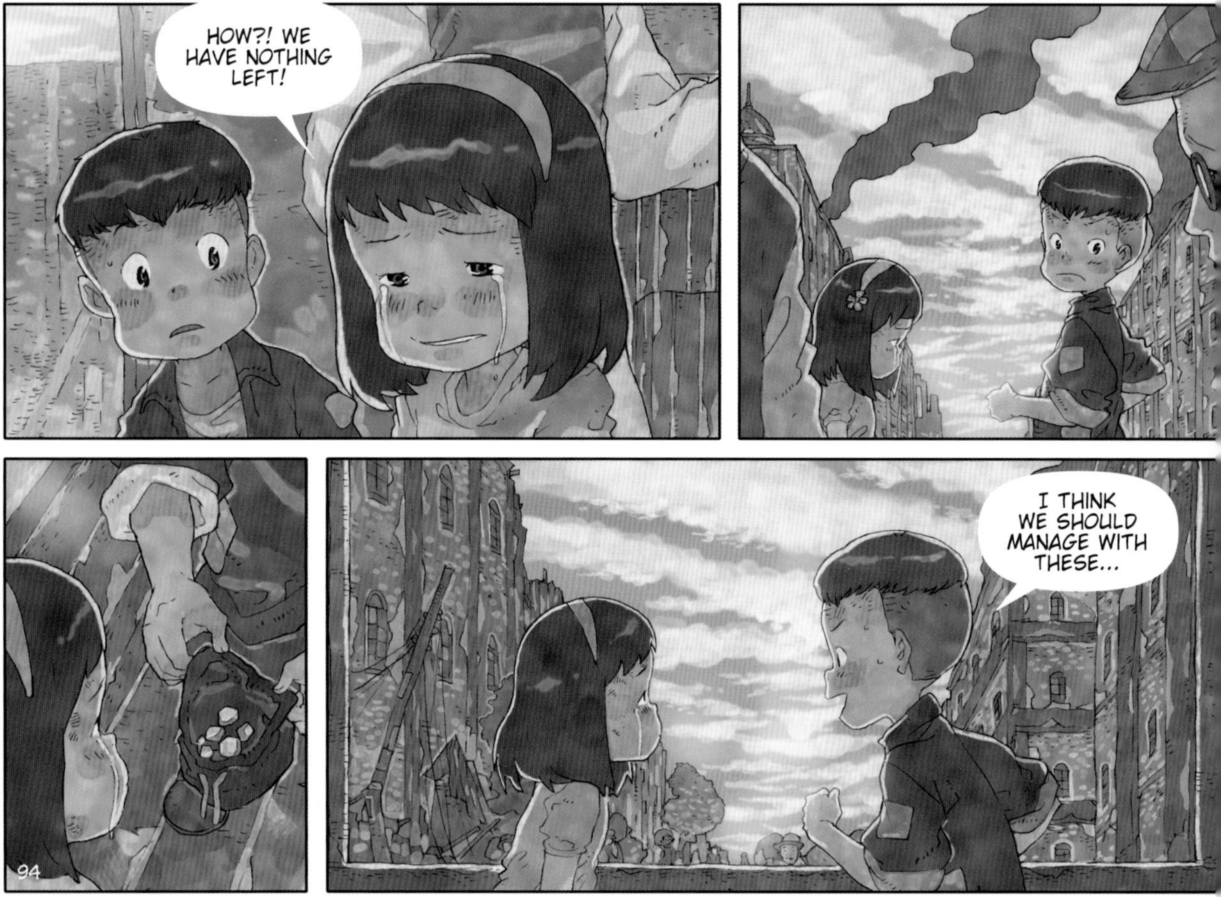
HOW?! WE HAVE NOTHING LEFT!
I THINK WE SHOULD MANAGE WITH THESE...